# Gone but
# Not for
# Garden

The Goddess of Greene Street Mysteries
By Kate Collins

A Goddess of Greene St. Mystery

# Gone but Not for Garden

## Kate Collins

Kensington Publishing Corp.
www.kensingtonbooks.com

This book is dedicated to my sweet little Lily, my beloved Shih-Tzu, whom I miss terribly. You will always be in my heart, my darling Lily.

# Acknowledgments

I would like to thank Dispatch Operator Paul Sweeney for his expertise in crafting a key part of the danger scene.

I would like to thank my editor, Elizabeth May, for her patience and understanding.

I would like to attribute much of the key plot planning to my son and excellent personal editor Jason Eberhardt.

I would also like to thank my daughter Julia, as always, for her continued love and support.

# PROLOGUE

*Thursday evening*

Mayor Charles E. Sloan strode out onto the stage and took the microphone off its stand. He flashed his pearly white smile and waited for the crowded ballroom to finish their applause. "Thank you, everyone, and welcome to the final night of our Small Business Association fashion show. I see the association chair and coordinator of this event, Fran Decker, standing in the wings. Fran is the owner of Fabulous Fashions. All her outfits are created by local designers and will be for sale after the show. The proceeds will go to help small businesses all across our fine community, because as you know, nothing is more important to me than keeping Sequoia small. Fran, step out and take a bow for all the hard work you've done."

He waited until the clapping stopped to say,

"Folks, we have a great show lined up for you, with summer fashions from some of the best designers in town, and models whom I'm sure you'll recognize. We have Ms. Carly Blackburn, PTA president and campaign coordinator, Mrs. Hope Louvain, the wife of our esteemed chief of police, Ed Louvain, and my beautiful wife, Eleni Sloan, who can't wait to show you the outfits she's modeling this year.

"To get things started, I'd like to introduce our emcee and fashion consultant from New Chapel, Indiana." He pointed in my direction, but the audience couldn't see me. I was standing just offstage behind a curtain set up in the large banquet room of the Waterfront Hotel. It was my first year officiating the event. I'd done quite a few shows before but none in Sequoia, Michigan.

The mayor waited until I was beside him to introduce me, as he'd done the previous evening. Then, as he led the audience in a round of applause, he handed me the microphone and strode offstage and into the audience.

"Good evening," I said, absolutely loving the way my voice boomed over the loudspeakers. "As Mayor Sloan said, we have a great show lined up for you. So, let's get things started."

As the clapping subsided and the upbeat music began, I glanced at the notecard in my hand. "Our first outfit, modeled by Eleni Sloan, is from designer Martinique. This fun and flirty jumpsuit comes in a gorgeous coral floral print. The lightweight organic rayon fabric is flowy and breathable—perfect for a day at the beach or you can dress it up with wedges for dinner! The leg slits will make you feel pretty and sexy—perfect for that special summer night out."

I watched as Eleni crossed the stage and started down the runway, smiling at the women who *oohed* and *aahed* over her outfit. She was tall and fit, with dark features emboldened by a palette of smoky makeup and thick, curly black hair. At the end of the runway, she pivoted smartly and walked back, exuding confidence. I liked confident women.

"Thank you, Eleni," I said. "And our next outfit is modeled by Hope Louvain. This tropical floral jumpsuit by artist Jane Strayer has an elegant vee neckline and is fully lined. The waist tie is removable and can be wrapped in multiple ways, tied in the front or the back. This all-in-one wonder can be dressed up with your favorite heels or, for a more casual take, paired with platform sneakers and a denim jacket."

Hope was cute and short. Her outfit suited her, but the extensions she'd clipped into her short, blond hair didn't match. I had to hold my breath as she hobbled across the stage and down the runway, where she pivoted, faltered slightly on top of stiletto heels, and returned amid another round of applause. "Thank you, Hope," I said.

"Our third outfit, modeled by Carly Blackburn, is by designer Flora Smith, a pretty gauze dress with lace insets and pin tucks. It has a plunge halter neckline, open back, and an A-line silhouette, a smart but casual dress to wear to any summer event."

I looked down at my notes as I waited for Carly to emerge from the curtain. When she didn't appear, I said into the microphone, "Sorry. There must be a snafu backstage. Are you enjoying the show so far?"

The audience applauded. I glanced to my left but still didn't see anyone waiting to walk onstage. I waited a moment, hoping Fran was simply fixing a loose strap on Carly's dress. At the side of the stage, I caught sight of the audio technician, but he merely shrugged. I blocked the bright stage lights with my hand and looked out into the audience for Charles Sloan, but he, too, was gone.

I began again. "As I said, our next outfit is modeled by Carly Blackburn . . ."

And again, no one appeared.

I stood there staring down at my notecards, wondering whether I should go backstage to find out what was going on when Eleni Sloan ran out from behind the curtain. "Someone call 911. There's been an accident!"

My fingers instinctively reached for my phone. As I rushed past the curtain, I could see the models standing off to the side of one of the dressing rooms, where Carly's legs were sticking out beneath the curtain. I pulled back the flap and saw her lying on her side. No one else seemed to be calling for help, so I did.

"Hello? Yes, we need an ambulance. The Waterfront Hotel in Sequoia, Michigan. Please hurry." I listened to the instructions given by the woman over the phone, and when she had finished, she asked for my name.

"Jillian Ophelia Knight Osborne."

\* \* \*

I sat down on a folding chair and tapped my fingers impatiently. The police had told me not to leave. They had grouped all of us who were involved with the show in one area next to the stage and were calling each of us individually to question us. I wasn't sure why we were being interviewed—what kind of accident could cause all this fuss?

I glanced at my watch. I wanted to be back in my hotel room by ten so I could get to bed early. I planned to check out by eight o'clock the next morning so I could be home by nine thirty, when Harper's play group met. She was at the adorable age of eighteen months, and although I hadn't even been gone two days, I missed her terribly.

A policeman came over and ushered me to a table, where an overweight man with a sour face was seated. He looked tired and dumpy in his wrinkled overcoat and awful brown suit.

"I'm Detective Walters," he said. "Have a seat."

I sat down across from him and folded my arms across my expensive designer top.

"Who was responsible for dispensing the water bottles to the models' dressing areas?" he asked.

"That would be me."

He wrote it down, then looked straight at me. "Did you at any time open any of the water bottles?"

I stared at him, puzzled. "I opened mine. Why would I open anyone else's?"

"That's what I'm asking you."

"Believe me, I only opened mine. I put the rest in each of the three curtained dressing rooms and left, just as I did yesterday evening."

"Where did you get the water?"

"I stopped at a mini-mart about two blocks from here."

"Was it necessary to supply the models with water?"

"I wouldn't have done it otherwise."

"Is that a yes?"

This man was way too serious. "That's a yes. It's what I do at every fashion event. And that's all I have to say because I really need to get to my hotel room now."

"I'm going to have to instruct you not to leave town."

"What?" I rose in indignation. "I can't stay here. I have a baby at home."

"Who's taking care of the baby now?"

"Not that it's any of your business, but my husband, the father, is."

"So the baby is in good hands."

"That's not the point."

"State your full name for the record."

I sat down again. "I don't understand what's going on. Why can't I leave town?"

"You were backstage before the event."

"So?" I sat forward, my fingers on my knees, and said in a confidential voice, "We're not talking about a murder here, are we?"

"That's still to be determined. Now state your name for the record."

I huffed impatiently. "Jillian Ophelia Knight Osborne." I leaned over to see what he had written. "No. That's Osborne with an *e* on the end—and no *u*."

I huffed again. The man couldn't even spell. "Can I go *now?*"

"Yes, you may go. But don't leave town."

I rose and put my purse over my shoulder. If he thought I was going to stay in Sequoia, he had another think coming. In fact, forget about staying until morning. I was going to leave tonight.

Take that, detective sour face.

# CHAPTER ONE

*Sunday morning*

My cousin Drew led me away from the celebration in the conference room to the front of the big barn, where a young, redheaded woman was waiting by the checkout counter.

"Athena Spencer?" she asked.

"That's me."

"It's a pleasure to meet you." She shook my hand, her vivid green eyes exuding warmth and confidence. "Abby Knight Salvare. Bloomers Flower Shop. Have I got a case for you."

I stared at her in surprise. "A case? Involving your flower shop?"

The woman was a few years younger than me, more than a few inches shorter than me, pretty, and just brimming with energy. She smiled brightly. "I'm sorry. I meant to say *murder* case. My husband,

Marco, and I have a detective agency in New Chapel, Indiana."

Maybe it was her short stature, or her green and yellow floral sundress, or the smattering of sun-kissed freckles across her cheeks and nose, but the woman standing before me didn't look any older than twenty-five. It was surprising to hear her impressive résumé. "I see. Well then, it's nice to meet you, too, Abby."

"I'm sorry to be so forward, but I feel like already know you."

Another surprise.

"The reason I'm here is because I'd like your help," she said.

"*My* help?"

"You're locals. You know this town. And I understand you own a detective agency, too," Abby said.

"Yes, yes, I do," I stammered. "Actually, my partner, Case Donnelly, and I own it. The Greene Street Detective Agency. But how did you find us? We've only been open a few days."

"Research," she answered, setting her deep yellow purse down on the counter and pulling out several sheets of printer paper. "My husband is a pro at it. He found these articles in your local newspaper about the cases you've solved." She shuffled through the papers and showed me the story written after Case and I had solved the double homicide, the news story that had first given me the nickname *Goddess of Greene Street*. "He also read that you worked at your family's garden center. So here I am!"

"Athena, do you want some cake?"

I turned to see my bubble-headed younger sister, Delphi, standing in the conference room doorway, where a surprise party was underway celebrating my most recent success at catching a murderer, which, after taking a step back to appreciate the accomplishment, would've been three cases solved in less than three months. Clearly, our reputation was starting to spread. "I'll be there soon," I replied to Delphi and turned back to my guest.

"I'm sorry if I'm interrupting," Abby said. "Why don't I come back later?"

"How about at two o'clock this afternoon?" I suggested. "We close at two on Sundays, so there won't be any interference."

Abby gave me her bright smile again. "Perfect. I'll go have lunch somewhere in the meantime."

"I'd recommend the Blue Moon Café," I told her. "It's just one block down and around the corner. Good food at reasonable prices."

"Thanks. I'll see you at two." She started to walk away and then paused before she reached the door. "So, *this* is the famous statue," she said, putting her hand on the tall *Treasure of Athena* that greeted customers as they walked into the garden center.

"That's her," I said.

"She's beautiful."

Standing at over six feet tall, my namesake wore a traditional flowing toga gathered over one shoulder with a clasp so that the material draped down over her small, firm breasts. Another layer of material swirled down from her waist to the sandals on her feet. Her hair was swept up beneath a helmet that covered the top of her head. Her arms were bare and slender, but her strength was evident.

One hand rested on her right hip; the other hand was outstretched in greeting. She was the goddess of war and wisdom, strong, courageous, and independent, things I strove to be.

My *pappoús* had famously purchased the statue at the Talbot estate sale, which had ultimately led me straight into a double homicide investigation. He'd originally wanted to put it in his diner's front entrance, but the statue had been too large for the Parthenon. So, my dad and I had gladly welcomed it to Spencer's.

As Abby left the store, Case came out of the conference room and put his arm around my shoulders. He was dressed casually in a light green polo shirt and khakis, his wavy dark brown hair intensifying the color of his golden-brown eyes. "Everything okay?"

"I think so."

"Who was that?" he asked.

I glanced over Case's shoulder to see several customers enter the store. "I'll tell you about her later. Let's go wrap up this party. We're starting to get busy."

We returned to the conference room, a long, narrow room just up the hallway from the office where I worked at Spencer's Garden Center. The room was full of members of my big, zany Greek family, including my parents, three sisters, one aunt, one uncle, one cousin, and my grandparents, who'd taken time away from their diner to be there. Also in attendance were Officer Bob Maguire of the Sequoia Police Department, my sister Delphi's current flame, and Lila Talbot, the silent partner in the Greene Street Detective Agency.

"Now we can cut the cake!" my mother cried, and with the long, sharp knife in her hand, she began to cut slices into the three-layer cake with the strawberry pink frosting on it that said, *Three Cheers for the Goddess of Greene Street!* Case had given me that title after the first murder case I'd solved, the press had reported it, and it had stuck.

Lila, Case, and my family had surprised me with this little party. After a tumultuous day yesterday, where my life had been in grave danger, today had started as though nothing unusual had taken place. I'd felt a huge letdown all morning. And then they'd surprised me with this.

"Here's your cake," my sister Selene said, and thrust a plate into my hands. She looked at her wristwatch. "I've got to cut out. I have a client coming in soon."

Selene was a hairstylist at Over-the-Top Hair Salon. She, my sister Maia, and I were all named after Greek goddesses; Selene, the oldest at thirty-six, after the moon goddess; Maia, twenty-eight, after the goddess of the fields, which was fitting since she was a vegetarian; and me, thirty-one, after Athena, the goddess of war and wisdom. My mother, Hera, had been named after the mother goddess, and so she had carried on the tradition with us. Delphi, at twenty-five, was the exception. She was named after the Oracle of Delphi.

"I'm going to head down to the office," Case said. "How about dinner tonight? On the boat. I'll make spaghetti, and you can tell me all about the redheaded stranger."

I suppressed a little shiver of excitement at the thought of being alone with him. Case was a very romantic, very masculine man, but he was also something of a loner. "It's Sunday, remember? Big, family dinner on Sunday? You're always invited, you know."

He paused, as though having an internal debate. "I'll let you know later." He glanced around to see if anyone was watching, then leaned in to give me a quick kiss before striding toward the door. I watched him go with a contented sigh.

Case had come to Sequoia from Pittsburgh to collect his family's statue, the *Treasure of Athena*, and ended up being charged with a murder involving the statue. After we'd worked together to find the real killer, we'd gone on to solve two more homicide cases. Now Case had his private investigator's license, and together we had opened up the Greene Street Detective Agency.

Tall, fit, and handsome, Case had admitted to staying in Sequoia because he liked me, even going so far as to say he wanted me to be a partner in his detective agency. That was fine by me, since my job working as bookkeeper for my dad at our family-owned-and-operated garden center didn't occupy that much of my time.

"Athena," my dad said as I forked a piece of strawberry cake into my mouth, "enjoy your party. I'll go help Drew on the sales floor."

"I'll be right out," I said with a mouthful.

My dad had created the job for me when I moved back home with my ten-year-old son, Nicholas, after my marriage had ended. The job provided me with income, and the relaxed schedule allowed me to have breakfast and dinner with my son and take time off for school events. During our busy summer season, I also helped customers in the garden center with selection and design. I didn't have any formal training, but I did have a passion for it. Plus, I'd practically grown up at the garden center, learning all about horticulture from my father.

At a tap on my shoulder, I turned to see Delphi rubbing her forehead. She was dressed in one of her quirky outfits, today a purple and black–striped tube top with a gauzy black skirt and her favorite purple flip-flops. She waited for a young couple to walk away and then said, "Athena, I had a vision a few minutes ago. It was about the red-head who came in earlier. Who was she?"

Delphi's visions were well-known in our family. Being named after the famous Oracle made her believe she had the gift of foresight. After years of teasing and eye-rolling, we'd given up on taming our sister's otherworldly grandeur and had come to appreciate Delphi for who she was—comic relief. Oddly, her predictions were right about 25 percent of the time. In fact, her last prediction had helped save my life, so I felt like I should pay attention to her.

"She's Abby Knight Salvare, a private detective. What did you see?"

"I saw a red flame."

"What does that mean?"

"The red flame could be Abby, but it could also mean danger. I'm not sure. Just keep that in mind." With a satisfied nod, she turned and walked away.

The party dwindled quickly as most of my friends and family had to get on with their day. And so, too, did my workday begin.

\* \* \*

At two o'clock on the nose, Abby Knight stepped inside the big barn my grandfather Spencer had converted into a garden center and looked around. I had come up to the sales floor to watch for her, and now I walked toward her with a smile.

"There you are," she said in a friendly voice.

"Come back this way," I said, and led her toward the conference room just as my dad locked the front door, closing the shop early as we did on Sundays.

We took seats across from each other at the long, walnut conference table, where she folded her hands and smiled at me. "Where to begin," she said.

"Can I get you a cup of coffee before we start?" I asked.

"No, thanks. I had two cups at the Blue Moon, and I'm already jittery." She took a breath. "Okay. Here it is. Have you heard the news about the fashion show murder that happened this past Thursday evening?"

"I didn't know it had been classified as murder. The last I heard, one of the models collapsed and died backstage."

Abby pulled her purse open to retrieve her cell phone.

As she scrolled through her phone, I continued. "These past few days have been a whirlwind. When did the news break about the murder?"

"This morning." She handed me her phone. "Here, take a look."

I scrolled through the article as Abby spoke. "The murder victim was a woman named Carly Blackburn. The article states that she'd been poisoned sometime before the show."

"Poisoned how?" I asked, still scrolling through the story. "I don't see it here anywhere."

"Actually, that's the only piece of information I managed to draw out of my cousin. She was practically in hysterics when I talked to her over the phone. Jillian was the emcee for the event. She was also in charge of the models, making sure they had everything they needed for the show, including water. Unfortunately, one of the models died after drinking poisoned water."

"And the police think your cousin did it," I finished.

"They're holding her now on suspicion of murder." Abby held her fingers an inch apart. "I have a feeling they're this close to charging her with premeditated murder." She sat forward. "I know my cousin. She may be something of an airhead, but she would never willingly hurt anyone. So, what I need from you and your partner is help getting Jillian the defense she needs, not only by pointing me toward a good attorney, but also by working with me to find the real killer."

Before handing Abby's phone back, I spotted a name I recognized. Eleni Sloan, former president of the Greek Merchants Association and wife of one of the most beloved, powerful people in town, Mayor Charles Sloan. Eleni had been one of the models in the fashion show.

I continued reading and found a quote by another prominent woman who had modeled for the show. "Did you read what Hope Louvain said?" I asked Abby. "She told the reporter that your cousin and Carly were longtime enemies, dating back to their college years."

"Yes, I read it. She publicly threw Jillian under the bus, which is definitely not helping my cause."

"Hope Louvain and Eleni Sloan are very influential people in this town," I told her. "And according to this article, they both seem to believe Jillian is guilty. Going up against them is not going to be easy."

"That's another reason I came to see you," Abby said.

"Why me?"

"Because you're good at what you do. Marco told me all about the Talbots," Abby explained, "and Pete Harmon, so I know you're not afraid to take on powerful people. And by the way, I don't expect you to work for free. I'll pay whatever your going rate is."

Wow. This would be our first official case. I was practically salivating at the idea. "I'll have to run it by my partner first," I said, "but I think he'll be on board. Let me get my iPad so I can take notes." I pushed back my chair, hurried down the hall to the office, snatched the iPad off the desk, and hurried back. Abby was under the assumption that I wasn't afraid to take on powerful people, and over the course of the past few months, I had worked very hard to overcome those fears. But this situation was different. These women were well-liked, respected. Eleni was one of the original founders of the Greek Merchants Association, and more importantly, a good friend of the family.

Hope Louvain was an award-winning middle school teacher, not to mention she was also married to Sequoia's chief of police. I was going to have to tread very carefully.

"Okay," I said, opening the tablet, "what do you know about the case?"

She sat back. "I don't know much. According to the article, there were three models—the police chief's wife, the mayor's wife, and the murder victim, Carly Blackburn. There was also a woman mentioned in the article who provided the models with clothing for the show."

"Fran Decker," I said. "She owns a women's boutique a few blocks from here." I typed in the names of the women at the show before continuing. "Where is Jillian now?"

"In jail," Abby answered. "Which is why I need a good defense attorney."

"I think I know someone who can help. Has she been charged with anything?"

"Obstruction of justice," Abby replied.

I glanced up from my notes in surprise. "How?"

"Jillian was told not to leave town—and then she left town. It wasn't the smartest thing to do, but that's Jillian. So, the police picked her up and brought her back to Sequoia."

"And the only evidence the police have against Jillian is that she handed out the water bottles?"

"I don't know all the evidence they have, but I do know she purchased the water, and the bottles were in her possession until she delivered them to each dressing room."

"Have you seen Jillian yet?"

"Not yet. I was hoping you could help me get in to see her."

"I think I can make that happen. When would you like to go?"

"As soon as possible."

"Let me make a phone call. I might be able to get you in tomorrow afternoon."

Abby smiled in relief. "That would be great."

"Where are you staying?"

"At the Waterfront Hotel, where the murder took place. Do you know it?"

"Maybe a little too well. It's a beautiful place, but you might want to steer clear of a man named Mitchell Black. He's not the most helpful when it comes to his father's hotel."

"See, you're helping already. I knew coming to you was the right decision."

I hoped she was right about that. I smiled at her comment and stood. "My phone is in the office. I'll make that call and be right back."

Once again, I hurried up the hallway, dashed over to my desk, and grabbed my phone. I opened my recent call list and found Officer Bob Maguire's number. After explaining my situation to him, I was delighted to hear he could get Abby and me into the jail the next day, skipping all the red tape that would've required twenty-four hours to process.

Next, I placed a call to my once-upon-a-time boyfriend Kevin Coreopsis, who had gone to New York after college and returned home just this past year to become a defense attorney. As a new lawyer in town, I guessed that Kevin would be more than willing to take Jillian's case.

After I finished with my phone calls, I returned to the conference room and sat down with a smile.

"Good news. I have a contact on the police force who can get us into the jail tomorrow afternoon, and I've lined up my friend Kevin Coreopsis to handle Jillian's case. He's going to go to the jail to meet with her tomorrow after our visit."

Abby pressed her hands to her heart. "That's wonderful! What a huge relief. Does this mean you'll work with me on the case?"

"I still have to run it by my partner, but I can definitely help with your jail visit. Why don't we meet at our office tomorrow at one o'clock? I'll write down the address for you."

"That would be perfect."

I jotted the address on a green sticky note and gave it to her. She tucked it in her purse, pushed back her chair, and rose. "I won't keep you any longer. It is Sunday, after all."

"Is your husband going to join you here?" I asked, as we stepped into the hallway.

"No, Marco's holding down the fort at home. We have two pets to take care of."

"What about the flower shop?" I asked.

"Bloomers will be fine," Abby answered. "I have a great staff."

"You're welcome to have dinner with my family this evening, although I have to warn you, it's a big, crazy, Greek family and quite a noisy gathering."

"That's very kind of you, but I think I'll just enjoy the hotel amenities and maybe do a little internet sleuthing."

"Good luck," I told her.

She held out her hand. "See you at one o'clock tomorrow."

* * *

I couldn't wait to tell Case about Abby's visit. I texted him and learned he'd left the office and gone home, which to Case meant the *Pamê*, the small houseboat he was buying from my grandfather. "I'll be there in ten minutes," I told him. "I have exciting news."

After closing the garden center, I locked the door behind me and set off down Greene Street to Oak, the cross street that took me out to the harbor. My pappoús's boat was docked at the southern end of the harbor on the last of three piers along the wide, wooden dock, directly across from the section of Greene Street known as Little Greece.

I used the short plank to cross onto the boat, stepping down into the back. The flat-backed stern had a blue vinyl, U-shaped seating area surrounding a plastic table for outside dining. Up a step and toward the cockpit were the swivel seats for fishermen, and beyond that the helm. A deck on either side of the boat led to the bow, where a sundeck could be used for tanning or cooling off after a swim.

I crossed the stern to the center door that led belowdecks and rapped twice. "Hello, I'm here," I called.

"Come on in," Case called back.

I walked down the five steps into the small living room. There was a built-in sofa, also in blue vinyl, across from the galley, with two white plastic chairs and a small, square white Formica table in the middle that was bolted to the floor. Beyond that was a tiny bathroom followed by a cozy bedroom tucked into the front of the boat.

My pappoús had purchased the boat decades ago, and for years our family had enjoyed it for weekend getaways. As we grew older, the boat was mainly used by Pappoús for fishing, but he had given that up as his arthritis progressed.

"Wine?" Case asked, holding out a bottle of cabernet.

"It's a little early, don't you think?"

"Not when family is visiting for Sunday dinner," he joked.

I sighed. "Bring the bottle."

He poured me a glass, took one for himself, and settled onto the sofa. I settled next to him and took a sip of the wine.

Case's arm slid behind my neck, and I let my head fall back against it. "Tell me about your visitor today," he said. "I'm guessing that's your exciting news."

I took another sip of wine. "Her name is Abby Knight Salvare. She and her husband, Marco, have a private detective business in New Chapel, Indiana."

"Where is that?"

"It's about an hour and a half southwest of here. I wrote about New Chapel when I worked for the newspaper in Chicago."

"Why did a private detective come to see you?" Case asked.

"Because she needs our help with a case."

"She needs *our* help? That's surprising."

"Not really. We know this town better than she

does. We know the people. We have connections. Abby seemed to know all about us and the cases we've solved. She and her husband really do their homework."

"Sounds like we may need to do a little homework of our own," he said. "I'll have to look into this detective team, see what kind of history they have." Case reached over for his laptop stuffed between two blue vinyl cushions and opened it up. "What did you say their names were?"

"Abby and Marco Salvare. I think she said it was the Salvare Detective Agency."

Case typed it in, then silently scrolled for a while. "Wow," he finally said. "This news article says that they've solved twenty-four homicide investigations. That's quite a record." He looked up from the screen. "How did they find us?"

"Abby's husband did some research and found articles about the cases we've solved." I took a drink of wine. "They even knew about Pete Harmon."

"Harmon? That news broke yesterday."

"Marco's very good at research," I said. "Sounds a lot like you."

Case continued scrolling through the pages of search engine hits about the private detective team, stopping periodically to read through an article. "Marco was an Army Ranger. Now he owns a bar and runs the detective agency. Interesting."

"And Abby works with flowers. She and I have a lot in common. They're like a version of us from a different town."

"A better version of us," he said.

"Not better. Just more experienced." I finished

my wine and set the glass down, a nervous excitement tingling the tips of my fingers. "What do you think? Do you want to help them with this case? She said they'd pay us the going rate."

"Working with a top-notch detective team would certainly give us legitimacy," he said.

"And experience."

"That, too." Case shut the laptop. "I think we should take it."

"Me, too."

He leaned toward me for a kiss. "We're in business, Goddess."

I leaned back with a relieved sigh. "Abby wants to go see her cousin in jail as soon as possible, so I suggested tomorrow afternoon. I've already called Bob Maguire, and he said he can get us in without having to go through all the red tape. Do you want to go?"

"Absolutely."

"I told Abby I'd meet her at the office at one o'clock."

"Perfect."

"Now, about dinner with my family tonight . . ."

Case scratched his chin. "You know, I think I'll skip dinner and stay here to do research on the murder."

"Seriously?"

"We want to be prepared, right?"

I stood up. "Case, it won't take all evening to read a few news articles, and you can't do any more research than that until we learn more from Jillian."

Case swirled the wine in his glass, watching as it circled the sides.

"And Nicholas will be really disappointed if you don't come."

Finally, he glanced up. "I don't want to sit next to your uncle Giannis."

"You don't have to."

"And I don't want a coffee-grounds reading from Delphi."

"Deal."

"All right. I'll come to dinner." He pulled me back down, practically into his lap. "But I think we should come back here afterward to watch the sunset together."

At the thought of that, my heart fluttered. We kissed for a long moment, then I pulled back to say softly, "I would love that." Before any more kissing derailed my plans, I rose and walked to the door. "See you at five."

At five o'clock on the dot, Uncle Giannis, Aunt Rachel, their sons Drew and Michael, and my aunt Talia and uncle Konstantine arrived, all talking at once. Case showed up shortly afterward, slipping in quietly amid the noisy chatter. Counting the seven of us Spencers, plus Case, Yiayiá, and Pappoús, we were sixteen in all.

Mama, Nicholas, and I had set up two long tables on the patio behind the house and loaded them with food. There was grilled lamb, *pastitsio* (Greek lasagna), two whole chickens roasted with crispy, lemony potatoes, a cucumber, feta cheese, Kalamata olives, and tomato salad.

The temperature outside was perfect, and the open patio gave the family more space to relax and enjoy their dinner. I loved eating outside. It felt less claustrophobic. The loud noises didn't resonate quite as much, and with our family, the noise was inevitable.

While we'd been outside setting up the food, Yiayiá had been in the kitchen finishing the *spanakopita*. They'd been practically falling off the platter when she'd brought them out, so Niko and I had secretly popped a few of the scrumptious little spinach and feta triangle-shaped pastries into our mouths before the rest of the family had arrived.

My mom and dad sat at opposite ends of the long table, Mama closest to the back door for quick access to the kitchen, with my grandmother, whom we called Yiayiá, next to her. I sat at the far end near my father. Case sat next to me, and my son, Nicholas, who now called himself Niko, sat across from me. Delphi was seated farther down, glaring at me.

Because Case had joined us, Delphi was forced to sit next to Uncle Giannis, who had the unseemly habit of talking with his mouth full. I smiled back at her and lifted my shoulders.

"Tell us again how you figured out who murdered the photographer," Uncle Giannis said to Case.

"Actually, it was Athena who figured it out," Case replied.

My mother's voice boomed proudly from the far end of the table. "My daughter the hero."

My dad raised his glass of Greek wine, and we toasted to our success.

"Wouldn't that be the heroine?" Selene called

out. My sisters Maia and Selene were also seated at the far end, so they practically had to yell to be heard.

"Hero, heroine . . ." Mama smiled at me. "She's my brave girl, that's all. Niko, you should be proud of your mama."

Nicholas shoveled a bite of chicken into his mouth, looking alarmed that he was put on the spot. "Very proud," he mumbled.

"So, then tell us," Uncle Giannis said after finishing his first glass of wine. "How did you solve it?"

I gave them a condensed version of the murder investigation, leaving out the part where I was almost choked to death by a camera strap, and hoped that it would settle the topic for the evening. Although my mother was proud, she was also leery of my new private investigation endeavor. I didn't need to give her any more reason to fear it.

"What's next on your agenda, Case?" Aunt Talia asked. "Anything else in the works?"

Case glanced over at me. "Well, we had an inquiry today."

"Already?" Mama asked. "I trust it's nothing dangerous."

"Of course not," I answered, trying to avoid the subject. "Just a simple inquiry."

Delphi's eyes grew wide. "That's why the mysterious redheaded woman came into Spencer's today."

My mother leaned in. "What redheaded woman?" Everyone else quieted.

I shot Delphi a glare and then said as vaguely as possible, "Her name is Abby Knight Salvare. She's a private detective from New Chapel, Indiana, and she wanted to pick my brain on a case she's involved in."

"She wanted to pick your brain?" Mama asked with a lift of one eyebrow.

"She's heard about the cases we've solved," I said and shrugged as though it was no big deal.

"Thenie," Delphi said with a serious glance, "you should know Abby's aura is yellow—a fiery yellow—and that's a very bad sign. It spells danger for her and anyone around her."

"I thought you said you saw a red flame," I said. "Now it's a yellow aura."

"Athena," Mama scolded. "Listen to your sister."

"The red flame was my *vision*," Delphi insisted. "The fiery yellow was her *aura*." She huffed at me. "You still don't understand."

"Delphi," I countered, "Abby is a respected private eye. Of course she's going to encounter some danger in her work, but that doesn't mean this case is dangerous. It's a straightforward investigation."

"Enough talk about danger!" Mama ordered. "The fact of the matter is, Thenie, that you work too hard."

"How did this become about me?" I asked.

"Between the garden center, and Niko, and investigating the photographer's death," Mama said, "and before that, the Talbots and helping Selene, you haven't taken any time off for yourself. John, tell your daughter she's working too hard."

My dad reached over and patted my arm. "Take a little time off, Thenie. Delphi can help out more at the garden center. In fact, the county fair started today. Business always slows down during the fair. Why don't you and Case take Niko? Have some fun."

"Yes," Mama said, now directing her attention toward my new partner. "Case, why don't you take my daughter and her son to the fair?"

Case, who up to that point had managed to keep himself out of the spotlight, finished chewing his roasted lamb and slowly wiped his mouth with a cloth napkin. After resting the napkin back onto his lap, he looked at me. "Sure, why not? When would you like to go?"

Clever. He had quickly turned the conversation back over to me. After looking around at the faces who were now suddenly very interested in my answer, I shrugged. "I'll think about it."

At that, everyone started talking, all chiming in with their ideas of what to do at the fair. Then my grandmother rose from the table, all five-foot-two of her, and banged a serving spoon onto the table-top until all conversation halted.

"Athena," she said in her raspy voice, "you work too hard. I say you must make time for your lover."

My mouth dropped open. I glanced at Case and saw him staring at his plate. Niko giggled. Maia choked on her water. Selene had to cover her mouth, and Pops looked up at the sky. I noticed Delphi giving me a chiding smile.

Mama tugged on my grandmother's arm until she sat down, then Mama said, "What Yiayiá means is that you need to take time for your *loved* ones. Take a break from all this work, go to the fair, spend some quality time with your son. Right, Mama?"

"She heard me," was all Yiayiá would say.

I was so embarrassed I couldn't look at Case. At that moment, I just wanted the ground to swallow me up. The only break in the silence was Uncle Giannis chomping away.

"You have to take Niko on the Ferris wheel," Aunt Talia said from the far end of the table.

"And the Tilt-a-Whirl!" Cousin Drew chimed in.

"I can't do the Tilt-a-Whirl," I said, and pointed to my stomach.

"Then Case can take me on it," my little Nicholas said, beaming at Case.

"You bet, buddy," Case replied.

"Don't forget the Arabian horse show," Uncle Giannis said.

"And elephant ears!" Selene said.

"Caramel corn!" Maia added.

Delphi raised her hand. "How has no one mentioned cotton candy yet?"

"When can we go, Mom?" Nicholas asked. "Tonight?"

"You're better off going in the middle of the week," my mother said. "Less crowded then."

The chatter started again, everyone talking about their favorite parts of the fair, so I resumed eating. I could feel Case's gaze on me, however, and I knew he sensed something was up. I looked down at my food and said nothing, but the truth was, I didn't want to go to the fair.

# CHAPTER TWO

"We still have time to catch the sunset," Case said.

We were standing on the front porch in the evening dusk, light from the nearby windows casting a soft glow around us. The rest of the family were still sitting around the table on the back patio, everyone stuffed to the max after having their fill of baklava and vanilla ice cream.

I rubbed my neck, still feeling the aches and pains from my struggle with a killer just one night before. After a long, covered yawn, I was sure Case didn't need to hear my answer. "I'm sorry," I said. "I'm so tired and full. I just want to crash into bed."

He reached over to massage my shoulders. "I understand. Get some sleep and feel better. But before I go, let's talk about the fair."

"We don't need to go to the fair, Case. That was just my father's suggestion. I'm not actually a fan of the fair. It's always hot and crowded . . . and smelly . . . and who knows if the rides are safe."

"Don't be a stick in the mud, Athena. We need to go for Niko's sake. What child doesn't love the fair? Who can resist an elephant's ear, or hot corn on the cob dripping with butter? My mouth is watering just thinking about it."

"Is this for Niko's sake or for yours?"

"For all three of us. We deserve to have some fun."

I walked to the edge of the porch and stared up at the stars, waging a war in my head. Did I want to go to the fair? Absolutely not. I'd been forced into going with my family every year, even as a teenager. It wasn't just the rides or the food, or the disgusting smells of animals wafting out from the pavilions that had turned me off, but the crowds of people. People everywhere, moving in every direction. People staring at me and bumping into one another. It made my nerves sizzle.

Did I appreciate the pressure from my family and Case? Not one bit. I was Nicholas's mom. I should be the one who decided whether to go. But how could I ignore the hopeful look in my son's eyes? How could I ignore my family? Or Case? My conscience said I couldn't.

Case came up behind me and put his arm around my shoulders. "It's just one night."

With a resigned sigh, I said, "You're right. I owe it to Nicholas."

Case lifted my chin with his fingertip. "It'll be fun, our first fair together. Come on. Don't look so sad."

I forced a smile. "Is that better?"

"I think a kiss would be even better than that."

He dipped his head down, and his lips met mine, softly and tenderly, for a long minute. He pulled back and smiled at me, touching the tip of my nose. "Now, go back and tell Niko we're going to the fair this week. He'll be overjoyed."

"Thanks," I said. "I'm sorry for being such a bummer tonight. And I'm sorry if my grandmother embarrassed you."

He leaned over for one more kiss. "Maybe she was right."

As I watched Case drive away, I had a sudden inspiration for my blog, so I jogged straight upstairs and went to my room to write it.

For the past several months, I'd been writing a daily blog anonymously, mainly because the topic was usually family related and I didn't want them to know I was skewering them. I'd developed a large following over those months, including my mom, my sisters, and even my dad. Unfortunately, my dad had accidentally stumbled upon the fact that the blogger was me, and Delphi suspected as much, but neither one had given me up. The rest of the clan were convinced it was someone within the Greek community, and it had become a topic of discussion at my grandparents' diner in the mornings. So I purposely made the blog topics vague so my identity would remain anonymous.

So far, so good.

I opened my laptop and began.

### IT'S ALL GREEK TO ME
*Blog by Goddess Anon*

*Oh, That Family!*

> "There's nothing that makes you more insane
> than family. Or more happy. Or more exasper-
> ated. Or more . . . secure."—Jim Butcher

*I don't know who Jim Butcher is, but he sure hit the nail on the head. Families know exactly the right thing to say or do to exasperate you. They also know how to make you laugh—and drive you nuts, something I experienced just recently when we butted heads on a personal matter. What it comes down to is this: Does my family really know what's best for me? Do I trust my family enough to go against my own instincts?*

*I guess the whole "who's right" dilemma depends on how I'm feeling at that particular moment, and my most recent experience with a family decision did not leave me feeling very happy, even though I knew what they were pushing me to do would ultimately be in my best interests. Still, there are times when you have to go with your gut feeling no matter what the family thinks, if only for your own peace of mind.*

*With that said, however, there is security in being with a family that loves me so intimately and deeply that they would risk my ire. Even if they drive me batty, they are still my family, and I would be lost without them.*

*May I never take them for granted.*
*This is Goddess Anon bidding you* antio sas.

\* \* \*

*Monday*

The morning started out the way mornings usually did, with a stop at my grandparents' diner, the Parthenon, for breakfast. When Nicholas and I arrived, my sister Maia was sitting at a booth, with my mom looking over her shoulder, both reading something on Maia's laptop. Delphi sat beside Maia, staring at her phone.

Mama glanced around, saw us, and waved us over. I paused in front of the kitchen's pass-through window to say good morning to my grandparents.

"*Tí kánis?*" I called. How are you?

My grandmother shrugged. "Well enough." My grandfather gave me a thumbs-up.

My mom was wearing her standard hostess outfit—a blue blouse "the color of the Ionian Sea" with black slacks and flats and her stack of gold bracelets. All the waitresses wore the same color blouses with black skirts or slacks, complementing the blue background of the Parthenon's murals. Each of the two side walls had a huge Greek mural on it, one of the Parthenon itself, the other of the Acropolis.

Deep-red booths lined the dark golden walls, and ancient black-and-white linoleum covered the floor. The long, faded yellow lunch counter with its red leather–cushioned stools separated the diner into two halves, each side with booths and tables that were almost full. Behind the yellow counter was the wide pass-through window that always showed Yiayiá and Pappoús hard at work in the galley kitchen at the back.

"Hello, my little Niko," my mother crooned, "my

little *glykiá mou.*" My sweetie. She hugged him and then turned to give me a peck on the cheek. "*Kaliméra,* Thenie."

"Good morning to you, too, Mama," I said, and slid into the booth beside Nicholas. "I'll have a bowl of oatmeal," I told her

"An egg and cheese *omeletta,*" Nicholas said, using my grandfather's word for omelet.

"I've already put your orders in," Mama said, then slid into the booth beside Maia, putting her directly across from me. "You need to read Goddess Anon's blog today, Thenie," she said. "It's all about the importance of family."

"Actually," I said, "I read it this morning."

My two younger sisters looked up from their screens. Maia spoke first. "You actually read the blog?"

"That's a first," Delphi added.

Mama raised her eyebrow. "And?"

"And I thought it made a good point about a person being able to decide things for herself."

"But ultimately, the family decision is what's for the best," Mama argued.

"What about you, Mama?" I asked her. "Do you decide things for yourself, or do you wait for a group decision?"

Mama stared at me for a moment, clearly caught off guard. "Well," she said at last, "I suppose I decide for myself. But what Goddess Anon was ultimately saying was that family decisions come out of love."

"Even though they may be misguided," I added.

Mama scowled at me, then rose from the table and came back with the coffeepot to fill my mug.

"Have you given any more thought to taking some time off?"

"Yes," I said. "Don't worry. We're going to take Nicholas to the fair."

"But now you're working with this redheaded woman on a new case. How does that leave time for other things?"

"Mama," I said with exasperation, "I have time to work on a case and work at Spencer's, too."

"Leaving little time for your son," she fired back.

"Not true!" I replied.

"Mom," Nicholas said in a whisper, "you and Yiayiá are getting loud."

"Sorry, Niko," I said, and put my arm around his shoulders. "Thanks for the heads-up."

Instead of letting it drop, Maia asked, "So, Thenie, what kind of case is it?"

It was the question I'd been hoping no one would ask. I knew Mama would not be pleased.

"It's a murder investigation," I said.

"The model's murder?" my mother instantly asked.

Our food came then, so I waited until the waitress had gone to say, "Yes."

"You know Eleni Papadakis is involved," Mama said. "*Our* Eleni."

"It's Eleni Sloan now," I corrected. "She's married to Mayor Sloan, remember?"

"You know what I mean," Mama said. "She's one of us. You shouldn't get involved."

I paused with a spoonful of oatmeal in front of my mouth. "Because she's Greek?"

"It wouldn't look right," Mama said.

"I've investigated several members of the Greek Merchants Association, and you had no problem with that. What other excuse are you going to use?"

Mama huffed. "I still say you're stretching yourself too thin. Let Delphi take over some of your duties at Spencer's."

"Hey!" Delphi said. "I already do a lot. Besides, Bobby and I have started ballroom dance lessons, so I'll have to leave early some days."

Mama turned her full attention to her youngest daughter, whose wide-eyed expression relayed a sudden realization of her mistake. Never give Mama information unless you want it dissected. "Dance lessons! Why do you want to take dance lessons?"

Delphi shrugged. "We want to learn how to dance."

"Do we need a family vote on that?" I asked, purposely being snarky.

Mama frowned at me. "Don't get smart, young lady. I think Delphi can make her own decision."

"Exactly my point," I said. "Some things don't need a family to decide."

With a huff, my mother got up and left. The rest of us finished our breakfasts in pleasant silence.

After we'd eaten, Nicholas and I stopped by the pass-through to pick up two breakfasts to go, one for my dad and one for my cousin Drew. We walked the four blocks down Greene Street to Spencer's and went inside through the big red doors into what used to be a large barn. The doors had been retrofitted with large glass windows, making the entrance more inviting, and there were long windows across the front and sides of the store. This allowed a generous amount of natural light into the garden center and made the statue of Athena shine in the entryway.

My grandfather, Sam Spencer, had taken the old barn and transformed it with a new arched ceiling, lots of windows, fresh paint on the walls, and aisles for all the gardening supplies anyone could ever want. Besides the gardening supplies, Spencer's had flower and vegetable plants, and all the way at the back, sets of patio furniture, including a long oak-plank table we used for the Greek Merchants Association meetings that met monthly at Spencer's.

Directly in front of us was the statue, *Treasure of Athena,* who beckoned to everyone who walked in the door. To the left was the checkout counter, and behind it was a door that led to the office. A short hallway led to a bathroom, conference room, and kitchenette, where we ate our lunches in inclement weather. Otherwise, we took our food out the back door into the open patio area, a large cement pad outlined by a string of white lights and swaying paper lanterns where more outdoor furniture was displayed. There was also an outdoor cabinet for supplies, including a jar of peanuts and a few shiny toys we kept on hand for Oscar, the baby raccoon who'd been abandoned by his mother.

Beyond the patio area were rows of shrubs, roses, large landscape plants, and saplings, filling the one-acre space all the way back to the white picket fence. The fence separated Spencer's from a lane that ran behind all the shops on Greene Street and was where the trash containers were kept.

I found my cousin Drew unpacking a box of rose fertilizer and handed him his breakfast container. Drew was a hard worker, full of pep and energy, although his stomach was seemingly bottomless. He quickly dropped the fertilizer and popped open the lid.

"Wash your hands first," I told him.

I left Nicholas there to help Drew, then headed back to the office to find my father.

The office was a generously sized room filled with a big oak desk, two wooden chairs that faced the desk, a console table against the opposite wall that held a Keurig coffee machine, and a minifridge for coffee creamer, water, and snacks. My father was sitting at the desk drinking his morning coffee, so I set his breakfast container down and went to make myself a cup.

"I smell pancakes and sausage," Dad said, pulling the container toward him.

"That was for Drew," I said. "You get grapefruit and toast. You know what the doctor told you."

He looked inside the foam container and then closed it again. "I wasn't hungry anyway." He turned back toward the computer and moved the mouse. "Interesting topic in your blog today."

"Pops, be careful. Delphi will be here any minute."

"I thought you said she knew about your secret identity."

"She thought she knew, but then when I confirmed it, she accused me of trying to trick her."

He moved the mouse again. "There," he said. "It's closed. And I got the point of your blog."

"Good, because Mama didn't get it."

My dad leaned back in the swivel desk chair. "Thenie, it's your decision, of course, but your mother had a point, too. You can and should take some time off. Delphi can certainly do more around here."

"Thanks, Pops. And actually, I may need more time off for this case. It's a big one, with high-profile people involved."

"I was just reading an article about the murder in the news this morning. The mayor's wife, Eleni Sloan, is one of the high-profile people, I believe, as is the police chief's wife."

"Yep. They were the other two models in the fashion show. And because Eleni Sloan is involved, Mama is not happy about me helping with the case."

"I believe it. She and Eleni grew close when Eleni was the chair of the GMA."

"Well, she's just going to have to get over it. I'm not going to tell Abby Knight that I can't work with her because my mother isn't happy. And I'm not going to start making my decisions based on what the family thinks I should do, either."

"Thenie, don't get so worked up. No one is trying to run your life. We're just suggesting you take a little time away from work. Take Niko to the fair. Have some fun. Life is too short to work yourself to death."

"I get that, Pops. Don't worry. I'll take a step back here at Spencer's as long as you trust Delphi to take over some of my duties. But I'm still going to do investigative work."

"Mom?"

I turned to see my son poking his head through

the doorway. "Drew said there was something here for me. Hi, Grandpops."

"Morning, Niko," my dad said. "Yes, there is something here for you." He reached for a plastic grocery bag on the desktop. "Elissa Reed dropped this off for you early this morning."

Nicholas opened the bag, and his eyes lit up. "She found it!" He pulled out a bright yellow rubber dog bone that rattled when shaken. "This is Oscar's favorite. I'll have to go show him. Thanks, Grandpops!"

Nicholas scooted out the door and took off for the back patio. Oscar's toys had started to disappear after Nicholas introduced his new friend, Denis Reed, to our adolescent raccoon, who had made his home in the garden center out back. Unfortunately, Denis was so envious of Nicholas having a pet raccoon that he began taking Oscar's toys, wanting to adopt a raccoon of his own. Elissa had apparently just discovered another missing toy and brought it back.

My dad checked his wristwatch. "Looks like I'd better turn over the computer to you and get ready to open for the day. And don't give a thought to Delphi taking over some of your duties. She's a lot more competent than she lets on."

I took a sip of coffee and sat down at the big desk, opening the accounting app on the computer. I paused for a moment to reflect on all the changes in Spencer's since I'd moved back home. I'd convinced my dad to hire Cousin Drew for the summer to handle the extra business we always had from May through September, I'd rearranged the store's aisles to be more practical, and I'd accessorized the outdoor furniture area to stage the setting for potential buyers. And though I'd also taken over the accounting and purchasing end of the business, and worked with customers on landscape design, none of my duties had been enough to keep my curious mind occupied.

Working on murder investigations with Case had been a godsend. But I had been putting in some very long days doing both jobs recently. Maybe I could step back with no guilt. Maybe Delphi would step up and surprise me. And maybe, just maybe, I'd actually enjoy going to the fair.

At ten minutes before one o'clock, I paused outside the redbrick building at 535 Greene Street and glanced up at the sign that now hung suspended from the brick: *The Greene St. Detective Agency*. Heaving a happy sigh, I opened the door between two businesses, the Greene Street Deli and Majestic Jewelers, and proceeded up the stairs to the second floor.

I stopped in front of a door with a frosted glass pane and turned the handle. The door opened onto a reception area furnished with a sleek gray modern desk and a row of gray chairs facing the desk. To the right of the reception area were two offices side by side. The first office was Case's and had a window that looked down on Greene Street. The second office was identical to the first and was mine. My office was furnished in light oak and Case's in a rich dark walnut wood.

"Hi," I said, standing in Case's doorway. He sat

at his desk with his back to the window, facing his computer monitor. He glanced over the top of the monitor and smiled. "Come on in."

"You look busy."

He smiled. "We just got another job."

"Really?" I joined Case in front of his computer to read the email he had pulled up.

"There's a new company opening up in Sauga-tuck," he said, "a big operation, and the CEO wants me to do background checks on people applying for management positions."

"That's great, Case! Two jobs in two days. When do you start?"

"Well," he said gently, "that's the bad news. I have to travel to Saugatuck this morning, so I won't be able to go to the jail with you."

I sat down, surprised by the news. "That's almost two hours away. When will you be back?"

"It's more like an hour and twenty minutes, and I'll be back today. I just don't know when. Why, are you concerned?"

"I'm not concerned."

"Really? Because your face is telling a whole different story."

"I need your help, Case. I'm not the professional. You are."

"What are you worried about? Abby will be with you."

"Exactly, and she's counting on both of us to help her with this case."

Case sat back in his chair. "Is that why she came to see me first at the detective agency?"

"She did?"

"No," Case answered, smiling. "She came to the garden center to see you. The Goddess of Greene Street."

A knock at the outer door made us pause.

"Maybe that's Abby now," I said. "And I get your point. I just feel more comfortable when you're around."

"I wouldn't have taken the second job if I didn't have complete faith in you," Case said, rising from his seat.

We walked out of his office into the reception area, leaving our conversation unfinished. Case opened the door to find Lila Talbot leaning against a large, ornate oak frame, breathing heavily.

"Did you carry that all the way up here?" I asked, as Case picked it up and moved it into the reception area.

"I practically dragged it," she said, following us inside. "I didn't realize how heavy it was until I got it out of the van."

Case set the four-foot-tall frame next to the painting leaning against the wall behind the reception desk. The painting was a rendering of the Statue of Athena that Elissa Reed had painted for the Save the Dunes art auction. Lila had outbid everyone and graciously donated the painting to our business.

"It should hang right there," Lila said, pointing to the large bare space above the reception desk. "It'll be the first thing people see when they walk in." She reached into her oversized purse and pulled out a tape measure, a small hammer, and a package of picture hangers. "I came prepared."

Lila was a spoiled, forty-year-old former beauty pageant winner and drama queen who had been married to Grayson Talbot Jr., the wealthiest man in Sequoia, who was now cooling his heels in jail. Of medium height with blond hair that she wore in a high, swinging ponytail during the day and long and silky at night, Lila was dressed in her usual tight T-shirt and yoga pants, today's outfit in neon pink and black. Because of a generous divorce settlement, Lila was now the wealthiest woman in town and had bankrolled our detective agency. In return, she asked to be included in our investigations, which sometimes, but not always, worked to our advantage.

"Abby's going to be here any minute," I said, as Case measured the wall.

"Five minutes is all we need," Lila countered.

Case fitted the painting into the frame and nailed it in place. He marked two spots on the wall and pounded in the picture hangers. Then Lila and I hoisted the painting up while Case guided its placement on the hangers. I had to contort my body to squeeze behind the frame to make adjustments.

"To the left!" Lila commanded. "To the left!"

"It's as far to the left as I can get it," I called.

"Just a little more," Lila said.

I pushed my body farther behind the frame and pulled the metal wire with all my might. My back muscles tensed, and my backside stuck out toward the front door just as I heard someone knock.

"Hello," I heard from behind.

I pulled myself free of the canvas and felt my

cheeks flush. "Come in, Abby," I called. "We're almost done."

We maneuvered the metal loops on the back of the painting onto the picture hangers, then as Lila and Case worked to straighten it, Abby stood beside me studying the painting.

"It's beautiful," she said. "The artist certainly did the statue justice."

"Thank you!" Lila said with a smile. "That's why I bought it." She dusted off her hands and extended one. "Hi, I'm Lila Talbot, Case and Athena's partner. I don't believe we've met."

"Abby Knight Salvare," Abby said, taking her hand.

"What can we do for you, Abby?" Lila asked.

"I've come to ask for your help."

Lila's eyes widened. "*My* help?"

"Our help," I corrected.

Lila looked at Case. "Do we have a new client?"

"We do." Case put an arm around Lila's shoulders. "Come with me," he said, leading her into his office. "I'll explain everything."

# CHAPTER THREE

As Abby and I left the office and headed for the jail, she said, "What a charming town. And this is the famous Greene Street."

"Famous?"

"Aren't you the Goddess of Greene Street?"

I blushed. "It's just a nickname Case gave me. I guess it stuck."

"Deservedly. Marco and I read about the double murder case you solved that earned you that title. We also learned that Case had been suspected of the murders and you cleared his name. Well done!"

"Thanks," I said. "But it doesn't compare to all the cases you've solved."

"It's just helping innocent people stand up for themselves. That's what we do."

We cut down a side street over to White and proceeded to the jail, chatting about our lives and how our towns compared, until we came to the big brick building that housed the jail.

"This is it," I said.

Abby sized it up and took a deep breath. "Let's do it."

Inside the four-story redbrick building we stopped at the bulletproof-glass window to state our purpose. We had to slide our IDs through the opening, put our purses and cell phones in a locker, then pass through a metal detector. Fortunately, they let me take my iPad with me.

We were escorted into a wide, white-walled room that contained a long gray Formica counter, a clear plastic partition that separated the visitor side from the inmate side, and a row of black vinyl chairs with half walls dividing each cubicle. Large holes had been cut in the middle of the clear plastic partition for conversation. We sat down in one cubicle and waited for Jillian to arrive. We were the only visitors in the room.

Within a few minutes, a jail guard ushered her in. A tall beauty with long, copper-colored hair and a sprinkling of freckles across her nose, Jillian had the same green eyes and heart-shaped face her cousin had. She sat down in a black chair and leaned forward on her hands, looking pale in her orange jumpsuit. "When am I getting out of here?"

"Your lawyer will be here"—I checked my watch—"any minute now. He can tell you what's going to happen next. We wanted time to talk to you first."

"This is Athena Spencer," Abby said. "She and her partner, Case, own a detective agency here in Sequoia. Athena knows her town. She has connections that are going to help us."

"Thank heaven for that," Jillian said with a sigh. "I have to get home to my little angel."

"Jillian," I said, redirecting her attention, "your attorney's name is Kevin Coreopsis. He's smart and professional, and I think you'll like him. I've worked with him in the past."

I didn't mention that Kevin and I had recently dated. My mother had set us up, and it hadn't gone well. Kevin had been looking for something serious, and I'd had no intention of getting involved with anyone. I also didn't mention that Kevin had once worked for Grayson Talbot Jr., the man I'd helped put in prison after he'd tried to bury me under a building. Since then, Kevin had made up for his wrongdoings and we'd managed to work together amicably, so there was no reason to muddy up the waters with that little piece of info.

"You can't begin to understand what I've been through," Jillian said to her cousin. "I was questioned for hours!"

"I'm so sorry, Jill," Abby said. "I'm doing everything I can to prevent that from happening again."

"You know what I need right now?" Jillian asked. "A hug."

"I wish I could give you one," Abby said.

Jillian plucked at her shirt. "Can you believe this horrid outfit? Orange is definitely not my color."

Abby and I laughed at that.

Jillian frowned. "It wasn't a joke."

Abby looked at me. "Do you want to start?"

I gazed at her in surprise. "You want *me* to start?"

"Sure."

"Um. Okay." I didn't want to seem nervous, but I was. After learning about Abby Knight and her record of solving crimes, I suddenly felt out of my league questioning her cousin.

I retrieved my iPad and opened a new Word file labeled *Jillian.* "Why don't you start by describing your movements from the time you arrived at the Waterfront's ballroom until the show started?"

"My movements?" Jillian asked.

"Where were you before the show started?" Abby explained.

Jillian leaned back in her chair, more relaxed now. "Oh. I was in my hotel room."

"After that, Jill," Abby said, "describe what you did when you left your room. Be specific."

"Okay. My hotel room was on the third floor, so I took the elevator to the ground floor and headed to the ballroom at the rear of the building. The runway was already set up, so I circled it, walked up a small flight of stairs, and went backstage through a big curtain."

I typed diligently, trying to squeeze every detail in as quickly as Jillian spit them out. Abby waited a moment before continuing. "Describe the back-stage area."

"There were three dressing rooms off to the left side, not even dressing rooms, really, just little wooden, curtained boxes with dirty tilting mirrors and folding chairs inside. It was very low-rent."

"What did you do next?" I asked.

"I grabbed three water bottles and set them on the chairs inside the dressing rooms for the mod-els, just like I did the first night."

After typing her words, I looked up at her through the glass. "The first night?"

Jillian nodded. "The fashion show took place

over two nights. Carly died on the second night. Thursday night."

I made a note. *Fashion show was two nights. Carly poisoned on second night.*

"Was anyone else around when you set out the water bottles?" Abby asked.

Jillian thought for a moment. "There were hotel staff setting up the tables in the ballroom."

"What about backstage?" Abby asked.

"There was a sound technician behind the curtain when I first got there. I remember him because he asked me to test the microphone. And then the woman in charge of the fashion show came through the backstage door and said hello to me. Her name was Fran."

"Fran Decker," I told them, typing it into the iPad. "She's the chairwoman of the Small Business Association. They're the ones who put on the show."

"Why was Fran backstage?" Abby asked.

"She was bringing in the wardrobes," Jillian said. "There was a long metal rack standing behind the dressing rooms where all the clothes were hung. She said she was there to help the women adjust their outfits if they needed it."

"And the models weren't there yet?" Abby asked.

"No. Not at that time," Jillian answered.

I noted it and added, "What about the water bottles? Where did you get them?"

"I stopped at a little market and purchased a small case."

"Why do you bring water with you?" Abby asked.

Jillian shrugged. "Just to be nice, I guess. It gets hot under the stage lights. From my experience, models often refuse to eat before the show, but they appreciate the water."

"Was it a new case?" I asked. "Did it look tampered with in any way?"

"My bottle was a pain to open," Jillian said, "so I would say it was a brand-new case. No tampering."

"What did you do after you put the water into the dressing rooms?" Abby asked.

"I went out into the ballroom and sat at one of the empty tables. There was plenty of time to spare, so I had a video chat with Harper and Claymore, just like I did on the first night."

"Harper is her little girl," Abby explained to me. "Claymore is her husband."

I added their names to my notes. "What did you do with the remaining water bottles?"

"I only brought three with me," Jillian answered. "I left the remaining three bottles in my hotel room for the second night."

"Let's focus on the second night," I continued, "the night of Carly's murder. When you put the water in the dressing rooms, was anyone in the immediate vicinity?"

"No one was near the dressing rooms. But on the second night, one of the models came in early."

"How early?" Abby asked.

"I had just sat down to call Harper. So maybe forty-five minutes early?"

"Do you remember which model?" I asked.

Jillian cocked her head, thinking. "Eleni? She had dark hair with dark eye-makeup and tanned skin."

"That sounds like Eleni," I said.

"Did she go straight to her dressing room?" Abby asked.

"She went backstage. That's all I know."

"And the other two models came in while you were on your FaceTime call, right?" Abby asked.

"Right. About fifteen minutes after Eleni arrived, I saw the petite blond woman walk in. She was wearing heels that were way too high and blond extensions that didn't really match her hair color."

"That must be Hope Louvain," I told them.

"Yes, her name was Hope," Jillian said. "She was a fashion disaster from head to toe."

"Did Hope go backstage?" Abby asked.

Jillian nodded. "She almost tripped going up the little staircase on the side of the stage. I was worried she would trip during the show."

"What about Carly Blackburn?" Abby asked. "When did she come in?"

"I didn't see Carly come in." Jillian's eyes lit up. "But I did see her leave the stage a little while later. She stomped down the stairs, shouting into her cell phone. It sounded like a heated argument. Maybe that has something to do with the murder."

Abby watched as I typed in the information, then asked, "Do you know whom she was arguing with on the phone?"

Jillian shook her head. "She left the ballroom, so I have no idea." She leaned forward to say in a whisper, "I didn't even recognize Carly when she showed up the first night. She used to have this beautiful complexion with a thick head of dark amber hair, but her hair looked much thinner, and her skin was caked with makeup. I remember thinking how she hadn't aged well."

"So, you knew Carly before?" I asked.

"Yes. We went to Harvard at the same time. Abby, do you remember the sorority I wanted to join?"

"No, Jill. I don't."

"Well, Carly thought I was trying to flirt with her boyfriend, which wasn't true. *He* was flirting with *me*. But anyway, that started a whole big fight between us, and she managed to blackball me from the sorority. We never spoke after that."

Which meant there was bad blood between them, a convenient motive for the prosecutor. "Did you ever see Carly after your college years?" I asked.

"Not at all."

"Did you tell anyone about your feud with Carly?" Abby asked.

Jillian didn't answer her cousin right away. She sat sheepishly in her orange jumpsuit, tapping her fingers together.

"You did, didn't you?" Abby said.

"I might have mentioned something to Hope on the first night. I was stewing when I realized I would be working with Carly, and Hope seemed very eager to hear my story. I didn't think it was a big deal at the time."

I typed it in, then asked, "When did you distribute the water bottles on the night of the murder?"

"Oh, at least an hour before the show started on both nights."

Abby glanced at me. "That would have given someone enough time to get into the dressing room and tamper with the water before the show began." She turned to her cousin. "Jill, are you sure you saw Carly leave the backstage area?"

"Yes," Jillian said confidently. "About half an hour before the show started. I remember because I was curious as to whom she could've been arguing with."

"Did you see Carly return to the stage?" I asked.

Jillian shook her head. "After I finished my phone call with Harper, people started showing up to take their seats in the audience. I didn't really notice much after that, but I do know that all the models were in their dressing rooms fifteen minutes before the show started. That's when I went backstage to go over my notes."

"When Carly left the stage," I asked, "was she carrying a water bottle with her?"

"Um, she might've been, but I didn't notice."

"If Carly took a drink of her water before she left the stage," Abby said, "the poison could've had roughly half an hour to get into her system. What we need to know is what kind of poison it was and whether that was enough time for it to work. Otherwise, she might have been poisoned before she left home."

"Wouldn't she have been able to taste the poison?" I asked.

"Some poisons are tasteless. That's another question we need answered."

"I can call my contact on the police force," I told her, "and ask him to check the detective's file to find out."

"That would be very helpful." Abby turned to her cousin. "Walk us through what happened. How was Carly found?"

"I don't know," Jillian answered. "I was on stage waiting for her to come out, and someone cried out to call 911."

"Why did you call 911 if you were onstage?" Abby asked.

"Because no one else did. It was like everyone was polarized."

Abby paused. "Polarized?"

"No one was moving," Jillian explained.

Abby put her hand out for me to stop writing. "She means paralyzed."

"No," Jill insisted. "Frozen, like the North Pole."

Abby rolled her eyes at her cousin's remark and smiled at me. "Just write paralyzed."

"Well, they were frozen," Jillian continued. "Even when I ran backstage, no one was moving. Eleni was bent over Carly's body, and Hope was standing next to them."

"Did you get a close look at Carly?" Abby asked.

"Not a close look, no. But I saw her. She was curled into a ball. Her eyes were wide, and it looked like she'd thrown up. It was awful."

"I'm sorry, Jill," Abby said.

Jillian dropped her head. "Why do they think I did it?"

A female guard approached the cubicle. "There's an attorney here to see Jillian, but only two people are allowed in here at a time."

"I'll leave," I said. I finished typing my notes and slid the iPad into my purse.

"I'll take more notes if I learn anything else," Abby said. "Do you want to meet up later to discuss plans?"

"Sure," I answered. "At the office?"

"Why don't you come over to the Waterfront Hotel and check out the ballroom?" Abby suggested. "There's supposed to be a beauty pageant tomorrow, so the stage is still set up."

"That sounds like a plan."

"Thank you, Athena," Jillian said with a brave smile. "I think you and my cousin will make a good team."

I smiled back at her. I hoped she was right.


Spencer's was slow when I got back, so I called Case with a progress report. But after a few rings, I got his voice mail. I figured he was busy in Saugatuck, so I didn't leave a message. I stepped into the office to find Delphi sitting behind the desk with her feet up, drinking a cup of coffee.

"Is this what happens when I'm not around?" I asked.

"Relax," she said. "There's nothing to do."

"Then why did I see Dad out front washing the windows?"

She put her feet down and sat forward. "He is?"

"Delphi, I really am going to need you to take over some of my responsibilities here," I said, filling my coffee mug. "I'm going to be putting in more time than I thought on this new case, and you can't let Dad do all the work."

"What do you want me to do?"

"Order inventory, organize the daily receipts, keep Niko busy, close up shop if Dad's busy, and make sure the barn stays neat and tidy."

"That's a lot of work," she said, blowing steam from her mug.

"Trust me, it's not that bad."

"I can't close up every night," she explained. "Bobby and I have dance lessons on some evenings."

"How about tonight?"

Delphi sipped her coffee for a minute, thinking. "I can close tonight, but I'll only agree to that as long as you let me give Abby a reading."

I sat across from Delphi, who seemed strangely comfortable behind my desk, and countered, "Abby might not want a reading."

"It'll be her decision, of course," my sister said. "Just don't try to talk her out of it. Oh, and one more thing. You can't judge me on how I handle your responsibilities. I'll do them the best I know how. Okay?"

"Fine. Just make sure everything runs smoothly."

Delphi smiled. "I can do that."

As soon as she left, I took her place behind the desk and used my cell phone to put in a call to Bob Maguire.

"I'm on duty," he said, "so I have to make this quick. What can I do for you?"

"I'm working on a new case, Bob, with a private investigator from New Chapel. Her cousin Jillian was the emcee at the SBA fashion show last Thursday when Carly Blackburn was killed."

"I know all about the case. I was the one who had to go pick Jillian up in Indiana. She's a chatty one, that girl, and also kind of mean. She called me Officer Stringbean."

I had to suppress a chuckle. I'd known Bob since high school, when he was the class clown, a tall beanpole of a kid with orange-red hair and ears that stuck out. So, I completely understood the nickname. I could also understand Jillian's frustration. Being picked up by the police is embarrassing at best.

Bob continued, "I'm assuming you want me to do something to put my job at risk so you can solve the case and become a hero. Does that sound about right?"

He had a point. "Actually, I was just wondering if you could find out what kind of poison was used to murder Carly."

"Oh, is that all?" Maguire asked facetiously. "You know what you're asking me to do, right?"

"Bob, I understand it's risky, but I really need your help on this. Just find out the name of the poison, and that's it."

"In other words, you want me to sneak into Detective Walters's office and read through his case file."

"Is that the only way?" I asked.

He sighed. "Let me ask around, see what I can do."

"Thanks, Bob. I really appreciate it. Have fun at your dance practice." I waited for his answer, but there was silence on the other end of the phone. "Bob?" I looked at my phone to see if the call had ended, then put it back to my ear. "Officer Stringbean?"

"How did you find out about dance practice?" he asked finally.

"Delphi told me."

I heard another long sigh. "Is that all she told you?"

"Yes. Why? Is there something else I should know?"

He cleared his throat and answered, "Nope."

"What's wrong? Are you not enjoying your lessons?"

"Let's just say I have two left feet, and I'm not proud of it. But Delphi is loving it, and that means a lot."

"You're a champ, Bob. Thanks for everything. And if you feel like it's too risky to find that information, I understand."

I hung up with him and went to the sales floor to see that things were quiet, so I went back into the office and placed another call to Case. This time he answered.

"Hey, are you still in Saugatuck?"

"On my way back now," he answered. "Good news. I can do most of my work from the office, so I can still help with the investigation."

"That is good news!"

"How was the jail visit?" he asked. "What did I miss?"

"It was interesting. I learned there were four people backstage before the fashion show, not including Abby's cousin Jillian. One of them was the victim. The others will all need to be interviewed."

"Three suspects?"

"That's what it seems," I said. "Also, I'm going to meet up with Abby after dinner this evening to check out the venue. She said it's set up for a beauty pageant, so it should be similar to the fashion show event. We're meeting at six thirty at the Waterfront Hotel. Do you want to come?"

"You bet. I can swing by and pick you up at six fifteen."

"It's a date. Oh, I almost forgot. I just called Maguire and asked him to find out what kind of poison was used. He seemed reluctant to help."

"Of course, he was," Case said. "Giving out sensitive information could be detrimental to his career."

"But he's done it before."

Case laughed. "Yep, when he was trying to impress the family. Now that he's secured a relationship with Delphi, I'm sure he's more concerned with keeping his job."

"He said he would look into it."

"Why don't we go see Detective Walters ourselves and see what he'll divulge? Now that we have our license, maybe he'll help us out."

I didn't have the best relationship with Detective Walters. He was a good detective, but he was stubborn and sometimes a little too quick to close cases. I understood Case's point, though. It wasn't fair to continue pressuring Bob. "I guess it wouldn't hurt to try."

"We can go tomorrow whenever you can take a break from work."

"I asked Delphi to take over some of my responsibilities, so I can go anytime. How about noon?"

"Sounds great," he said. "What are you up to this afternoon?"

"Well, Delphi is closing the store tonight, so I'll work here at Spencer's until it's time to take Niko home. You can pick me up at the house."

"Don't work too hard," he joked. "I'll see you this evening."

* * *

Case picked me up in his newly purchased dark-green Jeep at six fifteen. I climbed in through the opening—he had removed the doors—and buckled myself in, double-checking the seat belt. I looked over at him, saw his mouth curl up at the corners, and returned his smile. Even though I hated the fact that his Jeep had no doors and was still convinced that I could fall out at any sudden turn, I did enjoy the ride, and he knew it.

I tucked my long hair behind my ears and checked the mirror only to discover that my lipstick looked dull, and the blush seemed to have faded from my cheeks.

Case gave my knee a quick squeeze. "You look beautiful as always."

I felt a blush return. Case was so good for my ego. "Thanks."

On the drive to the Waterfront Hotel, I couldn't help but recollect one of our recent cases, which happened to involve the hotel owner's son and daughter, twins Mitchell and Mandy Black. Spoiled, selfish, and perfectly suntanned, Mandy had been one of our top suspects in the scandalous murder of her groom-to-be. After accusing my sister Selene of the crime, Mandy had spent most of her grieving period at the hotel's luxurious pool sunbathing with her bridesmaids. She had eventually been cleared of the crime and had even helped us solve it by handing over a key piece of evidence, undermining the stringent demands of her overprotective brother.

Her twin brother, Mitchell, was the general manager of the hotel and had also been a strong suspect in the murder case. Exceedingly clever and as pale as could possibly be, Mitchell was the complete opposite of Mandy. His manner was stiff, his speech elitist, and his fuse was extra short. Mitchell had eventually been cleared of the crime as well, but not before Case had all but accused him of the murder. Because of that, he had banned Case and me from the hotel, promising to call the police if we ever set foot on the property again.

Thinking back to that now, it gave me pause. "Do you think Mitchell will give us any problems?" I asked as Case squeezed the Jeep into a tight parking spot. Given that the vehicle had no doors, he didn't need much room to park.

"I was just wondering the same thing."

"We haven't been back since your swan dive into the pool to avoid him," I said.

"Maybe he's not working here anymore. From what I recall, he wasn't doing a very good job managing the place. And it's not like he needs the money."

I checked the passenger mirror again, pinched my cheeks, and combed out my hair with my fingers.

Case sighed. "Athena, you look perfect."

I laughed. "Right. Perfectly windblown."

He took my hand. "You seem self-conscious today. What's going on?"

After a brief pause to consider his question, I pushed the visor back into place and looked over at him. "Abby's just so put together."

"And you're not?"

"She's got that beautiful red hair with the cute bob, and she can get away with wearing bold, bright colors. Then there's me, with my boring, straight hair and my khakis and white button-down. I just feel drab in comparison."

"No one's comparing you."

I unbuckled the seat belt. "I am."

"Well, stop it."

Easy for him to say.

I climbed out of the Jeep and met up with Case as we walked toward the hotel entrance. The sweet-smelling, cool, conditioned air burst out around us as the automatic doors opened. We stepped inside and glanced around. The hotel was just as elegant as I'd remembered. A large golden chandelier hung from the high ceiling over the reception hall. Behind the counter was a tall glass waterfall, filling the room with the relaxing sound of flowing water, accompanied by soft classical music.

We passed the gift shop, where Case and I had previously found our disguises to sneak into the hotel pool area. And just as I pulled out my cell phone to notify Abby of our arrival, Case said quietly, "We've been spotted."

I looked across the room and locked eyes with Mitchell Black.

# CHAPTER FOUR

Mitchell was just as I'd remembered—the slim-fitting pin-striped suit, the thin, hard-lined lips, and the matching scowl. He strode across the room, leaving behind a group of waiters who looked as if they'd just been chastised. He side-stepped the marble table beneath the chandelier and pointed his finger at us.

"You," he commanded, "are not permitted anywhere on these premises. Get out before I phone the police."

"Hold on, Mitch," Case said calmly. "We're not here to stay."

"You're correct about that," Mitchell snapped back. "Nor will you eat at our restaurant, swim in our pool, or speak to our guests."

Case remained calm. "Listen, I never got a chance to apologize for our last encounter. I know I came on a little strong—"

"A *little* strong? You outright accused me of murder," Mitchell sputtered, "among other things."

"And I'm sorry for that," Case continued. "Let's start over. As you know, there's been a suspicious death in the ballroom of your hotel, and we've been asked to help in the investigation."

"*You've* been asked?" Mitchell mocked. "Two inept amateurs playing detective? I don't believe you. Who on earth would ask for your help?"

"I did," came a woman's voice from behind me. She stepped forward and practically wedged herself into the middle of our little huddle. Abby Knight Salvare was taking control.

"Who are you?" Mitchell asked.

"I'm a guest at your hotel." She paused to add, "A paying customer with an active Yelp account."

Mitchell heard the implied threat and immediately backed down.

"I've asked Case and Athena to help me investigate the murder." Abby held out her business card and introduced herself. "Abby Knight Salvare. Salvare Detective Agency."

Mitchell took her card, gave it a quick once-over, and shifted his eyes between the three of us, finally landing back on Abby. "I'll need to verify that you're staying with us, and if so, these two will be *your* responsibility." He started toward the reception desk.

Before he could take three steps, Abby called, "Do you know there is a broken lock on the ballroom's back door?"

Mitchell halted.

"More importantly," she continued, "do the detectives know that that particular door leads to a hallway where the killer could have easily gone in and out without being noticed?" Her words were loud enough that most of the guests could hear.

Mitchell turned around with his hands facing out, hoping to silence Abby. He walked toward us and in a hushed tone asked, "What are you implying?"

"I'm just asking a question," Abby replied.

"I know of no such broken lock, and if you're trying to implicate me or my hotel in this horrid situation, then you'll be hearing from my lawyer."

"Your lawyer or your father?" Abby asked. "Isn't this his hotel?"

"How do you know that?" Mitchell sputtered.

Abby smiled confidently. "You don't have to be an inept amateur playing detective to find that out."

Flushed with embarrassment, Mitchell said sullenly, "Show me the broken lock."

Abby led the way with Mitchell fast on her heels. The ballroom was located past the row of golden elevators, past the large, open dining room, at the far end of the hallway. The double ballroom doors were already opened, with hotel employees inside setting the tables for the upcoming event.

We wound through the tables, the sound of plates clattering and silverware clinking all around us. The ballroom was just as fancy as the rest of the hotel, with high, ornately decorated ceilings and dark-red draperies flowing around the corners of the room. Centered at the far end of the room was a stage. Mitchell followed Abby up the side stairs, across the stage, and into the backstage area, with Case and me trailing behind.

"I've already spoken with one of the workers," Abby said, "and he told me the backstage area is set up the same as for the fashion show. Is that correct?"

"It is," Mitchell answered. "And if this is the door of which you speak, then you are mistaken. The lock isn't broken. The mayor's security guard asked me to keep this door unlocked so he could more easily perform a security sweep before the show. Someone must have forgotten to pull the latch, that's all." Mitchell reached up, his tight suit pulling at the seams, until his fingers found the latch and pulled it down. There was a soft *click*, and the door closed and locked on its own. "There. Now, if you'll excuse me."

"I do have a few more questions," Abby said. "If you don't mind."

Mitchell straightened his jacket. "Keep them succinct, please."

"This hallway leads out to a back parking lot," Abby said. "I'm assuming that lot is for employees and deliveries."

"Correct," Mitchell stated.

"Do you have security cameras in the hallways?" Abby asked.

"No, but there is a camera at each hotel entrance. The detectives have already confiscated the files for those cameras, so I would suggest leaving that work to the professionals."

"What kind of event is happening tonight?" Case asked.

"The Junior Miss Sequoia Beauty Pageant is tonight. We host the event every year."

"And you're certain that this backstage setup

hasn't changed since the fashion show?" Case asked.

"Yes," Mitchell answered. "The detectives cordoned off the ballroom during their investigation. We haven't been allowed back in until today, which is why we're pressed for time. So I must insist that you expedite your investigation."

"We'll be quick," Case said. He turned to Abby. "Any more questions?"

"Not right now," she replied.

"Thanks, Mitch," Case said as Mitchell turned to leave.

"You can thank me by never coming back," Mitchell responded tightly.

As he exited the stage, Abby turned to us and smiled. "That Mitchell is quite a character."

I let out a quick laugh. "You noticed?"

"Does he always talk like that?" Abby asked.

"You mean down his nose?" Case answered. "Pretty much."

The three of us studied the backstage area, where I noticed that the back door that had been unlocked during the fashion show was right next to a folding table set up along the wall. Next to the table was a large wastebasket. There were brooms and mops leaning against the wall, ropes hanging from the ceiling that controlled the tall stage curtains, and several tools lying in one of the corners. Nothing looked out of the ordinary.

I followed Abby to the dressing rooms, which were off to the left of the backstage area. The simple frame structures were just big enough for a person to change clothes in, closed off by a red curtain hanging from a dowel rod. Attached to each curtain was a green index card with the model's name on it.

Abby swept open one of the curtains to reveal a folding chair and a tall, standing mirror inside. All three dressing rooms were identical.

Abby went to the curtain marked with Carly's name and looked inside. "It doesn't look like the detectives dusted for prints in here."

I walked around the outside of the three dressing rooms and came back. "You know what I noticed? Jillian told us she hadn't seen anyone near the dressing rooms, but she wouldn't have seen someone standing *behind* the dressing rooms."

"Or waiting outside the unlocked hallway door," Abby said.

"But how would the murderer know Jillian was going to deliver those water bottles?" I asked.

Abby thought about it for a minute and then said, "Someone could have seen Jillian deliver the water on the first night and saw an opportunity."

We left the dressing room area to find Case testing the hallway door, which was now locked tightly. "We should've had Mitchell leave this door open for us," he said. "I'd like to go down the hallway and take a look at the door that leads to the parking lot."

"I've already checked it out," Abby said. "The employee exit is locked from the outside, but not from the inside. Anyone could've easily walked out, but they would've needed an employee security card to get in."

"Unless someone let them in," I said.

"Good point," Abby said. "In that scenario, it would mean our killer would've had help."

"Let's re-create the scene," I said as I walked to the side of the stage. "Jillian came up these stairs into the backstage area with three bottles of water. She saw Fran working with the wardrobe and saw an audio technician behind the curtain. Then she went to the dressing rooms, where she placed one bottle of water in each of the rooms. She said that was about an hour before the show started. She also told us the first model to arrive was Eleni, and that she had arrived about forty-five minutes before the show."

"If Eleni is our killer, that would've given her fifteen minutes to slip into Carly's room and poison the water before the other models arrived," Abby said. "My husband and I have just recently dealt with a poisoning case, and depending on what kind of poison was used, the effects will start anywhere between fifteen minutes and an hour after it was ingested."

"Then we need to speak with Fran or this sound guy to find out if they saw Eleni entering or leaving Carly's dressing room," Case said.

We heard a noise and turned to see an audio technician just outside the stage area setting up a microphone for the beauty pageant. His shirt had the Waterfront Hotel logo on it.

"Maybe that's him now," I said. "How should we approach him?"

"Excuse us," Abby called, walking over to him. "Were you setting up the microphones before both nights of the fashion show?"

Without looking up, the man said, "Yep."

Case leaned toward me and said quietly, "I guess that's how."

I was increasingly impressed with how confident Abby was. Case and I joined her.

"Were you backstage at any time before the show?" Abby asked.

"Yep."

"On both nights?"

"Both nights," he replied.

"We're focusing on the night of the murder," she told him. "Did you see anyone backstage on Thursday night?"

He fidgeted with a microphone and a cord for a moment, then a loud blare sounded, echoing throughout the empty ballroom. He tested the microphone by answering Case's question. "I saw a redhead and a brunette." His voice boomed over the speakers.

I didn't have my iPad ready to take notes, but I stored away his response. The redhead would've been Jillian, and the brunette could've been Fran. Abby must've been thinking along the same lines.

"Did you happen to get either of their names?" she asked.

"Nope," he said. The man stood and anchored the microphone in its stand, then gave Abby a lop-sided smile. "You mind testing this for me?"

Abby looked at the man quizzically. "How would I do that?"

"Well, you got any more questions, go ahead and just ask them right into that mic."

She turned her puzzled expression toward Case and me. The audio tech hopped off the stage and walked into the middle of the ballroom. He looked up at the speakers on either side of the stage and then gave a thumbs-up to us. "Go ahead. Ask away."

"This guy is a hoot," Case said quietly.

Abby was shorter than the microphone stand, so she had to pull the mic down, closer to her mouth. "Did you notice anything out of the ordinary on Thursday night?"

The man gave her a thumbs-up, then walked back to the stage, hopped up, and readjusted the microphone stand. "Just a bunch of flowers stuffed into a trash can in the backstage area."

"Why does that stand out?" Abby asked.

"Seems out of the ordinary, don't you think? A perfectly good bunch of flowers? I don't know where they came from, but they were still there after the detective came around. I told him to take a look, but he didn't care much what I had to say, so I took the flowers home to my wife."

"Do you know who the flowers were for?" I asked.

"Nope."

"Do you know where the flowers came from?" Abby asked.

"No, but my wife might know," he said. "There was a tag on the stems."

Abby walked over and handed him a card. He read it and looked up at her. "Private detective, huh? Like Magnum P.I.?"

"Yes," she said. "Just like that. Would you be able to get ahold of your wife and find out where the flowers were purchased?"

He pocketed her card. "I can ask her tonight after she gets home from work."

"That would help a lot," Abby said. "Please give me a call when you find out."

As the audio tech left the stage, I said, "Why would the detective ignore the flowers?"

"I don't know," Abby answered. "They could be a lead."

Before we left the backstage area, Case used his phone to take photos, and then we climbed down the stairs to the ballroom floor.

"The hotel's restaurant is just down the hall," Abby said. "Who's hungry?"


We were seated at a table in front of a large wall of windows with a view of the outdoor eating area and the swimming pool, and beyond that, Lake Michigan. The indoor dining room was mostly empty, with most of the diners preferring to eat outside during the summer months. As we waited for our food to arrive, Abby said, "I'll keep in touch with the audio technician. Once we find out where the flowers were purchased, the florist should be able to help with the sender's identity."

She paused as the waitress topped off our coffees, then, as Abby laced her cup with cream, she continued, "But I can't stop thinking about the backstage exit. If the mayor was worried about security, why did his team leave it unlocked?"

"Maybe because it didn't matter," Case said. "The back exit leads to the parking lot, but the door to the parking lot is locked from the inside, like you said. No one could get in without an employee security card."

"Athena," Abby said, "you mentioned that some-one could've been working with our killer. If that's true, then we have a whole building full of employees who might have ties to this murder."

Case set his coffee down. "We'd have to canvass the entire staff. That's a lot of work for a theory with no leads."

"We might not have to," Abby said. "I'm going to try my best to get ahold of that security cam footage just to make sure we aren't missing any leads. Just keep that theory in mind."

"Another theory," I explained, "involves Eleni Sloan arriving early to poison Carly's water. The thing is, there's no motive to back that up."

"We'll have to learn more about Eleni and her relationship with Carly," Abby said as the waitress came with our food order.

We paused as our plates were delivered. I had ordered a yummy-looking taco salad with South-west dressing, Case had a full plate of ribs and mashed potatoes, while Abby settled into her crispy French bistro ham-and-cheese sandwich.

After a few bites in silence, I realized I hadn't asked Abby about her meeting with Jillian and her new lawyer. "What did Kevin Coreopsis have to say about Jillian being released from jail?" I asked.

Abby held up a finger while she finished a crunchy bite, then said, "He was able to get a bond hearing for Jillian tomorrow, so hopefully she'll be released tomorrow afternoon. He said the judge will probably let her go home, but under the condition that she has to return at the detective's request."

"Looks like we have our work cut out for us," Case said. "We have to make sure Detective Walters doesn't have a reason to bring Jillian back."

"Tell me about this detective," Abby said.

"He's been on the force a long time," I told her, "and he's not easy to work with. In fact, he's on the surly side. He really doesn't like us getting involved in his investigations."

"He did acknowledge us after we solved the last homicide, however," Case said in between bites of his messy rib dinner.

"Marco and I encountered the same situation in New Chapel," Abby told us. "The detectives eventually got used to us, but it helps to be established. Hopefully, the same will happen to you."

I gave Case a wry smile and wiped a spot of barbecue sauce from his mouth with my napkin. "I can't see Detective Walters being that cooperative."

Abby took a sip of coffee, then set down her cup and pulled a small notebook and pen out of her purse. "What do you know about the people who were backstage? Do you know them well?"

"I don't know anything about the victim, Carly Blackburn," I said, "except what you told us."

Case wiped his fingers on a napkin, pulled out his phone, and scrolled through his notes. "Carly was very active in the community," he replied. "President of the middle school's PTA, secretary for a philanthropic sorority, and the campaign manager for Mayor Sloan's reelection. She had one child, a son, and was divorced this past April."

Abby finished writing it down, then looked up. "Do we know anything about the ex-husband?"

"Not yet," Case said. "I'll do some more digging."

"Divorce records are public," Abby told him. "It might be smart to dig through those files as well."

"I'm on it," Case replied.

Abby readied her pen. "Who's next?"

"Hope Louvain," I said, "the police chief's wife."

"She's a teacher," Case said. "I found out that she's teaching over the summer at Sequoia middle school, so we know where to find her. She has two children aged eight and twelve, and that's all I have on Hope right now."

Abby wrote it down. "Got it."

"Then there's Eleni Sloan," I said. "She's the mayor's wife. She's Greek and owns a bookstore on Greene Street called The Garden of Readin'. I've been there a few times to pick up books for my son. Eleni is always there, so we know where to find her, too."

"You mentioned that she's Greek." Abby said. "Does that have any significance?"

"Just that she's well-known in the Greek community," I explained. "My mother is friends with her."

"She is also a member of several philanthropic organizations," Case said. "Most dealing with literature and the arts. She has a sixteen-year-old daughter. That's all I have on her."

"That takes care of the models," Abby said. "What about Fran Decker?"

"Fran owns a boutique dress shop downtown called Fabulous Fashions," I explained. "She's also the chairperson of the Small Business Association."

"She's married and has no children," Case added.

Abby noted it, then picked up her sandwich. "These women all sound perfectly normal."

"I agree," I said. "So, why was Carly targeted? Who was she, and what kind of enemies could she have made?"

"From what Jillian told us," Abby said, "Carly was not a very nice person, so she could have had any number of enemies."

"An enemy who would risk slipping into her dressing room to poison a water bottle?" Case asked. "That's a pretty serious enemy. We're going to have to find someone with a very strong motive."

"Or a very convenient opportunity," Abby added.

After we'd finished eating and the waitress had come by to refill our cups, I said, "Whom should we interview first?"

"Why don't we start with Fran Decker?" Abby asked. "She was backstage more than anyone, and she worked with all three models. What do you think?"

I nodded. "That's a good place to start. I'd suggest we stop by her dress shop midafternoon tomorrow. In my experience, business is usually slow at that time of day."

"How about three o'clock tomorrow?" Abby asked.

"I can do that," I said.

"You mentioned that Eleni Sloan has a bookstore," Abby said to me. "Is that anywhere close to Fran's shop?"

"It's within walking distance."

"Then we can talk to Eleni after Fran. How does that sound?"

"Sounds like a plan," I told her.

"I'll let you two handle the interviews," Case said. "I've got some work to do. But don't forget, Athena, we're going to try to talk to Detective Walters at noon tomorrow. Abby, would you like to join us?"

"I don't know," Abby said. "With three of us there, the detective might feel cornered, and then you'd get no help from him."

"We'll be lucky if we get any help anyway, but I get your point," Case said.

Abby finished her coffee and pushed back from the table. "I have some phone calls to make, and I want to see if I can get a copy of the hotel's security camera footage for the night of the murder. And then I think I'm going to call it a night."

"I'll be at the Greene Street office tomorrow bright and early." Case said. "Oh, and to make things easier"—he dug through his pants pocket, lifting out a key ring—"this is the spare key to our office. You can come by any time if you need a place to work. Just lock up when you leave. And feel free to use the reception desk while you're there."

"That's Lila's desk," I said to Case. "You think we should set her up there?"

"Lila has never claimed the reception desk," Case explained. "Besides, no one ever sits there, and it has a working computer."

"Abby, you can also make yourself at home in my office if you need to," I told her. "The reception desk is now officially Lila's."

Case rose and escorted us out, giving me his killer smile. "*You're* going to explain that to Lila," he said to me. "Not me."

We left Abby by the hotel elevators and headed out to the parking lot around the side of the hotel. "What do you say we go to the *Pamé* for a sunset cruise?" Case asked, as we climbed into the Jeep. "I have a bottle of champagne chilling in the fridge."

I climbed in through the open door, buckled my seat belt, then double-checked to make sure it was tight. I laid my head against the headrest and smiled as Case's hand covered mine. "That sounds tempting."

"But?"

I turned to face him. "But I haven't seen Nicholas all day."

"Bring him along. He loves the boat."

"I also have to check in with Delphi to see if she's doing okay with her new responsibilities. And I should probably talk to my dad, too."

Case pulled my chin gently toward him to gaze into my eyes. "Why don't you check in with them, spend some time with your son, and then join me on the boat later tonight? You deserve some time to relax."

I melted at Case's charming smile and warm

touch. "How about this? Once I get Nicholas tucked in, I'll come over."

"Perfect. And then tomorrow we can all go to the fair."

I gave him a kiss. "Don't push your luck."

As we headed back to my parents' house, my phone rang, and I saw Bob Maguire's name on the screen. I put him on speakerphone and said, "Hey, Bob. You're on speaker with Case. Do you have news for us?"

"I haven't been able to learn anything about the poison yet," he said. "Mainly, I'm calling to give you a heads-up about the case."

"That doesn't sound like good news," Case said.

"Here's the thing," Maguire told us. "Detective Walters is getting ready to retire, so this case isn't getting the attention it deserves. In fact, it seems to me like he just doesn't care."

"Maybe we can prod him a little tomorrow," I said.

"You're coming to the station?" Maguire asked.

"We have some questions for him," I replied.

"He doesn't like being bothered at work, Athena."

"What about lunch?"

"What about it?" Maguire shot back.

"He has to stop to eat, right? Where does he go on his break?"

"He has food brought in," Maguire answered. "But I should let you know that bothering Walters during lunch might be worse than bothering him while he's on duty."

"He's not my boss, Bob," I said. "I'm not afraid of him."

Maguire laughed. "That doesn't sound like the Athena I know. Where is this confidence coming from?"

"Just make sure Walters doesn't order any food," I told him. "We'll bring lunch."

"Okay, suit yourselves. All I can say is good luck," Maguire said. "You're going to need it."

# CHAPTER FIVE

Case pulled up in front of my parents' house and leaned over to give me a kiss. "I like the confident Athena," he murmured and kissed me again, his lips firm and gentle, his taste sweet.

I practically melted against him. "I like her, too."

He lifted my chin and looked deep into my eyes. "My beautiful, confident goddess, I'll see you tonight."

At that moment I did feel beautiful. And confident. "I can't wait," I said softly and leaned in for one more kiss.

I fairly floated up the sidewalk to the front door. After suffering through a loveless first marriage, I was thrilled to have found someone like Case, someone who cared about me, someone who made me feel safe, someone I could trust implicitly. I felt like one lucky woman.

Inside, I found Nicholas and my dad playing chess at the dining room table.

"Good thing you came home," my dad said. "This little scamp has beaten me twice." He rose and indicated his chair. "Why don't you take over for me?"

My father knew I was terrible at chess. "I don't know," I said slowly.

"I bet I can beat you, too, Mom," Nicholas said. "I've been practicing."

I looked at his proud little face, and my heart melted. "I bet you can't," I said and took my dad's place at the table.

Just then my mother ambled down the stairs with worry lines creasing her forehead. "Where have you been all day, Athena? We missed you at lunch, and then your father brings home little Niko saying that you'll miss dinner, too."

"I had dinner with Case and Abby," I told her. "You don't have to worry about me."

"I just worry that you work too much."

I gave my dad a pleading look, but he shrugged his shoulders. He knew better than to fight with Mama. "I'll take some time off soon," I promised.

"When?"

"When the case is finished," I said sharply, hoping my tone would end the conversation.

Mama folded her arms, clearly not willing to concede. "And what about the fair?" she asked.

"Yeah, Mom!" Nicholas said. "When are we going to the fair?"

Dad leaned close to my ear and whispered, "Checkmate."

I promised Nicholas we would go to the fair sometime during the week, and both he and my mom seemed satisfied. Nicholas and I played chess until nine o'clock, and then we went upstairs to Nicholas's room, where I read him another chapter in his current Harry Potter book. Sometime later, I came awake with a start and realized I'd fallen asleep on his bed. I crept back to my room and checked my phone to find several text messages and one missed call from Case.

*Sorry,* I texted back. *I fell asleep.*

*I figured you did,* he wrote back. *Get some rest. Kalinihta, goddess.*

*Night, Case.*


*Tuesday*

The next morning, Nicholas and I walked into my grandparents' diner to see my mom chatting with a tableful of women and my sisters Selene and Maia sitting at our booth having breakfast. We stopped to bid my grandparents a good morning, then Nicholas hopped onto a stool at the counter to talk with his great-grandmother and I joined my sisters in the booth.

"Morning," I said. "Why do you two look so bored?"

"No Goddess Anon blog this morning," Maia said.

Oh, no. I had forgotten to write my blog!

I sat back with a frown and contemplated the situation. The frustrations I'd once felt with my crazy family had diminished, and I was getting busier by the day. Other than to entertain my sisters and mother, did I need to write it anymore?

"Want your usual breakfast?" my mom asked, stopping by the table to fill my cup with coffee. She, too, looked bored.

"Yes, please."

I glanced across the table at my sisters. Selene was dressed for work at the hair salon, just a pair of jeans and a loose top, the color of which picked up on the new orange braid she'd fastened in her curly, dark hair. It was well-known that Selene changed her hairstyle almost every week, but this orange trend did not suit her olive complexion. She sat hunched over the table looking at her phone as she ate in silence.

Maia was sitting next to her, staring vacantly across the room, chewing mindlessly on her fruit plate. Had my blog really brightened their mornings that much?

"Good morning, everyone," Delphi called cheerfully and slid into the booth beside me. "Isn't it a glorious day?"

"Talk to Bob this morning?" I asked.

"Just now."

At least one of my sisters was happy.

Maia smiled at her across the table, a crafty gleam in her eye. "How are dance lessons going?"

Delphi handed me her purse to store at my side, glaring across at Maia the whole time. "You don't have to say it like that."

"Like what?" Maia asked innocently, although her tone had been jesting. After almost three decades of being sisters, it wasn't the words that mattered. It was all about tone. Even the slightest variation could be detected and picked apart by all four of us.

Mama walked up with the pot of coffee. "How are your s*ecret* dance lessons going?"

"Oh my God, why is everyone so interested in my life?" Delphi blurted. "And it's obviously not a secret if I've told everyone."

Okay. Words mattered sometimes.

"You never told us *why* you were taking lessons," Selene said, leaning in. "There must be a reason."

"Why must there be a reason?" Delphi exclaimed. "Why do you have an orange braid in your hair? It's not Halloween. Why does Maia have a stash of beef jerky in her closet? Is that part of a vegetarian diet? Do we all want to explain ourselves, or can I eat my breakfast in peace?"

Mama poured Delphi's coffee, the only sound breaking the tension her gold bangles falling down her wrist one by one.

Selene leaned back and combed out her orange braid with her fingers. "That's just mean."

Maia popped a grape in her mouth and stared down at her fruit plate.

"Girls, *irémise*," Mama told us. Calm down. "There's no need for hostility. Delphi, I'm happy for you, and Selene, your sister is right. With a hairstyle like that, you'll never find a man."

Selene rolled her eyes. "I'm not looking for a man."

"Well, good," Mama said confidently. "You don't

need to. *I'm* going to find the perfect man for you."

Selene turned to me for help, but all I could do was shrug.

Nicholas and I arrived at Spencer's about ten minutes before the doors opened at nine o'clock. Drew hadn't arrived yet, so I set his breakfast platter on the front counter and brought a bag full of bagels into the office. I found my dad sitting at the computer shaking his head. Nicholas came in and gave his grandpa a hug before dashing back into the garden center.

"What's wrong, Pops?" I asked.

"You're going to have to help Delphi with inventory," he said. "I tried explaining our process to her yesterday afternoon, but she just didn't get it. She ended up storming out of the office in frustration."

"It's pretty easy," I told him.

"It's easy for you," he said. "Maybe you could explain it better."

"I'll work with her this morning." I popped a pod into the Keurig machine and placed my mug beneath the dispenser.

Dad leaned back in the office chair and stretched. "What are your plans for the day?"

As I waited for my coffee, I went over the list. "I have to meet Case at noon to speak with Detective Walters, then I'll be working with Abby later this afternoon, so I'll be in and out today."

Dad stood and pulled the office chair out for me. "Sounds like a busy day."

By the tone of his voice, I could tell what he meant. He still thought I was stretching myself too thin. I grabbed my steaming coffee and stepped aside. Dad swiped his cup from the desk and placed it under the machine, replacing my pod with a new one.

"How many cups is that?" I asked him sternly.

"How long until you take a day off?" he replied as he hit the START button.

We waited in silence while the piping hot coffee filled his empty cup. I could see him watching me from the corner of his eye and knew he wasn't finished with the "busy day" conversation. I sat down behind the computer, still feeling the strain in my back from falling against a staircase while struggling with a killer just a few days earlier.

"I'm fine, Pops," I finally told him. "I'll take a day off when I need one."

He blew the steam softly from his cup and sat across from me. "You fell asleep in Niko's bed last night."

"How do you know that?"

"The light was on," he said. "I turned it off and tucked you both in."

Wow. I'd been in such a deep sleep I hadn't even noticed.

"You flinch every time you sit down," he continued, "and you didn't write your blog last night."

I let out a sigh. "Okay, I'm a little tired and sore, but it's nothing to worry about."

"What about Niko?" he asked me. "Are you taking him to the fair this week?"

"Yes," I answered honestly. "I'm not neglecting him."

"Thenie, I don't think you're neglecting him. You're a fine mother, and you've raised a fine son. I just want you to enjoy it while you can. Kids grow up fast."

"I understand."

"And I want you to take care of yourself. You might've grown up fast, too, but you'll always be my little girl."

I smiled at him. "I will, Pops."

After our heart-to-heart, we went over some numbers for the garden center, then we heard Drew and Delphi come in the front doors.

"Another day, another dollar." My dad took off his glasses for a thorough cleaning.

My cousin Drew stuck his head in the doorway. "Just a heads-up," he said while chewing a bite of pancake. "I literally just opened the doors, and Delphi is already doing a coffee-grounds reading for a couple who came in to buy hydrangeas."

"Where did she get the coffee?"

"She brought it from the diner."

My dad slipped his glasses back on and looked to me for help.

"I'll take care of it," I said, and went to find my sister.

Reading coffee grounds was Delphi's favorite diversion. Normally, she'd make a customer a cup of Greek coffee, a thick, sweet brew with a layer of fine coffee grounds at the bottom, then chatter away until the coffee was gone and only the grounds were left. At that point, she would give the cup a few swirls, creating a pattern in the grounds, then interpret them, kind of like a palm reading. Customers were usually intrigued by her readings, but some had been frightened. I tried to monitor them whenever I could.

I found Delphi sitting with a middle-aged couple at one of the patio tables in our outside garden area behind the store. Delphi was studying the bottom of her to-go cup, while the couple watched her curiously. I paused just outside a rose trellis to listen.

"I see a water sign and the letter *B*." She swirled the cup. "*BL*," she said. "Water and *BL*. Blue, maybe. Blue water. Are you going on a trip to the ocean?"

"No," the two said.

"Are you going out on Lake Michigan? Maybe for a boat ride?"

The couple looked at each other, then the woman said, "We weren't planning on it."

Delphi swirled the cup and studied the bottom again. "I'm also seeing the number three." She stared at the cup for a long moment, then looked up at them. "Just remember what I said and be very careful. I don't want to frighten you, but don't go near any large bodies of water in the near future. Your lives could depend on it."

The couple looked at each other, clearly confused.

"Thank you," the man said as the two rose.

Just as they started to go, Delphi halted them. "Didn't you want to see the hydrangeas?" she asked.

"We'll come back another time," the woman responded.

"I'll be here," Delphi said cheerfully.

She didn't see them glance at each other and roll their eyes.

As the couple headed back inside, Delphi saw me and came over. "Another successful reading. What's up?"

"You scared away the customers."

Delphi scoffed. "He said *thank you.*"

I pointed at her cup. "This is *your* coffee. Aren't you supposed to use *their* coffee for a reading?"

"They didn't have coffee, and I just felt something. I knew they needed a reading."

"But doesn't that mean you just read your own future?"

Delphi blinked twice, then scowled. "Why would I be afraid of water?"

"Delphi, listen. I need to teach you how to do inventory."

"Thenie, I can't take over all of your duties!"

"But you can take over the inventory. It's easy. Come inside, and I'll show you how."

Before I could turn around, Nicholas came running out of a large shrub area laughing in delight, with mud all over his arms, legs, khaki shorts, and sandals. He came to a quick stop on the gravel walkway when he saw me.

"Niko," I said, "what have you been doing?"

He looked at the ground. "Working."

At once Oscar bounded out of the bushes also covered in mud, the yellow rubber rattle in his mouth. The little gray-and-black raccoon ran up to my son, stood on his hind legs as if to show Nicholas his prize, then scampered away again.

"Working, huh?" I asked my embarrassed son. "How did you get so muddy?"

"There's a whole bunch of mud in the back corner by the fence," he said.

"Show me."

He led me through an area of tree saplings to the wooden fence that surrounded our acre of property. There in the corner was a sprinkler head sticking up out of the ground leaking water. I couldn't get close because of the muddy ground surrounding it.

"I'll have to tell your grandpop," I said. "Now, about that mud bath you just took, come with me."

He followed me to the toolshed near the back gate. Instead of a water hose, I found an old blanket folded up on the cement floor, and beside it a water bowl and more of Oscar's toys. "Niko, you shouldn't be messing around in here."

"Oscar needs an inside home, Mom. He loves it in here."

I gazed at my son, at his big brown eyes and his earnest expression, at his brown hair ruffled on top, at his arms folded across his chest, and my heart expanded with love. "Okay. But you're going to have to keep the shed clean. We don't want vermin inside. And no food. Just water."

He smiled brightly. "Okay!"

Outside the shed, I connected the hose to the faucet and had Nicholas hold out his arms while I hosed them off. I turned it on his legs and bare feet, but his shorts, unfortunately, got sprayed with water, too. "You're going to have to stay outside until your shorts dry," I said. "In this heat, it shouldn't take long."

"Okay. I'll just play with Oscar until they dry."

"Then stay away from this area or you'll step in more mud. I don't want you tracking it into the barn."

I left Nicholas looking for Oscar and went inside to find my father. He was standing at the cash counter talking to a customer, so I waited until he was free and then said, "One of the sprinkler heads is stuck, Pops, and it's making a muddy mess in the back right corner near the gate."

"I'll have to add that to the list of things to do," he said.

"I'll take care of it." I turned to find Delphi standing behind me with an oddly concerned expression on her face.

"Thanks," I said. "Do you know what to do?"

"I'll figure it out," Delphi answered. "And you were going to show me how to do inventory."

I glanced at my father, puzzling over Delphi's rapid change in mood. He raised his eyebrows in bewilderment.

"Okay," I said. "Let's go back to the office."

"Wait a minute." She turned to our father. "Pops," she said, "I'm sorry I threw a fit yesterday. I can do better. And don't worry about the sprinkler head. I'll make sure it gets fixed."

"Thank you, dear heart," he said.

I worked with Delphi in the office for an hour. She was surprisingly cool about it and willing to learn. Then I helped on the sales floor until almost eleven thirty, when I had to leave and head down to the detective agency.

Inside our new office, I found Case sitting at his desk working on the computer. Abby was seated across from him writing on a notepad. The late morning sun was shining through the slats of the blinds, highlighting Case's light brown hair, reminding me of how handsome he was.

He looked up at me and smiled. Abby turned in her chair and did the same.

"Anything new to report?" I asked the two of them.

"I learned something interesting about Carly's ex, Donald Blackburn," Case said.

I rubbed my hands together. "Tell me."

"I found a write-up of an interview Donald gave last year," he said, "in which he talked about the success of his riverboat casino and about his plan to eventually build a land-based casino on the outskirts of Sequoia."

"And that's interesting why?" I asked.

"Because I also searched public records and found the Blackburn divorce settlement," Case explained. "It turns out Carly didn't get a single dime from Donald's casino business, but she did receive a large parcel of land. And check this out. I looked up the address of that land. It's a twenty-acre empty lot near the Blackburn riverboat, the perfect place for a land-based casino."

"So you think Donald Blackburn intended on building his casino there?" I asked.

"It makes sense," Case replied, "except that Carly got the land in the divorce. So no casino."

"That's still a weak motive to kill his ex-wife. What was his plan? Kill her and take back her land?"

"Actually," Case said, sitting back in his desk chair, "that's not as far-fetched as it sounds. If she didn't have a will specifying differently, Donald would have been her beneficiary. If she were to die, he would get the land back, a motive for getting rid of her. So we need to find out if Carly drew up a new will after her divorce."

"And how do we find that out?" I asked.

"We'll have to talk to her family," he said, "her mother and father, a sister, a brother, or a best friend. Someone should know about a new will."

Abby raised her pen. "I'll research Carly's family. And I suggest we add Donald's name to our suspect list."

"But he wasn't at the fashion show," I said.

"Not that we know of," Abby said, "but I was able to watch the security cam footage of the hotel's employee exit. I saw two men exit into the parking lot on the night of the murder. One was wearing a black baseball cap and black T-shirt, and the other was a man dressed in a suit. One of those men could've been Donald Blackburn."

"Did you see their faces?" I asked.

"No, it was very blurry," Abby answered, "but it's a start. I also saw a woman bringing racks of clothes in, so I'm assuming that's the woman from the boutique."

"We'll have to ask Fran if she had an employee pass," I said. "If she didn't, then maybe the parking lot exit was left unlocked just like the backstage door."

Abby picked up her pen. "I'll add that to the list."

I glanced at my watch. "Case, we need to head over to the police station to talk to Detective Walters."

Case turned off his monitor and rose. "Let's go."

"Abby," I said, "I'll meet you here at three o'clock. We can walk down the street to Fran's boutique from here."

"In the meantime," Abby said, "I need to get

over to the courthouse for Jillian's bond hearing. Hopefully, she'll be released afterward."

"I'll keep my fingers crossed," I told her.

Case and I walked across the street to the plaza and headed for the food trucks. I ordered a beef hoagie for Detective Walters, then we walked to the police station a few blocks away.

"Listen," Case said on the way. "We have to be very careful in our approach with Walters. Why don't I do most of the talking?"

"What are you trying to say?"

He put his arm around my shoulder. "It's no secret that you and he have butted heads on more than one occasion. So let me try speaking with him man to man."

"*Man* to *man?*" I asked, feeling a prickle of annoyance.

"Think about it, Athena. Walters is retiring. He just wants to be done with this case, and here we come strolling in questioning him about his work. He definitely won't be happy."

"Fine," I said. "This was your idea anyway. My only contribution is the sandwich."

We had to go through security before we could go upstairs to the detective bureau, and there we found the detective on the phone, dressed in a crumpled white button-down shirt, brown pants, and scuffed brown shoes. We waited some distance away, and once he had finished his conversation, we walked over to his desk.

He eyed us warily and said in a dry voice, "To what do I owe this honor?"

"We brought you a surprise," I said, and set the food container on his desk.

"What is it?"

"It's from Fat Hoagies food truck on the plaza," Case explained. "Best in town."

"Look," Walters said, eyeing the container, "if you're here about the murder case, I don't want to hear it. We're handling the matter."

"By arresting the mother of a toddler whose only crime is wanting to be with her child?" I asked, then remembered I was supposed to keep quiet.

Case leaned over and popped the lid on the container. "Detective, we've looked into the case, and we've found several persons of interest, none of whom are Jillian Osborne. We understand you're getting ready to retire, but we really need you to take this matter seriously."

"Just hold up a minute," Walters said. "What makes you think I'm *not* taking the matter seriously?"

"Have you found any persons of interest other than Jillian?" Case asked.

"I don't give out information on a current investigation," he replied brusquely.

"I can understand that," Case said, "but I thought you should know that we've found several other people who—"

"I'm working on the matter," Walters ground out.

"That's a laugh," I muttered.

Walters shot me daggers. "*What* did you say?"

I couldn't keep quiet any longer. "What you're saying, Detective, is that you're going to force *us* to solve your last case. Some legacy *that* will be."

He rose in a furious huff and pointed at the door. "Get out of my office. Now!"

I put my hands on my hips and glared at him, all sorts of angry retorts on the tip of my tongue, but Case put his hand on my back and guided me toward the door. "You're not going to change his mind, Athena," he said quietly.

"Then I'm happy this is his last investigation," I said, throwing Walters a backward glare. He didn't notice. He was too busy unwrapping the hoagie.

# CHAPTER SIX

"It was worth a try," Case said on our return trip to the food trucks. "But what happened to me doing all the talking?"

"Your way wasn't working," I told him. "Besides, it doesn't matter who talks if no one is listening."

"True," Case said, taking my hand. "I wonder if Walter's replacement will be any more helpful."

That gave me pause. Who *would* replace Detective Walters? Then I remembered that Bob Maguire had mentioned something about the position. "Wouldn't it be great if Bob got the job? I'll have to ask him more about it."

"That would make our life a whole lot easier," Case said as we made our way back to the food trucks. "I'm going to order a hoagie for lunch. They look amazing. You?"

"I'll stick with my pizza," I told him.

The food trucks were located in downtown Sequoia at a plaza across from our office on Greene

Street. As soon as we had our food, I picked out a picnic table with a clear view of our building. The clouds had cleared away, leaving the sun shining brightly in the sky, glinting off the sign that read *Greene St. Detective Agency.*

As we ate, Case and I talked about the murder investigation. We discussed our next steps, and that I would be going back to Spencer's until it was time to meet with Fran. "What are you going to do this afternoon?" I asked him as we stood to throw away our trash.

"I need to do some work in Saugatuck."

"I thought you could do your work from the office."

"Most of the work, not all of it." He put his arm around my shoulder and pulled me close. "Don't worry. I'll be back early. I might even have time to play a few hands of blackjack at the Blackburn Riverboat Casino. I'm feeling lucky today."

"Are you going to talk to Donald Blackburn?"

"Maybe."

"Man to man?"

He gave me a forced smile. "Funny, but no. I just want to see his operation, get a feel for the place."

"Just remember, though," I teased, "I know how much money is in the petty cash drawer."

Case smiled and pulled his sunglasses down off his forehead before leaning in to give me a peck on the cheek. "Good luck with your interview."

At two o'clock I met with a couple who needed a landscape plan for their house, and after talking over their needs, I took them out back to select their shrubbery. I led them past the patio featuring a large selection of outdoor tables and chairs, past several rows of roses, until we came to the hydrangeas. They chose three varieties for color, two viburnums for height, and six boxwoods for edging. We drew up a plan, scheduled a day for delivery and installation, and suddenly it was nearly three o'clock and I needed to get ready for the meeting with Fran Decker.

I went in search of my father and found him unpacking bags of potting soil in the stockroom on the back side of the big barn. "Pops, I have to leave for a while. I'm not sure when I'll be back."

He pushed a bag up onto a shelf. "Thanks for the heads-up. Do me a favor and let Delphi know on your way out."

"Where is she?"

Dad wiped his forehead with the back of his work glove. "I have no idea."

"Have you seen Niko?"

"He's probably with Delphi," Dad said.

When Delphi went missing, it usually meant she was in the conference room giving a coffee-grounds reading to an unsuspecting customer, but this time the room was vacant. I searched the large indoor space, looked down every aisle, but the whole barn was empty. I didn't even see any customers.

Drew was sitting behind the cash register reading the back of a pesticide can, looking unbearably bored.

"Where is everybody?" I asked him.

"Probably at the fair. It's been slow all day." He

held up the can. "Have you ever read the ingredients in this?"

I heard a *thwack* coming from the entrance. I turned to look through one of the barn-door windows, but I couldn't see anyone there.

Another *thwack*. I looked out in time to see a bright green tennis ball bounce back to the sidewalk. I opened one of the big red doors and stepped outside just as the tennis ball came flying at me. I flinched instinctively but somehow managed to catch the ball.

Delphi stood a few feet down the sidewalk, looking surprised. Nicholas stood beside her, looking horrified. I heard the scampering of little feet and saw little Oscar running up the sidewalk at full speed. He leapt after the tennis ball in my hand, and I braced myself for impact as he landed in my open arms. The baby raccoon we had raised was growing up. I could feel the weight of him almost knock me backward. Oscar wrestled the tennis ball from my hand, jumped down, and ran to drop the ball at my son's feet.

Nicholas jumped for joy, clapping and hollering. "He did it, Mom! I taught him that!"

Delphi doubled over laughing. "Thenie, you should have seen your face."

"What in the world are you doing out here?" I asked, trying to hold back a sudden rush of anger.

Nicholas was immediately contrite. "I'm sorry, Mom. We were just playing."

"If you're going to play with Oscar, Niko, play in the back. Not out in front. He could run out into the street."

"Sorry, Thenie," Delphi said. "You were back there with customers, so we came out front."

"Go help Grandpa in the stockroom," I told my son. "He's the only one working around here."

"Yes, Mom," Niko said.

"Delphi, I'm leaving for a while. You're in charge of the sales floor."

"Don't forget," Delphi reminded me, "you're closing up tonight."

"I won't forget. Keep your eye on Niko, will you? No more playing around."

"You can count on me."

Could I, though?

The day was sunny and warm, and the light blue sundress and white sandals I'd chosen that morning were perfect. I walked down Greene Street to the 535 building and went upstairs to the detective agency, where I found Abby working on her laptop in my office. I sat down at my desk and waited for her to finish typing. "I talked with the detective," I told her, "and I have some discouraging news."

Abby looked up from the monitor. "Let me guess. The detective wouldn't talk to you."

"Oh, he talked," I said, "but he didn't have anything nice to say. So, unfortunately, Jillian isn't out of the woods yet."

"Speaking of Jillian," Abby said, "the judge set her bond, she posted it, and then she was released. Her husband picked her up, and she's on her way home right now."

"That's great! I'll bet she's relieved."

"She is." Abby closed the laptop and stood. "But *I* won't feel relieved until we find the murderer. From experience, I know how fast things can turn

around and head in the wrong direction, especially when the lead detective isn't cooperative."
She glanced at her watch. "Shall we go?"

We grabbed our purses and headed for the
door. "Just so you know," I said, as we stepped into
the hallway, "I've never met Fran Decker before.
How should we play this?"

Abby waited while I locked the office door, then
asked, "What do you mean?"

"This is my first official investigation. Until now
Case and I have had to take a very creative approach to our interviews because we weren't legiti-
mate PIs. Case still has nightmares about the
Greek fisherman disguise I made him wear."

Abby laughed as we headed down the stairs.
"Trust me, we won't need any disguises or creative
approaches. Tell you what, why don't you let me
take the lead on this one?"

"Sounds great to me."

We walked a few blocks going over some of the
questions Abby was going to ask Fran, then I
pointed to a small boutique across the street with
*Fabulous Fashions* in white letters arcing across its
large plate-glass window. "There's her shop."

We cut across the street and stopped in front
of the shop. "Are you okay taking notes?" Abby
asked me.

"Of course."

She reached into her purse and pulled out a
notepad. "Here you go."

I patted my tote bag. "I brought an iPad."

"Hi-tech," she said, slipping the notebook back
into her purse. "I still do it the old-fashioned way."

She opened the door, causing a bell to ring inside. I followed her into the shop, where we found a salesclerk helping a customer select some clothing. Another woman was standing behind a sales counter. She smiled as we approached.

"We're here to see Fran," Abby told her.

"She's in back," the woman said. "I'll go get her."

While she was gone, we looked at some of the clothing hanging on the round racks. "This is pretty," Abby said, pulling out a yellow sweater.

"That color looks nice with your hair," I told her.

She turned to admire herself in a full-length mirror hanging on the far wall. "That's what my husband says." She draped the sweater over her shoulders and checked the mirror again. "It's a good thing, too, because yellow just happens to be my favorite color."

I was about to pull out a pretty, blue summer dress when suddenly I found myself summoning the words of my so-called psychic sister. *Yellow aura.* Delphi had imagined Abby surrounded by a yellow aura, and there she was, wrapped in a yellow sweater. I chalked it up to coincidence.

The clerk came through a curtain in the back and walked up to us with a smile. "Fran will be right out."

We continued looking through the racks until a tall, slender woman with short white hair came through the curtain. Appearing to be in her early sixties, she wore a slim navy dress with navy heels and large oval glasses, looking every inch a smart, stylish businesswoman.

"Hi," she said with a smile. "How can I help you?"

Abby handed her a business card and gave Fran a moment to look at it. "I'm Abby, and this is Athena Spencer from the Greene Street Detective Agency. Do you have time to talk to us?"

Fran said in a whisper, "Is this about Carly Blackburn?"

"Yes, it is," Abby answered.

"Come with me." Fran led us to the back of the shop and through the curtain, where we found an area she had carved out as office space, a niche where she'd set up a computer and a filing cabinet. There was nowhere for us to sit, so we all stood.

"I hope you don't mind talking back here," Fran said. "I wouldn't want a customer to overhear. You understand."

"It's fine," Abby told her. "We won't be long."

Fran smiled again. Her smile was modest and warm with laugh lines creasing the corners of her eyes. "How can I help?"

"We'd like to ask you some questions about last Thursday evening," Abby said.

"Sure. Go ahead."

I pulled the iPad from my tote and opened a file marked *Fran*. With the device in my left hand, I did my best to type notes with my right while Abby fired away her questions.

"What time did you arrive at the hotel?"

"Let's see." Fran tapped her chin. "It was a little before six p.m. The show started at seven, but I arrived early to bring in the clothing."

"What did you do when you got there?" Abby continued.

"I wheeled in the dress racks and positioned them behind the row of dressing rooms. That took up my time until models started to arrive, and then I helped them with their outfits."

"Did you see Jillian Osborne backstage?" Abby asked.

"Yes. I saw Jillian around six, then she was pulled away by the audio man to test the microphone. After that she went out to the ballroom until the show started."

"Thinking back, do you remember anything unusual happening backstage?" Abby asked.

"Oh, yes," Fran replied, "there was a lot of tension between the models. It was incredibly uncomfortable. In fact, on the first night, I overheard Carly arguing with Eleni."

I quickly typed in her response with my free hand, but there was too much information. My fingers couldn't keep up, so I asked Abby to give me a minute, wishing I had accepted her offer to use the notepad.

When I'd finished, Abby continued. "Could you hear what the women were arguing about?"

"Something to do with the mayor," Fran replied. "Something about an affair."

Abby pulled her notepad from her purse and flipped to a certain page. "The mayor is Charles Sloan," she read aloud, as though reminding herself, "and Eleni and Charles are married." She looked up from her notes and asked Fran, "Carly and Eleni were arguing about Charles Sloan having an affair?"

"Yes, I heard his name mentioned several times, but I didn't stay long enough to hear anything else. I didn't want to eavesdrop."

I added the name of Sequoia's beloved hometown mayor, Charles Sloan, to my notes and high-lighted the word *affair*. Things were starting to get interesting.

"Was he at the fashion show?" Abby asked.

Fran nodded. "Yes. He gave the introduction before Jillian took over."

"Why would the mayor introduce a fashion show?" Abby questioned.

"He has just recently pledged his support to the Small Business Association, so we asked him to speak at our event. He drew in quite a large crowd."

"Did you see him before the show?"

Fran thought for a moment, then answered plainly, "I don't believe so."

I added a question to my notes: *Where was the mayor before the show started?*

"Did anything else happen on the first night?" Abby asked. "Anything that stood out to you?"

"Not that I can recall. We ended up having a great show."

Abby moved on to the second night, the night of the murder. "Can you describe the events leading up to the show on Thursday night?"

"Jillian came in like I said, and then Eleni came in a little after that. She wanted to make some changes to her outfits, so I helped her."

Fran's information lined up with what Jillian had told us.

"Had Jillian placed the bottles before Eleni arrived?" Abby asked.

Fran nodded. "She put out the bottles when she first got there. We chatted for a bit. She was very nice. I really hope you can prove she didn't poison the water."

"Me, too," Abby said. "Hopefully your information will help. I'd like to get a timeline of what happened after Eleni arrived. Do you know who came in next?"

"Carly came next," she told us. "That must've been about a half hour before the show started."

Abby leaned over to check my notes, then continued, "From the timeline you've given, Eleni arrived well before the other models. Was Eleni ever alone backstage?"

Fran paused to give the question careful consideration. I could tell where Abby was leading. If Eleni was alone, she would've had plenty of time to poison the water.

"I'm sorry," Fran answered, "but I wasn't keeping tabs on Eleni. I was going back and forth between my racks of clothes and the dressing rooms, getting ready for Hope and Carly."

"And you said the clothing racks were located behind the dressing rooms," Abby said.

"Yes, that's correct."

"Did you ever see Eleni enter Carly's dressing room?"

"No."

"In the time it took you to set up the other outfits," she said, "would Eleni have had time to slip into Carly's dressing room?"

Fran shook her head. "I don't know. I guess she could have, but I wasn't paying attention."

"When Carly came in," Abby continued, "did she and Eleni continue their argument from the previous evening?"

"No, from what I could tell, the two didn't speak to each other." Fran cleared her throat. "You seem to be very interested in Eleni. Do you think she had something to do with Carly's death?"

"We're interested in everyone who was backstage," Abby answered.

Fran cleared her throat again and said in a lower voice, "The reason I'm asking is, Eleni seemed to be upset when she first came in Thursday night. I know her fairly well, and I don't want to place the blame on anyone, but Eleni didn't seem herself. She's normally very outgoing and funny, always laughing, always smiling, but that night was different. She was quiet, and her eyes were red and swollen, as though she'd been crying. It wasn't the Eleni I know."

"And this was on the night of Carly's death?" Abby asked.

"Yes," she said confidently.

I typed it in.

"That's all the questions I have about Eleni," Abby said to both of us. "Athena, can you think of anything else?"

"I think you've covered everything," I told her.

"Then let's move on to Hope," Abby said. "We basically have the same questions. Was Hope alone backstage? Did you see her enter Carly's dressing room?"

"No, but when Hope came in, she was practically screaming at Carly. I remember that clearly, and I told the police about it because of the threats."

"What threats?" Abby asked.

"Carly kept repeating. 'You'll pay for that.' I'm not sure what she meant, but then Hope responded by telling Carly to watch her back."

My fingers were typing furiously, trying to keep up.

"Hope threatened Carly?" Abby reiterated.

"Yes," she answered. "Loudly. And I'm not the only one who heard it. Eleni was there, too."

Wow. Not only had Carly argued with Eleni on the first night, but she had also been fighting with Hope on the night of the murder. Abby was right. Carly did make enemies easily.

"What happened next?" Abby asked.

"Carly received a phone call and left the stage. I don't remember when she came back to get ready for the show, but she was there when it started."

"And that's all the information you have about Hope?"

"Yes," she said, "I don't know Hope very well, and I've come to believe that's a good thing."

"What do you mean?" Abby asked.

Fran shrugged. "I can't put my finger on it. She just seems a little . . . off-balance?"

"What happened after Hope left?" Abby asked.

"The rest of the night is just a blur of activity. Soon after that, the music started playing, the crowd began to filter into the ballroom, and then the show began."

After I finished typing, Abby looked to me for more questions about Hope, but I had none. I had numerous questions to ask Hope, though, like why she had threatened Carly. And if the police knew about it, why wasn't Hope being considered a suspect?

"Moving on," Abby said. "Did you see anyone else backstage at any time, before or during the show?"

"I did," Fran answered. "I believe he was a security guard. He walked through before the show, stopped me to ask a few questions, and then left."

"What did he ask you?"

"He asked for my name, my reason for being backstage, security type questions."

"Was that before or after Jillian arrived with the water?" Abby asked.

"I'm pretty sure it was after she arrived."

"We also have evidence that another man was backstage," Abby said. "He would've been wearing a black baseball cap and T-shirt and would've exited through the back door. Did you see anyone matching that description? This would've been right before the show started."

"Not that I remember. Like I said, it was just a blur at that point."

One of Fran's employees came into the back room and stopped at the door to the small office. "Everything okay?" she asked.

"Just fine, dear," Fran answered gracefully. "I'll be out soon."

Before leaving, the employee gave Abby and me a strong once-over, clearly confused as to why the three of us were crammed inside Fran's office.

"Just a few more questions," Abby said, "and then we'll let you get back to work. Did you notice anyone coming in or out of the backstage door?"

"Just me and the security guard."

"So, you were able to enter the hotel through the back entrance?" Abby asked.

"Yes. I parked in the employee lot and was given a pass to get into the building. It was a lot easier

than going in and out through the lobby with my
racks of clothing."

"And the only other person you noticed using
the back door was a security guard?"

"That's right," she said.

"Did he have an employee pass?"

"I can only assume he did," Fran answered.

Abby glanced at me. "Do you have anything else
you want to ask?"

"Yes," I said. "Do you know who found Carly's
body?"

"I believe Eleni was the one who called for
help."

"Where were you when Eleni called for help?" I
asked.

"I was behind the dressing rooms, preparing the
next round of outfits. I heard Eleni call out and
came to see what had happened." Fran shook her
head. "It was so sad. Carly had drawn her knees up
to her chest, and her eyes and mouth were open,
as though she'd been surprised. And there was a
puddle of vomit beside her. It was a terrible sight."

"I'm sure it was," I told her. "I'm sorry to bring
it up."

"I just hope I've been of some help to you,"

"You've been very helpful," Abby told her. "Thank
you."

"It's not a problem," Fran said. "Anytime."

As Abby and I headed back up Greene Street to
the detective agency, Abby said, "Good interview.
We got a lot of information from Fran. Now I'm
really curious as to the arguments the women had.
What intrigued me was the conversation between

Eleni and Carly mentioning an affair. That bears investigating."

I slid my sunglasses over my eyes. "I thought it was interesting that Carly argued with both Eleni and Hope."

"Jillian warned us about Carly," Abby pointed out. "It sounds like she made enemies easily, which makes our job all the harder."

"What about the threats made by Hope?" I asked.

"Would you read back what Fran said about them?" Abby asked.

I pulled out my iPad and looked through my hastily typed notes. "Here it is. Carly came backstage and told Hope that she would pay for that, whatever that means. And Hope replied with a threat of her own. She said that Carly should watch her back."

"I have a feeling," Abby said while rummaging through her yellow purse, "that Hope told the detective about Jillian's relationship with Carly to throw them off her trail." She retrieved a pair of sunglasses from her purse and shaded her eyes. "Given the threat she made to Carly, I'm moving Hope to number one on my suspect list. Let's try to talk with her soon."

We chatted for another ten minutes as we walked to the office and then climbed the inside stairs to the detective agency, where I found the door unlocked and Case at his computer.

"Win any money?" I asked as Abby and I approached his desk.

"Nope."

"Lose any money?" I quipped.

"I lost the houseboat and the deed to our building."

Abby set her purse down and looked at Case with raised eyebrows.

"He's joking," I informed her. "He doesn't own either one."

"I did find out that Donald Blackburn is at his casino every evening if we want to check him out," Case said. "How did your interview go?"

We pulled up chairs in front of his desk and filled him in on our meeting with Fran. He sat, quietly listening while Abby explained why Hope was her top suspect, and I made my case for Eleni having the most convenient opportunity and, possibly, a motive involving Eleni's husband.

"So," Case said, "the murder victim and Eleni were arguing about Mayor Sloan. And we know that the victim was the mayor's campaign manager. Maybe they had a dispute about how the campaign was being run."

"It's possible," I countered. "But given that Fran heard Carly and Eleni mention an affair, I have a different theory—two women fighting over a man. Carly was working with him, and Eleni was married to him. Not to mention Carly was recently divorced."

"A love triangle," Case said. "That's a strong motive."

"Fran mentioned that Eleni was acting strangely on the night Carly was poisoned," I said. "Maybe Eleni had just found out about an affair and took the opportunity to seek her revenge."

"Speaking of Eleni"—Abby checked her watch—
"it's after four now, and we want to be at her bookstore by five thirty." She stood. "If you don't mind,
I'd like to do some more research. Will you send
me your notes?"

"Of course," I said.

Case started typing. "I'll work with Abby to com-
pile a list of questions for Eleni."

"Perfect." I stood up. "That gives me time to
check in at the garden center and be back by five
fifteen. I'll see you both then."

When I got back to Spencer's, everything was
quiet. I saw only two customers in the store. My
dad was unpacking a box of garden gloves and
hanging them on an endcap, and my cousin Drew
was perched on a stool behind the counter scrolling through something on his cell phone.

"Where are Delphi and Niko?" I asked Drew.

"Niko is out in the back trying to teach Oscar a
new trick, and Delphi is in the conference room
with a couple she knows. You might know the
guy—Ken Brody. His uncle owns Majestic Jewelers."

"Is Delphi doing a reading?" I asked.

He chuckled. "I think so."

I went up the hallway that led to the office and
stopped just outside the conference room to listen.

"You have to love this ring," said the man, whom
I assumed was Ken Brody. "The wedding band
locks into the engagement ring from the back."

"Isn't it beautiful?" the woman asked. "Try it on."

"I love it!" Delphi exclaimed a moment later. "It's perfect."

I stepped back in surprise. Was Delphi picking out a wedding ring? Had Bob Maguire proposed?

"Athena," Drew called out from the other end of the hallway, "there's a customer on the phone with a question."

I shushed him, tiptoed away from the conference room, and went into the office to take the call. When I hung up, I noticed Delphi standing in the doorway. She went to the mini-fridge and pulled out a can of sparkling water.

"How's it going?" I asked.

She glanced at me oddly as she popped open the can. "Why? Is there a problem? Did I do something wrong?"

"No! Not at all. I just wondered how your day was going."

"It's fine." She took a long swig of water, eyeing me askance. "So, when did you get here?"

"Oh, um, just now," I stammered. "Just walked in, and Drew said there was a call for me."

"Hmm. I heard Drew call your name, but it sounded like he was near the conference room."

"That's weird," I said.

"Yeah, it is weird." Delphi looked at her can, trying desperately to act nonchalant. "So, you weren't near the conference room?"

"No," I tried to say convincingly.

"You didn't overhear anything?"

"Was there something I was supposed to have heard?"

"Nope," Delphi answered. "Nothing at all." She took another sip of water and walked out.

If she was about to get engaged, she sure was keeping it quiet. And I sure wasn't going to say anything about what I'd heard. Delphi had only known Bob about a month. I couldn't even imagine what Mama would have to say.

"Good luck, Delphi," I whispered.

# CHAPTER SEVEN

I returned to the detective agency at five fifteen to find Abby standing outside in front of the gift store two doors down, looking in its window. She saw me coming and turned. "Ready for our next interview?"

"I'm all set. The bookstore is up six blocks, in Little Greece. We have plenty of time."

"You have your iPad?" Abby asked. "Case emailed you the questions he wrote up."

I tapped my purse. "Got it right here."

As we walked, Abby said, "I spoke with Carly's mother and sister this afternoon. Both said Carly had made a will after her son was born, but she had not made a new will. Carly's mother was emphatic she would've known about it. Apparently, since Carly's divorce, she and her mother talked on the phone every night."

We stopped at the corner to wait for the light to

change, then as we crossed the street Abby said, "If Carly didn't have a new will, then, according to the original will, her son would've inherited the land at her death. And with Carly gone, Donald will undoubtedly get custody of the boy, which means he would have his land back."

"Which gives him a motive," I said. "He goes on the suspect list."

The sidewalks were mostly free of tourists, which was strange for such a warm day in my lakeside tourist town. Abby and I strolled casually, talking about our lives. I asked Abby about her flower shop, and she told me how she had come to acquire it. "After being ejected from law school," she said, "I didn't know what to do with myself. And there it was, like a jewel in a crown, the place where I'd spent several happy college summers working, Bloomers Flower Shop. The owner was in financial straits and wanted to sell the business, but fortunately, I had money left from the college fund my grandfather had set up, so I was able to assume her mortgage." Abby smiled. "It's been quite a ride, and I love every day of it."

"You're very lucky," I told her. "I love the garden center, but it's not my passion. I haven't quite figured that part out yet."

"It seems like solving mysteries may be your passion," Abby said. "From what I've seen so far, you're pretty darn good at it. You and Case make a great team."

Smiling at her remark, I said, "I wouldn't be doing this without him."

I glanced at the shop ahead of us. Above the big

front window was a sign in Greek-style lettering, *The Garden of Readin'. New and Used Books.* "And look. We're here."

"Would you like to take the lead?" Abby asked.

"Sure!"

"You can read the questions from your iPad, and I'll take notes in my notebook. Don't judge my handwriting, though."

"That's why I use the iPad," I told her. "You should see *my* handwriting."

"Marco has been telling me to start using a tablet for my notes, but with my luck the battery would run out in the middle of an interview. You can't go wrong with a pen and paper."

"The pen could run out of ink."

Abby stopped before opening the door and looked at me. "I've never thought about that before."

We entered the little shop and saw a young woman talking to a customer at the cash register. The shop had a center aisle with bookshelves on both sides. The lighting was dim, the sun coming in the window illuminating dust motes in the air.

While Abby checked out the shop, I walked up to the counter and waited until the clerk glanced my way. "Is Eleni around?" I asked. "I'm a friend."

"She's around here someplace," she said. "Eleni?"

"Back here," Eleni called from the rear of the store.

I followed Abby, noticing a strong tingle in my nostrils. I'd forgotten how terribly dusty the store was.

We found Eleni in the last row, unpacking a box

of books. She had on a pink print shirt and white pants with white sandals. Curly dark hair framed an oval face, heavy eye makeup coated the lids of her dark brown eyes, and deep red lipstick colored her lips.

"Athena!" she said with a smile. "What are you doing out and about? Are things quiet at Spencer's, too?"

"Very quiet today," I said.

"How's your mother?"

"Busy at the diner, as always."

Eleni gave Abby a curious glance, then said to me. "What can I do for you?"

"First of all," I said, "this is Abby Knight Salvare from New Chapel, Indiana. Abby and her husband have a detective agency there."

Eleni smiled at Abby and extended her hand. "Happy to meet you. Are you here for a vacation or on official business?"

"Business," Abby replied, "but I'm also enjoying getting to know your town."

"Eleni, as you've probably read in the newspaper," I said, "my partner, Case Donnelly, and I own a detective agency. Right now, we're working on a case with Abby concerning Carly Blackburn's death."

"Carly's death?" Eleni asked. "I thought the police had already arrested the woman responsible."

"That's why we're conducting a private investigation," Abby said. "My cousin is the woman targeted by the police, and I know for certain she's innocent."

"I'm sorry to hear that. How can I help?"

"We'd like to find out more about the events of last Thursday evening," I said. "That would be a great help."

Eleni leaned one elbow against a shelf and gave me a skeptical glance. "Go ahead, then."

I opened the iPad to retrieve Case's notes. "First of all," I said, "when did you arrive at the ballroom on Thursday evening?"

Eleni paused to think. "I don't know. I closed the shop and made my way over afterward. So, sometime after six o'clock."

Abby had pulled her notebook from her purse and was scribbling notes. I looked over to see what she had written but couldn't make out her handwriting.

I continued, even though Eleni seemed more interested in unpacking her box of dusty old books. "Who was there when you arrived?"

She slid a book onto the shelf. "Fran and Jillian."

"What time did the other two models arrive?" I asked.

"Hope and Carly arrived sometime after I did," Eleni said.

"Did you see a man backstage at the beginning of the show?" I asked.

She turned to gaze at me as though the question puzzled her, but then she smiled. "Oh, that was Ben, our security guard. He was there briefly for a walk-through."

"You have a security guard?" Abby asked.

"Actually," Eleni said, ruffling the pages of a book, "Ben works for my husband." She set the book on a shelf and leaned down for another. "Charles gave the introduction for the fashion show."

I let Abby finish writing her notes, trying to ignore the sensation to sneeze. After wrinkling my nose a few times, the sensation dissipated. "Why does your husband need a security guard?" I asked.

"Charles has had some serious threats made against him because of his campaign platform, so he hired a security guard to travel with him."

"What kind of threats?" I asked.

"Death threats."

"From whom?" I asked.

Eleni positioned another book on the shelf, then turned to face me once again. "We suspect they came from someone connected to one of the corporations trying to get a foothold in town. As you probably know, Athena, Charles's platform is to keep Sequoia small. We don't want big corporations to come in and take business away from all the local shops. More than likely, it's just a scare tactic, but Charles takes our safety very seriously."

"What were the threats, specifically?"

"I don't know the details," Eleni replied. "Charles handled that. But they must have been serious enough to warrant a full-time security guard."

"Who else knows about the threats?" I asked.

"Just those people who work closely with Charles. He doesn't want to scare anyone, and I'm sure he doesn't want it to go public."

"Did Carly know about the threats?" I asked.

"Carly was his campaign manager," Eleni replied, "so I assume she knew. And along those lines,

you might be interested to know that Donald Blackburn, Carly's ex-husband, had planned to build a
giant casino near the lake."

"Why is that important?" Abby asked.

"Because my husband quashed the deal. It wasn't
very long after that when the threats began."

Abby wrote it down, and I watched her under-
line the name *Donald Blackburn.*

"Did you see Donald at the show?" I asked.

"No," she answered. "And I doubt he would've
been welcome."

"So, Ben the security guard was at the show to
protect your husband," I said.

"Yes. And for my safety, too, of course. Ben was
told to make a thorough sweep of the premises
just to be safe."

"Do you know him well, this security guard?"

"Not well at all," she replied. "He was just hired
two weeks ago."

When Abby finished writing, I asked, "Did your
husband go backstage at all before the show?"

Eleni bent to retrieve another book. "Charles
came back briefly to wish me good luck."

"Did you notice any other men backstage?"

"No."

"What about a man in a black baseball cap and
T-shirt?" I asked.

"No," she answered again. "I didn't see anyone
like that."

I gave time for Abby to write, puzzling over the
mysterious man in the black hat that Abby had
seen on the security camera. How could he have
made it backstage without Fran or Eleni seeing
him?

"I'm not really sure what you're hoping to find," Eleni said. "There were only a few people backstage, and I can't help but wonder whether you're looking at one of us as a suspect."

I tried to reassure her, although I had to bend the truth to do so. "We're not even sure that Carly was poisoned at the fashion show. We're just trying to eliminate the possibility."

"I see." Eleni bent down to retrieve another book from the box on the floor. "Will this be much longer? I have several more boxes to unpack."

"I'd like to know more about Carly," I told her. "When she arrived backstage, did she seem to be acting normally?"

"I couldn't say," Eleni replied. "I was busy trying on an outfit in my dressing room."

"What about the first night of the fashion show?"

There was a subtle tensing of Eleni's jaw as she flipped through the pages of another book. I tried my best not to breathe. "Carly seemed fine," she answered.

I noticed her looking impatient, and I hadn't even started with the harder questions Case had written out. I tried to tread carefully. "Someone we've spoken with mentioned that you and Carly were seen having an argument on the first night," I said. "Would you tell us what the argument was about?"

"It wasn't an argument," Eleni answered hotly. "We were having a discussion."

"Then what was the discussion about?" I prodded.

Eleni unpacked another book. "That's none of your business."

Apparently, I hadn't trodden carefully enough.

"Excuse me. I'm sorry," Abby interjected, "but we're private investigators. This *is* our business. You were heard having an argument with Carly one day before her death. You've been very forthcoming up until this point, but I find it very odd that you chose this question to avoid."

Eleni placed one hand on her hip. "What are you insinuating?"

"I've been doing this a long time," Abby said, "and it's usually the guilty who refuse to help."

"*Guilty?*" Eleni glared at Abby, her nostrils flaring. "You must be joking."

"I'm dead serious," Abby told her.

Eleni pivoted and walked up the row, browsing the middle shelf with her index finger. "Accusations can be damning," she said, pulling a book from the shelf. She walked back over to where we stood. "Have you ever read Arthur Miller?"

I stared at her in bewilderment, but Abby merely said, "No, why?"

Eleni handed her the book. It was Arthur Miller's *The Crucible.* "It's about the Salem witch trials. You should read it, and maybe you'll learn to be more careful when accusing others." She pulled another book from the box at her feet.

Abby set the Arthur Miller book on the shelf. "Tell me what the argument was about."

"Like I told you, it wasn't an argument."

"Then what were you discussing?" Abby asked. "Your husband?"

Eleni stepped to the end of the row and glanced toward the checkout counter, where I could hear the clerk chatting with a customer. Then she stepped back into the row and in a hushed voice said, "My husband is a good man. He's been an excellent father and an outstanding mayor. So, when I learned that rumors were circulating about Carly and my husband, I politely asked her to resign as campaign manager. She wasn't very happy about that and proceeded to tell me so, just not as politely."

I waited a moment as Abby scribbled her notes before asking, "What was the rumor?"

Eleni studied the spine of an antique-looking Bible for a long moment, then finally sighed and looked away. "I was informed that my husband was having an affair with Carly."

My mouth dropped open in surprise. "Who told you that?"

Eleni shook her head sadly. "I shouldn't have listened to her—she's the biggest gossip in town—but she hears things. She has her sticky fingers in everyone's business. Plus, I knew Carly and my husband were working closely together on his campaign."

"Who told you?" I asked again.

"Hope Louvain."

I let that sink in while Abby jotted more notes. Was that why Eleni had been so quiet before the show? Was that why she'd been crying? Had Charles just admitted to an affair?

"When did Hope tell you about this rumored affair?" I asked. "Was it before the fashion show?"

"No," she said. "It was earlier in the week. She stopped by the bookstore to tell me."

"Did you have any evidence besides Hope's gossip that your husband was having an affair?" Abby asked.

"No, because it wasn't true."

"How do you know it wasn't true?" I asked.

"After hearing the rumor from Hope," Eleni replied, "I went to my husband's office one evening. It was late, but I have a key, and I was able to get in quietly without being seen. I watched Charles and Carly sitting in his office going over a speech. I stayed there for quite a while, and nothing happened. It all seemed perfectly innocent."

"Then you believe your husband wasn't having an affair?" I asked.

"It didn't appear that way," she answered, "but I still wanted Carly to resign."

"Why?"

"Because I was afraid Hope would spread the rumor and it would taint the campaign. I explained that to Carly and she was furious with Hope. I'm sure someone could've misread that as an argument, but I can assure you, Carly was not upset with me."

I glanced at Abby to see if she was wondering the same thing I was. Why would Hope go out of her way to spread a false rumor—unless the rumor wasn't false.

"How long had Carly and your husband been working together?" I asked.

"A few months," she said.

"Then how can you be sure the rumor wasn't true?"

"I do not believe my husband was having an affair with Carly," she said with fierce determination, "but I do believe Hope was trying to turn me *against* Carly."

"Why would she want to do that?" I asked.

"Hope was trying to use me to ruin Carly's reputation. Hope and Carly were bitter enemies, which I'm sure you'll find out as you continue your investigation."

Before I could move on to another question, Abby raised her pen. "Would you explain it to us now?" she asked.

"Only if this is off the record."

"We're not journalists," Abby informed her. "We share our information with the police."

"All I mean is that I don't want Hope to know you got this information from me. Her retaliations can be"—she took a deep breath and let it out—"harsh."

# CHAPTER EIGHT

"Y ou have my word on it, Eleni," I told her. "Whatever you tell us about Hope will not be traced back to you."

"Then I'll tell you what I know," Eleni said after another deep breath. "But I have to reiterate how sensitive this information is. It might not be something you'll want to share with the police, especially since Chief Louvain is involved."

"I understand," I said, although I didn't fully. I was simply agreeing with her to fast-track the conversation. Eleni had certainly aroused my suspicions about Hope Louvain.

"Hope and Carly both have boys in middle school," Eleni said quietly. "The boys have been in trouble numerous times for fighting after summer school, and I'm not sure how, but Carly had Hope's son expelled from school for bullying."

"Eleni?" we heard, then saw her clerk appear at

the end of the row. "I'll be leaving in about ten minutes. Should I start closing up?"

"Yes, Janine. Thank you." Eleni waited until she was gone to say quietly, "After Hope's son was expelled, she was so upset that she took a tire iron to the front windshield of Carly's Mercedes—and Carly was in her car at the time."

"Was she hurt?" I asked in surprise.

Eleni shook her head. "Fortunately, the windshield just cracked. This happened a week before Carly's death."

"Did Carly call the police?" Abby wanted to know.

"She sure did," Eleni said, "but it seems the incident report never got filed. Hope's husband made it go away. I only know what happened because I was in my dressing room when they fought about it."

Hope Louvain was quickly moving up my list of suspects. I flashed back to what Fran had told us, then asked Eleni, "Do you remember whether Hope threatened Carly?"

"Yes. Something to the effect of 'You'd better watch your back.' But then, Hope likes to threaten people. It wasn't anything new."

"Did you tell Detective Walters about Hope's threat?"

"Absolutely not," Eleni said. "I shouldn't even be telling you."

"Doesn't it seem a bit irresponsible to withhold that kind of information from the police?" Abby asked. "Especially when it could mean that someone innocent takes the rap?"

"The Louvains are not the kind of people you want as enemies," Eleni said. "I'm not going to put my family in danger, or my husband's career at risk. Hope is a violent woman, and Ed is like a pit bull when it comes to protecting his wife. He has more sway in this town than my husband does, so again, be careful when talking to them."

"Are you saying she would retaliate?" I asked.

"What I'm saying is, if you're looking for a suspect, you know where to start. With her husband there to back her up, I would imagine Hope had every reason to believe she could poison Carly and get away with it."

Abby seemed to be skeptical. "You just said that accusations can be damning, yet here you are accusing Hope."

"And you said it's the guilty who refuse to help, so here I am, helping."

Abby's cell phone rang, so she stepped away to answer it. Eleni glanced at her watch and said to me, "It's late, and I still have some things to do before I close up. I wish you luck in finding Carly's killer. Just remember to leave me out of it."

"I understand," I said. "Thanks for your help."

When Abby joined us again, Eleni pulled the Arthur Miller book from the shelf and held it out. "Would you like this?" she asked Abby.

"No, thanks," Abby said.

"I'd be happy to take it," I said. "How much?"

"No charge," Eleni said. "And tell your mother I said hello."

\* \* \*

Outside, the sidewalks were nearly deserted. I'd forgotten how dramatically business slowed down when the fair was in town. The sun was still hot and lingering in the summer sky, cooking the empty sidewalks. Normally, the shops would have their doors open with customers bustling in and out, but with the lack of tourism and abundance of heat, the shop doors were shut tight, and the hum of air-conditioning units buzzed loudly at every alleyway.

Abby squinted as we turned into the sun and said, "That was the audio tech on the phone. He said the flowers Carly received came from a florist shop called Back to the Fuchsia. Any idea where that is?"

"It's on White Street," I told her. "About two blocks south of here."

Abby pulled her sunglasses from her purse, a pair of cute oval frames in white with yellow sides, and slid them up her nose. "Let's head over there."

I checked my watch. Delphi would be leaving for her dance lessons in less than an hour. "You'll have to go without me," I told Abby. "Why don't we meet tomorrow morning to discuss our interviews and figure out our next steps?"

"Perfect," Abby said. "I'll see you then."

I texted Case about meeting with Abby the next morning and headed back to Spencer's. As I approached the building, I noticed through the windows that the lights inside were off. The only thing I could think was that my father had closed the store early due to lack of business, but when I tried the barn door, it opened smoothly.

"Hello?" I called into the empty, dark store. "Pops?"

The door closed quietly behind me. Long splinters of sunlight cast through the tall window at the front of the big barn, lighting up the outstretched arm of the statue of Athena, beckoning me deeper into the darkness. Past the statue, I called again into the expansive space. "Anyone home?"

I tried to convince myself to accept the simplest answer. Either the power had gone out or Dad had closed up early, but something in my gut was warning me otherwise. I walked toward the light shining in through the slender back door window, holding out my hands to keep myself from bumping into potted planters and backyard furniture. Luckily, I had been the one to stage the sales floor and by then could almost walk the store with my eyes closed.

Coming up to the back door, I could hear a soft, metallic pounding. I inched closer to hear my dad yell out in pain. At that, I burst through the double doors out onto the patio, ready for action, only to find my dad, Delphi, Nicholas, and Bob Maguire gathered next to the building staring at a big metal box nestled in the bushes.

"Son of a—" My dad jabbed his thumb into his mouth before finishing. He was kneeling next to the unit with a flushed face.

"What's happening here?" I asked as Nicholas jumped up to give me a hug.

"Grandpa's fixing the air conditioner," my son said proudly.

"Not exactly," Dad said, shaking out his sore thumb. "It's a generator, Niko."

Bob helped my dad to his feet, then knelt down in his place to take a look.

"A tree must have fallen on an electrical line," my dad explained. "The power went off about ten minutes ago."

"Bobby brought the generator from the shed, but it's not working," Delphi explained.

Bob flicked the switch on and off several times before the engine kicked over and the generator started rumbling. "There we go," Bob said. "Just a little rusty is all."

Oscar popped his head out from behind a row of boxwoods with his nose jabbing in all directions, clearly hoping this unlikely gathering would bring him his next meal. He disappeared when the generator came to a sputtering stop.

"We're out of gas," Dad said. "And unfortunately, I don't remember refilling the gas cans the last time I used them."

"We'd go get more, but we're going to have to leave," Delphi said, pulling Bob away from the group. "Our dance lessons start in ten minutes."

"I guess I'll go to the gas station," Dad grumbled.

"I'll get the gas," I offered. "I need a refill anyway. Bob, before you go, have you had a chance to check the detective's file about the poison?"

"No, I haven't," he said. "I know the lab results have come back, but I haven't had a chance to sneak a peek."

"That's okay. I understand."

"How did your lunch meeting with Walters go?" Bob asked.

"Unproductive," I said. "He's not going to cooperate with us."

"That's what I was afraid of. Looks like you're on your own."

"No shock there," I told him. "Maybe Walters's replacement will be better."

"Maybe you're looking at him," Bob said with a secretive smile.

"Are you serious?" Delphi asked.

"That's good news," I said.

"I'm up for the position, as are several others, including my former partner, Juan Gomez."

That wasn't good news. Gomez and I had butted heads on two different murder investigations. There was no love lost between us. "I'll keep my fingers crossed for you, Bob," I said.

"Keep your fingers crossed that we don't show up late," Delphi told him, leading him away.

"Come on, Niko," I said. "Grab the gas cans from the shed, and let's go."

On our way back from the gas station, Nicholas and I stopped for sandwiches. We returned with a sandwich for my dad, only to find him seated on the picnic table out back, feeding Oscar peanuts from his palm.

"Pops, you're going to spoil him."

"I think it's a little late for that, Thenie. Do you know he took up residence in the garden shed?"

I gave my son a pointed look and said to my dad, "I thought you might have something to say about that. Niko and I will clean that up right now."

"It's okay," Dad replied. "The shed's a great little home for Oscar. We'll just have to find a different spot to store the gas cans and pesticides."

Nicholas hopped onto the bench next to his grandfather. "Can we install a doggie door, too? That way we don't have to leave the shed door open all the time."

"That's a good idea, Niko," my dad said.

"We can discuss that later," I told them. "For now, we have to call an electrician."

"Already did it," Dad said. "We're not the only building without power, so it might be a day or two before we get it fixed."

"How are we going to operate the business without electricity?" I asked.

"That generator will run power to the office and the register and a few lights in the barn. That's all we really need."

"We need more than a few lights, Pops."

"It doesn't get dark until closing time anyway," he said, handing the bag of food over to my son. He got up with a groan and made his way over to me. "I'll just have to make sure we have plenty of gas to keep this thing running."

Nicholas squeezed in between us. "Can we fix up Oscar's shed now, Grandpa?"

I ruffled his hair, left the two to discuss the details, and took the gas cans over to the generator. After topping off the fuel, I flicked the switch, and the engine rumbled to life. Through the glass door window, I saw a string of lights inside the store light up.

I had just set the gas cans behind the shed at the back of our property when I heard my phone ringing in my pocket. It was Lila Talbot.

"Hello, partner," she sang out happily. "I'm calling a meeting at the detective agency tonight. What time are you able to meet up?"

"You're calling a meeting?" I asked hesitantly. "About what?"

"Just a general meeting," she answered. "We need to keep each other in the loop. That's what partners do."

Which meant she was feeling left *out* of the loop. I tried to suppress my sigh, but Lila caught on anyway. "Don't sound so put out. Case and Abby are already at the office, and I'm on my way. What time can you be there?"

After sending Nicholas home with my dad, I closed up the garden center as soon as I could. I shut down the computer for the night and stood from my desk, stretching and rubbing my stiff neck. Then I hoisted my purse over my shoulder and noticed it was heavier than normal. I set the purse on my desk, opened it, and pulled out the old copy of *The Crucible* that Eleni had given me. I thumbed through it, sneezed twice, and left the book for my dad. Maybe he would enjoy a good read. Minus the allergies.

I arrived back at the office to find Case and Abby sitting in Case's office. And of course, there was our silent partner, Lila Talbot, dressed like a model in a light-blue summer sweater and slim navy slacks, her blond hair braided on each side and pinned at the back of her head with a crystal clip. She had pulled one of the reception chairs into the office and placed it next to Abby's.

"Don't worry about being late," Lila said to me. "I know you're busy at the garden center, so Case and Abby have already caught me up to speed. Abby was just starting to tell us about visiting the flower shop after your interview with Eleni."

"I found out who bought the flowers," Abby said. "Carly's ex-husband, Donald Blackburn. I have the purchase order from the flower shop with his name on it."

"I knew it," Case said.

"Why would Carly's ex-husband buy her flowers?" Lila asked.

"The logical answer is to get backstage," Case said. "That would explain the man in the black cap and T-shirt leaving through the back exit. The Blackburn Casino employees wear a black baseball cap and black T-shirt."

Lila pushed back a loose strand of blond hair. "If this Donald is bringing Carly flowers, then he must've wanted to get back together with her. My ex-husband would always buy me flowers after a fight."

"If Donald had a reunion in mind," I said, "it obviously didn't work, because Carly threw the flowers in the trash."

"Ouch," Lila said. "That would hurt."

"Or maybe a reunion wasn't what he had in mind," Case said. "I did more research on Donald and Carly and learned that Carly had filed for full custody of their son, claiming verbal abuse. They had a court date set for the week after Carly's death. And Abby told me about Carly's will situation, so I'm going to say Donald definitely had a motive for murder."

"Then we need to prove that Donald was at the fashion show," Abby said.

"Doesn't the purchase order count as proof?" Lila asked.

"It proves that Donald bought the flowers, but not that he delivered them personally." Abby folded the purchase order into her purse. "I'll show a photo of Donald to the hotel staff to see if anyone remembers seeing him."

"Look up the Blackburn Casino's website," Case said. "His picture is listed under *Staff*."

"Thanks," Abby said, pulling out her phone.

Lila turned to me with a smile. "It sounds like you and Abby got a lot of information today. How close are we to nailing down the suspect?"

"Well," I said, "the good news is that there were a number of people backstage before and during the show, giving us several persons of interest."

"The bad news," Abby said, putting away her phone, "is that both women we talked to placed Jillian backstage before the show, too, which means they would have reported that to the detective, giving him more ammunition against her."

"Then we'll have to double our efforts to find the killer," Case said, tapping his pen on the desktop. "The info about Hope's temper tantrum with the tire iron was very interesting. It says a lot about her character and how far she would go to get even."

"And don't forget about Ed Louvain's cover-up of her crime," Abby said. "It makes me wonder what else he would hide for her. So I say we list Hope Louvain as our top suspect."

"And Fran Decker?" Case asked.

"I'm not putting her on my list," Abby answered. "I usually get a strong gut feeling about someone, and she didn't do it for me. She didn't seem to know Carly very well."

"I agree," I said. "She had no motive."

"Fran is a doll," Lila said. "I've known her for years. She wouldn't harm a fly. What about Eleni Sloan?"

"She's on the list," Abby said. "Eleni was the first model to arrive, and from what Fran told us, she would've had a window of opportunity to poison Carly's water bottle. The problem is, she has no apparent motive."

"Unless Hope's gossip is true," I said, "and Eleni lied to us."

Lila leaned in. "Just so you know, I've heard the rumors that the mayor has been unfaithful. However, I, for one, don't believe them."

"You've heard rumors about Charles Sloan?" I asked.

"The Sloans and I run in the same circles," she answered, "and I've always found Charles to be honest and sincere."

"Looks can be deceiving," Case said.

Lila leaned back in her seat and huffed in indignation. "You don't trust my judgment?"

"It's not you I distrust. It's politicians in general."

"Then let's put this rumor to the test," Lila said. "If you want to know whether Charles is likely to be unfaithful, let me suggest something. I'll go down to his campaign headquarters tomorrow morning to volunteer for his reelection campaign. He knows me. I can get close to him—you know, like, a little flirtation? Then we'll see how he behaves."

"Lila," I said, "you could be playing with fire."

"Sweetheart," she said, "if anyone knows how to douse a flame, it's Lila Talbot. Don't you worry."

I glanced at Case, but he said nothing. I couldn't imagine how Lila's little "flirtation" would help our investigation, but I knew her well enough to realize that once she set her mind on helping us, nothing would deter her. And maybe her plan would actually keep her out of our hair.

"Then go for it," I told her.

"I would also suggest we talk to the mayor and his security guard," Abby said. "They were both at the fashion show. They might have noticed something the women didn't."

"I'll contact the mayor's office and see what I can set up," Case said. "In the meantime, we need to interview Hope Louvain. She'll be working at the middle school tomorrow."

Sliding her purse strap over her shoulder, Abby stood. "We should head over to the school when the kids get out and talk to her then. I like to catch people off guard. It gives them less time to think out their answers."

"I'll find out what time Hope is finished and let you both know," Case said.

Abby stretched and tried to suppress a big yawn. "I'm going to head back to the hotel and see if any of the employees remember seeing Donald. Then I'm going to get some sleep."

"I'm going to take off, too," Lila said, rising. "I have a busy day tomorrow. First thing in the morning I'm going down to the mayor's headquarters, then after lunch it's my spa day." She wiggled her fingers. "Time to have these babies polished."

We waited for the two to leave, then Case walked me to the door, pulling me in close for a kiss. He leaned back to gaze at me. "Good work today."

"Thank you."

"Why don't you come back to the *Pamé* for a nightcap?"

I slipped my hands around his neck and leaned into him, very aware of the solidness of his chest, of his pulse beneath my fingertips. "I wish I could, but I want to spend some time with Nicholas, and I need some sleep, too. It's been a long day."

"I forgot to tell you," he said, holding me closely against him, "we got a new case today."

I leaned back to look at him. "We did?"

He smiled and pulled me in for another kiss. "The case of the missing love life."

"I'm sorry," I said between kisses. "We can solve only one case at a time."

"I have an idea," he said. "Let's take Niko to the fair tomorrow. That way we can get in some quality time with him earlier in the evening, and then later you can spend some time with me."

I shuddered.

Case gave me an exasperated look. "That's comforting."

"No, it's not you." I heaved a sigh. "You know one of the reasons why I was happy to leave Chicago? Because of the crowds. The endless crowds of people everywhere. That's what the fair reminds me of."

"But you promised Niko."

"I know I did."

"You can make it through one night," he told me. "I'll be with you the whole time. And it'll make Niko very happy, which will also make you happy."

I sighed again and leaned into Case, realizing there was no escape. "Okay. One night. For Nicholas. Happy now?"

"Ecstatic." He kissed me again. "And don't forget to write your blog tonight, Goddess."

### IT'S ALL GREEK TO ME
*Blog by Goddess Anon*

*Finding Your Happiness*

*We all want to be happy, and we also want to be successful, but can we be both?*

*I came across this list on a website and found it interesting enough to prompt a little self-evaluating. Read the list and let me know how you measure up.*

*Traits of happy, successful people:*

1. *They don't hold grudges.*
2. *They think outside the box.*
3. *They have a supportive tribe, thereby not wasting time with negative or toxic people.*
4. *They don't care about what other people think.*
5. *They don't people-please.*
6. *Fear doesn't hold them back. They're ready to take risks.*
7. *Passion is what drives them. They authentically believe in what they're doing.*

   *8. They live by their core values in both their profes-*
      *sional and personal lives.*
   *9. They finish what they start.*

   *I think I've got a handle on most of them, and I'm*
*especially strong on #2, #3, and #8, but there are a few*
*areas that need work. How about you?*
   *This is Goddess Anon bidding you* Antio Sas.

*Wednesday*

   The next morning, Nicholas and I arrived at the
Parthenon to find my sisters Selene and Maia making lists, with my mom looking over their shoulders. We stopped at the pass-through window to
say hi to my grandparents and put in our orders,
then joined my family at the booth, where they
were discussing Goddess Anon's latest entry.

   Sad to say, I had been so tired after reading
Niko a bedtime story that I really hadn't put much
thought into my blog. To my surprise, no one
seemed to notice.

   "I'm really strong on numbers one, four, and
five," Maia said.

   "For me," Selene said, "it's five, six, seven, and
eight."

   Mama clucked her tongue. "Neither one of you
mentioned number three—'they have a supportive tribe.' What do you call our family if not a
tribe?"

   "What's the tribe up to?" I asked, sliding into
the booth opposite my sisters. Nicholas scooted in
beside me.

"Hello, my Niko," my mom said, kissing him on the cheek. "*Ti kanis?*" How are you?

"*Poly kala,*" Nicholas said, trying his best to imitate a Greek accent. Very well.

"Did you read Goddess Anon's blog?" Selene asked.

"I haven't had time," I said.

"Read it," Maia said. "It'll make you think."

My mother made a show of looking around the diner. "I wonder where your baby sister is." When no one answered, she moved closer to where I was seated and pondered loudly. "I still haven't figured out why she and Bob are taking dance lessons. She's being very evasive, and it makes me suspicious."

When her passive-aggressive pondering still didn't garner a response, she finally got to the point. "Do you know what's going on with her, Thenie?"

"Nope," I said.

"Well, find out for me," she insisted. "Something is going on, and I want to know."

"Maybe they just wanted something fun to do," I said.

"No," Mama said, shaking her head. "It's more than just for fun. I know it."

"I know something fun to do," Nicholas said. "Let's go to the fair. When can we go, Mom?"

"How about tonight?" I asked.

"Cool!" he said. "Thanks, Mom. I mean *efxaristo.*"

I ruffled his hair. "*Parakalo.*" You're welcome. Thanks to my son, we'd gotten Mama off the subject of Delphi's lessons.

\* \* \*

As soon as I'd checked in with my dad at Spencer's, I went back to the office and read a text that had come in from Case. He told me what time school let out, and then I phoned Abby to schedule our visit. The call went directly to voice mail, so I left a message and started on my morning work.

At eleven o'clock, there was a soft knock on the door frame, and Abby stuck her head through the doorway. "Sorry to bother you at work. Are you busy?"

"Just finishing up," I said. "Come in."

"I got your message." She sat in one of the chairs on the other side of the desk. "Shall we head over to the school about fifteen minutes before two?"

"Definitely."

"I wanted to let you know what I found out," Abby said. "I've already shared the information with Case. I showed a photo of Donald Blackburn to six members of the hotel staff. Some of them remember seeing a man carrying flowers, but they couldn't identify Donald specifically, so I can't be sure it was him. However, I wasn't able to locate everyone who was there Thursday night because some of them weren't working today."

"So the delivery man is still a mystery," I said.

"I know it was Donald," Abby said. "I just need a way to prove it."

"Athena?" Cousin Drew said, peering in the doorway. "There's a woman here to see you. She said her name was Maureen Knight."

Abby's mouth fell open. "My *mother* is here?"

# CHAPTER NINE

A bby and I went out to the sales floor, where I
saw a slender, middle-aged woman with a short
light-brown bob smiling brightly at us. She was
wearing a large canvas sunhat and a blue print
shirt with beige pants and flats, looking very tour-
isty.

"Mom, what are you doing in Sequoia?" Abby
asked, giving her a hug.

"I should ask you the same, Abigail," her mother
told her. "I stopped by Bloomers on Monday, but
you weren't there. I had to hear it from Lottie that
my daughter was out of town."

"I'm sorry, Mom."

"You know, it's funny, though, because I've been
struggling to come up with a new art project for
the flower shop. When Marco told me about
Athena and the garden center, I had a brilliant
flash of inspiration." She turned toward me. "You

must be Athena Spencer." She stuck out her hand, and I shook it. "Maureen Knight," she said.

"It's nice to meet you."

"You have such a wonderful business here," she continued. "Exactly what I envisioned when I started my project, which reminds me, I brought you a gift. Wait right here, and I'll run out to my van to get it."

"Dear God," Abby said when her mother had left. "I'm so sorry, Athena. My mom considers herself an artist. She usually makes these wacky creations and then brings them to Bloomers for me to sell. I can't imagine what she's made this time, so just be prepared."

"It's no problem at all," I told her. "I'm kind of excited to see what she made."

"I was excited, too"—Abby sighed—"the first time."

In a few minutes, Abby's mom came into the garden center carrying a large box. I helped her carry it into the conference room, where she began to unpack it. She pulled out what appeared to be a tall mushroom about four inches wide on a three-foot-high stem. The mushroom cap was painted in a bright neon pink covered with large white spots, and the stem was painted a shiny white. Maureen set it down on our long table and pulled out another, the cap of that one painted in neon orange with purple spots.

I watched with a sinking feeling as she laid them all out. The stems appeared to be made from thin dowel rods. The caps looked like she'd cut off the tops of plastic fluted wineglasses and turned the plastic cups upside down to paint them and glue them onto the white rods. Each mushroom was painted a different neon-bright color with contrasting spots. This went on until she had unpacked six of them.

"This should give you a good idea of the rest," Maureen said with a big smile.

Abby's eyebrows shot up. "The *rest?*"

"They're very . . . pretty," I said lamely. I glanced over at Abby, who had a pained look on her face.

"Thank you," Maureen said proudly.

Delphi walked into the conference room and stopped short. "Sorry," she said. "I didn't know you had company." Her gaze landed on the mushrooms lying side by side on the table and instantly widened in surprise. She walked over to examine them, picking one up to look it over.

I held my breath. I never knew what was going to come out of my sister's mouth.

"They're gorgeous!" she exclaimed. "Garden stakes. I love them!"

"Thank you," Abby's mom said. "I made them."

"You made these?" Delphi asked, unable to keep the excitement out of her voice. "Did you bring them for us to sell? Because I can totally sell them."

"I did," Maureen said. "They're a gift for Athena for helping my daughter with her case."

Delphi rose and turned to me. "We can display them at the base of the statue. People will see them as soon as they walk in the door." She swung to Maureen. "Let me show you where they'll go."

As soon as Delphi and Maureen had left, Abby

said, "You don't need to display the garden stakes. My mom can be a little overwhelming at times."

"If you think that's overwhelming, you should meet *my* mother," I said. "And besides, Delphi thinks they'll sell. But please let me pay her for them."

"Are you kidding? She'd be offended if you tried to pay her."

Maureen returned by herself. "I love your sister," she said. "She's got such enthusiasm for her work. I'll bet she's a real treasure here at Spencer's."

"Yes," I said. "A real treasure."

"Mom, why don't we let Athena get back to work? I'll take you to this charming little coffee shop for a sandwich and some espresso."

"No need for espresso," Maureen replied. "Delphi is going to make us some authentic Greek coffee. She told us to wait here in the conference room." Maureen opened her arms to give me a hug. "Thank you so much for your help on Jillian's case. She's so relieved to be home."

"I'm glad that worked out for her," I said. "And it's been wonderful working with your daughter. I'm learning a lot from her."

"That's my Abigail. A born teacher, just like her mother."

"If you're hungry," I told them, "there's no need to wait for Delphi. I'll tell her you had to leave."

"It's okay," Abby said. "Greek coffee sounds really good. I'll meet you at the Greene Street office later."

I found Delphi in the kitchenette, where she was using a special coffeepot to make the coffee.

"Delphi," I said sternly from the doorway.

"Yes?" she answered without turning around.

"Why is it necessary to give Abby's mom a reading?"

"The reading isn't for Abby's mom," Delphi explained, looking at me over her shoulder. "You said I could give Abby a reading. You promised."

"I promised not to talk her out of it."

"Then keep your promise and let me do a reading." Delphi filled both cups and waited for the grounds to settle.

"Please don't scare them," I pleaded. "Whatever you see, whatever visions you have, if they're not happy ones, keep them to yourself."

"That's not ethical," Delphi scolded.

She was worried about being ethical? I tried not to laugh. "Delphi, please. If you see anything important, come to me first."

"Fine." She picked up the cups. "But it's still not right."

I went back to the office and sat at my desk just as Nicholas came skipping into the room. "Mom, you've got to come see what I taught Oscar."

"Can it wait a little bit?" I asked him.

"No, you have to come now. You'll never believe it."

I stood back up with a groan. Nicholas led me through the store and out the back door all the way to the shed in back, where Oscar was cleaning his face with his little paws.

"Look, Oscar," Nicholas said, shaking the yellow

rubber rattle. He tossed it into a row of low ever-green shrubs. "Oscar, fetch!"

Oscar rose on his hind legs and sniffed the air. Then he ran toward the row of shrubs, disappeared behind them, and returned a moment later carrying the rattle in his mouth. He dropped it at my son's feet and looked up expectantly. Nicholas held out his palm, and Oscar ate the peanuts in it.

"Wow!" I said. "That's impressive."

"Oscar's smart for a young raccoon," Nicholas said, running his hand down Oscar's furry back. "I should show him at the fair. We could have a booth in the small animal tent."

"I think Oscar might be a little overwhelmed if we took him to the fair," I said. "He might get spooked and try to run away."

"You're probably right," Nicholas said, "and I don't want to spend the whole evening in a tent. I want to go on rides! Do you think *Thea* Delphi can go with us? She's fun."

"I think Aunt Delphi has dance lessons this evening, but you can ask her."

"Thanks, Mom. I can't wait!" He gave me a kiss on the cheek, then skipped away with Oscar at his heels.

At two fifteen, I arrived at the detective agency to find Abby sitting in the reception area talking on her phone. She ended the call and smiled. "Either my husband misses me, or he's just really bored at work."

"Maybe it's both," I said. "How long are you able to stay in town?"

"I'm not leaving until Jillian is in the clear," she said. "So, if Marco misses me, he'd better come visit. Shall we head over to the middle school?"

We walked down the inside staircase and out onto the sidewalk, where Abby paused. "If you don't mind, I'd like to drive. I'll take you for a ride in my Corvette."

"Sounds like fun," I said.

Abby pointed up Greene Street. "I'm parked around the corner."

"Case normally drives," I told her. "And he has the doors off his Jeep, so this will be a treat. It's not fun going to an interview with windblown hair."

"I wouldn't worry about that."

We turned the corner and walked down Oak Street, where she stopped beside a vintage banana-yellow convertible with its top down, exposing a black interior.

She saw my surprise and said, "Don't worry. I have lots of extra hair ties."

"At least it has doors." I opened the door and slid inside, admiring the classic interior. "My dad would love this car."

Abby handed me a hair tie. "This little beauty was actually what brought Marco and me together. Just after I bought the 'Vette, it was involved in a hit-and-run, which Marco witnessed. That investigation led us to a murder case, which started our first investigation."

"You should invite Marco to join us. I'd like to meet him."

"I'm hoping he'll be able to take a day off soon. We'll see."

Abby drove north on Greene Street, the wind sweeping through the convertible. Regardless, I found myself enjoying the ride. The middle school was only a few more blocks away, so we didn't have much time for conversation, although one big question had been on my mind all afternoon.

"So," I tried to say casually, "how was the Greek coffee Delphi made for you?"

"It was delicious," Abby answered. "My mom and I both enjoyed it. Delphi is adorable. I wish I had a sister. I have two older brothers."

"I'll trade you," I said. "Three sisters for two brothers."

Abby laughed. "It's a deal."

I found myself breathing a whole lot easier knowing that Delphi hadn't mentioned anything about her psychic visions to Abby. Come to think of it, Delphi hadn't come back to the office to tell me about her reading, either. I hadn't seen her the rest of the afternoon. Was she avoiding me? I quickly shook that thought from my head as we approached our destination. I would have to deal with Delphi later.

"There's the school," I said, pointing to the long, one-story building coming up on the right. "There's a parking lot on the far side."

Abby turned down the side street and into the parking lot, pulling into one of the visitor spaces. She turned off the motor and looked at me. "Let's do this."

"Should I take notes?" I asked.

"Sure, but don't hesitate to ask questions," Abby said. "You're good at thinking on your feet. I like that."

I removed the hair tie and got out of the 'Vette, patting my purse to make sure I'd remembered the iPad. We walked into the school through the front doors and stopped at the office to tell the secretary why we were there. She wrote down our names and then used an intercom to call Hope.

"I have an Abby Knight Salvare and an Athena Spencer here to see you. They say they're private detectives working on the Blackburn case."

"I'll be right down," came the reply.

In a few minutes, an attractive woman with short, silky, blond hair strode into the room. Looking to be in her late thirties, she wore a short-sleeved light-blue blouse with brown slacks and white sneakers. It was an odd outfit. I couldn't help but think back to Jillian's description of Hope as a fashion disaster. If this was any indication, Jillian had been spot-on.

"Hope Louvain," she said, extending her hand.

"Abby Salvare," Abby said as she shook it. "This is Athena Spencer."

"Spencer . . . Spencer," Hope said. "From Spencer's Garden Center?"

"That's my family's business," I said.

"Oh, wait! You're the Goddess of Greene Street?"

"That's me," I said.

"And you're investigating Carly's murder?"

"We both are," I told her.

"Now it makes sense," she said. "Come with me."

As we proceeded down a long hallway, I tried my best to make small talk. "How's summer school going?"

"It's fine. I enjoy it. I work with kids who have a

hard time with chemistry during the normal school year. These poor kids need the extra attention."

As it turned out, Hope Louvain did not just make small talk—she *talked*.

"Especially the Bernards' youngest boy," she continued. "You should have seen his report on the periodic table. What a disaster. I mean, who doesn't know that the chemical formula for water is $H_2O$? I think it's a learning disability, honestly, but Mrs. Bernard won't admit it."

She led us into her classroom, where I saw walls filled with colorful chemistry posters and inspirational artwork, and even a section filled with teacher awards. She motioned for us to sit in a pair of wooden chairs at a round table near her desk. "But you didn't hear that from me. Please, have a seat."

"We appreciate your meeting with us on such short notice," I said.

"It's not a problem," Hope answered. "To be honest, I'm fairly certain the police are wrong to accuse Jillian Osborne. I'd like to see the real killer put behind bars."

I pulled out the iPad and opened a new Word file. "I'm going to take notes, if you don't mind."

"Not at all," Hope said. She had fair skin and a pretty smile with bright white teeth. She scooted the chair out from her desk to face us, leaned back, and crossed one leg over the other.

"To start with," Abby said, "set the stage for me. What time did you arrive on Thursday?"

"Around six thirty."

"Whom did you see backstage when you got there?"

"Let's see." She looked up at the ceiling. "Fran . . . Eleni . . . Jillian . . . I think that's all."

I entered the names and looked up to see Hope watching me type. I adjusted the iPad slightly so Hope couldn't see.

She smiled pleasantly and continued. "Oh, and I saw Charles Sloan pop backstage to see his wife, too."

"How long was he backstage?" Abby asked.

"Just a few minutes," Hope replied. "Not long enough to poison Carly, if that's why you're asking."

"Okay," Abby said hesitantly. "Moving on. Did you see a security guard?"

Her thinly plucked eyebrows rose in interest. "You mean Charles's security guard?" Hope leaned in closer to ask, "Have you talked to Eleni yet? Has she told you why they hired a security guard?"

I waited a moment to see if Hope was going to continue, but she paused, as well, waiting for our answer. I looked at Abby, who seemed confused herself.

"We can't give out that information," Abby finally replied. "How do you know the security guard is working for the mayor?"

Hope waved her hand. "Oh, everyone knows. And don't believe a word Eleni told you about him. Charles isn't in any danger. It's all for show. He just wants to look like a big deal while the fair is in town, so he hires some muscled goon to follow him around in a suit. How pathetic is that? Like anybody really cares what the mayor of a rinky-dink town is doing."

Abby gave me a quick glance, as though she

found Hope's statement odd. I typed a note with the same sentiment.

Abby tried to keep the conversation moving forward. "Did you see the security guard backstage?"

"I saw him before the show started," Hope answered. "He wasn't doing much. Then again, it was all for show."

"Was he near Carly's dressing room?" I asked, trying to help Abby keep Hope focused.

"Not when I saw him," Hope said. "I saw him on the first night, too, in the back hallway for a while. Then he was standing in the crowd during the show." She cocked her head, suddenly realizing where our line of questioning was headed. "But if you're wondering whether it's possible that he poisoned Carly, he had plenty of opportunity to do so."

I typed in more notes. It was becoming clear that Hope was truly worthy of her awards. She was smart, and clever, although a bit too chatty for my liking. I kept that in mind as Abby continued.

"Did you have any interaction with Carly during the first night of the fashion show?" she asked.

"Oh, no," Hope replied. "It was so busy there was no time for interaction."

"What about the second night?" Abby pushed.

Hope glanced up as though she were thinking. "I don't recall any," she finally answered.

Which was the exact opposite of what we'd been told by Eleni. She'd told us that Carly and Hope had been threatening each other. I wrote a note about it and underlined the words *Someone is lying*.

Abby glanced at my notes and continued. "Had you ever met Jillian before the fashion show?"

"No, but Carly told me all about her. She said Jillian had always been jealous of her, and she didn't want her at the show."

"When did Carly tell you this?" Abby asked.

Hope started to speak, then paused as though she'd caught herself. I could practically see the wheels in her head spinning. She finally said, "This would've been on the first night."

"So, you did talk to Carly before the show," Abby said.

"On the first night, yes," Hope answered. "When I said that I didn't interact with Carly, I meant on the second night. But the first night we talked quite a bit."

I noted Hope had quickly changed her story.

"I understand you knew about the friction between Jillian and Carly," Abby said.

"Yes," Hope answered. "I heard it from Carly."

Abby gave her a skeptical look. "Carly told you about it herself?"

Hope looked down at her blue polished fingernails. "Actually, I overheard Carly telling Fran."

"Then you didn't talk to Carly about Jillian," Abby said. "Correct? You overheard her talking to Fran, and then you reported that information to the police."

Hope's face immediately flushed with color. "You don't have to be snippy."

"Well," Abby said, "you're giving me several different versions of the same story."

"The police asked me what I knew, so I told them what I'd heard. That's all you need to know."

I typed in Hope's answer and looked over at

Abby. I could tell by the tensing of her jaw that she wasn't happy, but she didn't push the subject.

"How did you know Carly Blackburn?" Abby asked.

"We were both in the same philanthropic organization," Hope said.

"Had you worked on committees together?" Abby asked, as I typed.

"A few times."

"Were you and Carly friends?" Abby prodded.

"Um." Hope shifted as though she were uncomfortable. "I wouldn't say *best* friends." Her eyes widened. "Oh! You know who else I saw backstage? Carly's ex-husband, Donald Blackburn. He was trying to disguise himself in a hat and glasses, but he wasn't fooling anyone. I knew he was there to win Carly back. He was carrying a fancy bunch of tulips."

Abby gave her another skeptical look. "Tulips? At this time of year?"

"Roses, whatever," Hope said. "He was carrying a big bouquet, the kind that desperately screams *take me back.*"

That answered the question of our mystery man.

"But then I saw those same flowers in the trash can at the back of the stage," Hope continued. "You can draw your own conclusions."

Abby waited until I was done typing, then asked, "What was *your* conclusion?"

"You know, now that I think about it, maybe he didn't want her back. Maybe he wanted her dead. Maybe the flowers were an excuse to get backstage and poison her."

"What time did you see Donald?" I asked.

"Right before the show started," Hope answered.

I typed in her comment about Donald being the killer, but also added that she'd changed subjects when questioned about her relationship with the murder victim.

"What about Fran?" Abby asked. "Did she have any connection to Carly?"

"Poor Fran," Hope said, her lower lip turning down in sympathy. "Her little boutique is about to go bust. I've heard the fashion show was her last chance to bring in some business. People just don't like her styles, I guess. I like the clothes, but personally, I wouldn't wear them. With that said, I don't think she deserves to go out of business." Hope sat back and waved one hand. "But that's life in a small town. It's hard owning a business. That's why our mayor is so popular. He's standing up for the little guy, the shop owners."

"That wasn't my question," Abby said.

"You know Carly worked for the mayor on his campaign, right?" Hope said, as though she hadn't heard Abby. "Carly was his campaign manager. I'm sure that's why she was asked to model for the show."

Abby and I exchanged glances, and I knew we were thinking the same thing: Eleni was right about Hope. She was definitely a gossip. "That's still not an answer," Abby said. "Did Carly have any connection to Fran? Did they serve on any committees together? Belong to the same clubs?"

"Not that I'm aware," Hope said. "It's my opinion that Carly was only in the show because of the mayor. She worked very closely with him, if you know what I mean."

"I'm not sure I do," Abby said. "Are you accusing the mayor of having an affair with Carly?"

Hope's mouth curved up in a secretive smile. "Well, I'm not actually accusing anyone of anything. I'm just saying they worked closely together, and knowing the mayor's history—and how Carly liked to flirt—it wouldn't have been long before the sparks started to fly."

I paused with my fingers on the keypad. "The mayor's history?"

"Oh, you don't know about the mayor?" Hope leaned in, glancing over at the doorway to be sure we were alone. "Well, get this. I heard the mayor was caught having an affair a few years back with a female employee. I won't give any names—because I'm not like that—although I do know the woman. Poor thing. She was gutted when he dumped her."

"How did the affair end?" I asked.

"Somehow word got out and spread around town like wildfire. And just like that"—she snapped her fingers—"it was over. And yet, for some reason, the news never made it to the paper. But then, I'm sure the mayor and his team made it go away."

"Did Eleni know about her husband's infidelity?" Abby asked.

"Oh, I'm sure of it," Hope replied. "I'm surprised Eleni stayed with him. It wasn't the first time Charles had been caught with another woman. Even before he was the mayor, when he was an attorney, he would be seen having dinner with women other than his wife."

I was highly skeptical of Hope's story. In a small town like Sequoia, it would've been suicide for Charles Sloan to be seen out to dinner with another woman. And surely that news would have made it to the paper.

"Did you tell Eleni that her husband was having an affair with Carly?" Abby asked.

Hope smiled enigmatically. "Let's just say news spreads fast around here."

"So, you're saying you didn't tell Eleni," Abby probed.

"My lips are sealed."

I highly doubted that. "Do you have any proof the mayor was seeing Carly?" I asked.

"You know, Athena," Hope said, "with some men you don't need proof."

Obviously, she didn't have proof. Hope's credibility was sinking quickly, and her cloying smile was bothering me. It made me wonder what sort of gossip she would spread about Abby and me as soon as we left.

I was about to ask Abby if she'd gotten all the information she needed when she took a sudden shift in her line of questioning.

"Do you know anything about Carly's broken windshield?" Abby asked.

Hope's smile instantly dissolved. "No," she said curtly.

"Are you saying you had nothing to do with it?" Abby asked again.

"I know nothing of which you speak," she answered smugly. "And I suggest you change the subject."

"One more question before we change subjects,"

I said. "If I speak with one of my friends on the police force, will I hear a different story?"

"Ask away, Athena. I have friends on the force, too." She smiled coyly, obviously thinking she was untouchable because of her husband.

"Let's change subjects, then," Abby said.

"Yes." Hope raised one eyebrow. "Let's."

Abby leaned in. "Tell me about your son. I understand he got into some trouble."

Hope's lips thinned. She sat forward and put both feet on the ground. "What about my son?"

"He was expelled from middle school," Abby pushed.

"Excuse me?" Hope said. "What does that have to do with Carly's death?"

"Shall I lay it out for you?" Abby asked calmly.

Hope's eyes narrowed. "I wouldn't if I were you."

"Oh, really?" Abby responded.

"You don't want to get on my bad side," Hope told her.

"That sounds like a threat to me," Abby said. "Some might even call it bullying. Interesting. Isn't that why your son was expelled from school?"

Hope slammed her palm against the top of her desk. "Don't you dare go there."

I sat back in my chair, suddenly concerned for our safety, but Abby leaned in closer and continued. "Carly was responsible for getting your son expelled, wasn't she? And then you confronted her and took a tire iron to her car's windshield."

"Stop it," Hope said bluntly.

"But that wasn't enough," Abby prodded. "You were seeking revenge. So you got to the fashion show early, dropped some poison into Carly's water bottle . . ."

"Stop right there!" Hope demanded. "Don't you dare accuse me of murder. This thing between Carly and me"—she took a breath to calm herself—"my son wasn't the problem. That Blackburn boy, he's the real troublemaker. And with a cheating, lying mother like Carly, the poor boy never stood a chance." Hope stuck her finger in Abby's face. "And if you keep asking questions about my son, you'll be hearing from my husband. Trust me, you don't want that."

Abby kept her eyes locked on Hope, whose finger was still directed at Abby's face. I couldn't get a read on Abby's expression, but her cheeks flushed red, and her nostrils flared. I sat farther back in my chair, suddenly feeling like I was sitting next to a pressure cooker.

Abby's fingers curled into her palms, and with steel in her voice, she said, "I'd like you to take your finger away from my face."

Hope didn't move. It was a showdown.

# CHAPTER TEN

"You leave my son out of this," Hope fired back.

Before the fingers became fists, I decided to step in. "We won't bother your son, Hope, but we need to follow up on any leads, so I suggest you talk it out with us, not threaten us."

Hope dropped her finger and sat back. "Who told you about Chip?"

"Is that your son?" Abby asked.

"Yes. And I want to know who told you he was expelled."

"Let's just say it was gossip and move on," Abby told her. "Gossip seems to spread like wildfire around here, doesn't it?"

Hope crossed her arms over her chest and looked away. "We're done here. Don't bother coming back. And don't expect any more help from me."

Abby glanced at me. "Do you have any other questions?"

I read over the answers I'd typed in. "I can't think of any."

Abby rose, and so did I. "Then I think that will do it for now."

Hope didn't say a word, so we left.

On our way back to Abby's 'Vette, I said, "Hope was really defensive about her son."

Abby agreed. "If Carly was indeed behind Hope's son's expulsion," she said, "and it seems like she was, then Hope has a motive for murder."

"It's hard to imagine a woman killing another woman because her son was expelled," I said.

"I've seen people kill for less." Abby slid into the driver's seat, and I climbed into the passenger seat. "Look at it this way," she said, starting the engine, "Hope's a teacher at the school, and her husband is the chief of police. It would be awfully embarrassing for them to have their son get into that kind of trouble."

"The question in my mind," I said as I put the hair tie back in, "is whether Hope was alone backstage long enough to poison Carly's water bottle."

"If I remember correctly," Abby said, "Hope's dressing room was right next Carly's. It wouldn't take long for Hope to steal the bottle while Carly was out, bring it into her dressing room, poison the water, and slip the bottle back into Carly's room, especially if nobody was really paying that much attention."

"It would take a lot of nerve," I said. "And by the way, you handled yourself pretty well when Hope put her finger in your face."

"I don't take well to bullies, and Hope's actions definitely fall into that category. And thank you for throwing water onto the fire. That could've gotten ugly."

"Did you notice how eager Hope was to throw everyone else under the bus?" I asked.

Abby nodded. "My inner radar was going off like crazy."

"Your inner radar?"

She smiled. "It's just a gut feeling I get. Like the way Hope used her husband as a shield, and the way she gossiped about everyone. There's more to that story, and I think it warrants further investigation."

"Hope said something about Carly's son being a liar," I said. "What do you think she was talking about?"

Abby turned the corner. "Probably about the bullying. Unfortunately, Carly isn't around to defend the accusation."

"But Donald is," I said. "Maybe he can enlighten us."

"That's what I wanted to remember," Abby exclaimed. "Hope confirmed that Donald was at the show. That's something I need to share with Detective Walters. I'll give him a call today, and hopefully he'll follow up on it. In the meantime, we need to write up a list of questions for Donald."

I pulled my iPad out of my purse. "I'll start that list right now."

"When do you want to go see him?" Abby asked.

"Let's check with Case."

When we got back to the office, Case was working on his computer. "How did the interview go?" he asked, looking up.

"Hope wasn't very helpful," I told him. "We

heard a lot of gossip, especially about the mayor. According to her, he was having an affair with Carly when she died."

"Does the info ring true?" he asked.

"Nothing about Hope rang true." Abby sat down in front of Case's desk. "I don't trust her word on anything."

"It's hard to believe her," I agreed and took a seat beside her. "If Charles Sloan had been seeing other women, it would've been all over the local news."

"However," Abby said, "there is such a thing as hush money. He might have paid the other women to keep quiet."

"Let's suppose that's true," Case said. "What if Carly threatened to expose their affair anyway?"

"For what reason?" I asked.

"Maybe to force him to leave his wife," Case said. "Maybe to blackmail him. Who knows? But we have to consider it as a possibility."

"Have we considered the security guard?" Abby asked. "He was backstage twice—once before the show, according to reports. And we know he works for the mayor."

"Then you're saying he could've poisoned Carly's water for the mayor," I said.

"We can't rule out that possibility," Abby answered.

"Were you able to set up an interview with the mayor?" I asked Case.

"I've called three times, and each time I was told I would be contacted with a date and time. I think we're going to have to show up in person."

"Maybe we can do that tomorrow," I said.

"Okay, it's on the calendar." Case sat back in his chair. "What about a motive for Hope?"

"Hope and Carly were strongly at odds over their sons," I said. "Hope was furious that Carly had managed to have her son expelled. She got very defensive when Abby pressed her on the issue. She jabbed her finger in Abby's face and threatened her."

"She *threatened* you?" Case asked.

"She threatened to send her husband to talk to us," Abby said. "And I believe she would."

"Then that's something we should consider," Case told us. "The last thing we need in this business is to have the police chief as an enemy."

"We can't back down from a bully," Abby insisted. "That only gives Hope and her husband more power."

"Then at least tread carefully," he said. "For the sake of the agency."

"We can do that," I told him.

"So, what's next on the schedule?" Case asked.

"We need to interview Donald Blackburn," I said. "How do you recommend we go about doing that?"

"Donald has an office at his casino," Case told us. "He walks the floor with the pit bosses in the evenings. We might have to catch him that way. I've called several times with no response, but I can keep trying."

"I'd rather catch him off guard," Abby said. "Why don't we head over to the riverboat after supper?"

"We're taking my son to the county fair this evening," I said. "You're welcome to join us."

Abby pondered the offer for a moment. "I absolutely love the fair, but I have some more work to do. What about tomorrow evening?"

"I'll put it on the calendar." Case reached for the keyboard. "Let's plan on going around eight."

"I need to check with Delphi," I told them. "I might have to close at Spencer's."

"Then let's meet back here tomorrow afternoon," he suggested. "We can solidify plans then. Athena, what time are we leaving for the fair tonight?"

"How about six o'clock?"

"Perfect. We can grab some fair food before we hit the rides."

My stomach was already turning.

As we drove up to the fairgrounds that evening, Nicholas was practically jumping out of his seat with excitement. Through the relative darkness of the highway, the bright, shining Ferris wheel loomed over the midway like a beacon—or, in my view, like a giant bug zapper, beckoning the poor, unwitting insects to their doom. I tried to match my son's enthusiasm but found myself compiling a list of reasons why we should leave the fair as early as possible.

"Look at that one, Mom!" Nicholas cried.

I turned around to find him sticking his head out of the Jeep's rear door, pointing high into the sky as a teetering tangle of metal beams swung back and forth, reaching a dizzying height, leaving the patrons momentarily suspended upside down.

I had to look away. "Nicholas, sit down. Is your seat belt still on?"

He sat back down. "Yeah, don't worry."

Case reached over, put his hand on my knee, and said very quietly, "Are you sure you can handle this? You seem rattled already."

"It's too late now," I whispered, as Case followed a line of cars turning into the entrance. He had to use two hands to steer his way across the lumpy, grassy field surrounding the fairgrounds.

"It smells like the fertilizer at Spencer's," Nicholas said with a giggle, covering his nose. "*Lots* of fertilizer."

I had to agree. The smells of the fair were wafting through the open Jeep doors. "That's horse poop," I said. "There's a horse show tonight." I looked back at my son. "Are you hungry yet?"

Case and Nicholas both laughed.

"I'm starving," Case said. "How about you, Niko?"

"I want to go on rides!" Nicholas answered. "Where should we go first?"

I listened to the two talk as Case wove through the grassy field, looking for a spot to park. Afterward, as we made our way to the front gates, the grass transitioned to mud, which then turned into loose gravel, and finally, to blacktop. I swiped my shoes against the ground while Case paid our entrance fees, then I pulled out some cash and gave it to Nicholas so he could buy tickets at the first ticket booth we saw.

"Where to first?" Case asked me.

I motioned to the right, where a wide expanse of blacktop led past the exhibition halls, the source of the fertilizer smells. "I think we should avoid that area if we plan on keeping our appetite."

Off to the left was the midway, where the terrified screams and loud-as-locomotive carnival rides competed with the hard-thumping music blaring over the loudspeakers. "Let's save the rides for later, too."

I pointed forward, where food stands lined the thoroughfare. A woman holding a cotton candy bag the size of a small child knocked into me as she passed. She turned to glare at me, as if my slender frame was the problem. I glared back.

"Mom," Nicholas said excitedly, "I got twenty tickets!" His infectious smile stifled my sour mood.

"Let's get some food first and then play some games on the midway," I said.

Nicholas caught sight of a pirate ship practically sailing straight over our heads. "Pirate ship first!" he called out.

Case and I followed him through the gates onto the midway, then I held the tickets and Case's phone while they waited in line. Across from the ride was an empty bench, so I quickly snatched a spot away from the crowd to wait. Out of the corner of my eye, I caught sight of something surprisingly familiar—a thick crop of long black curls bouncing through the crowd. Then I caught a glimpse of a bright pink-and-white tie-dyed skirt and knew it had to be Delphi.

Yep. The matching pink flip-flops gave it away. Without thinking, I followed my sister, whom I noticed was holding hands with her beau, Bob Maguire. I struggled to catch up, continually interrupted by clusters of people who seemed to pop

up out of nowhere. When I did finally catch another glimpse of Delphi, I saw the couple walk into
a big brown brick building near the fairground's
back entrance.

I caught up with Delphi inside the building. She
was bent over a desk filling out a form. "Delphi!"

Hearing her name, she turned. Bob turned, as
well, both giving me a startled look. Delphi spoke
first. "Athena. Hi."

"Athena," Bob said with a grin.

"Delph, you're supposed to be helping Pops at
the store. What are you doing here?"

"We just came to"—she paused and turned to
Bob, stuttering a bit before answering. "We—we
aren't staying long. Besides, Dad and Drew are
closing the store early. There were no customers.
Everyone's here."

I glanced up at a sign posted above her head in
big, old-fashioned letters that read *COUNTY FAIR
DANCE CONTEST*. My eyebrows drew together in
confusion.

Delphi noticed my expression. "Okay, yes, we're
entering a dance contest," she fired at me, "and I
was hoping to keep it a secret from the family."

"Wait a minute," I said. "*This* is your big secret?"

"What are you talking about?" Delphi asked.

"I heard you with a young couple in the conference room yesterday. You were talking about engagement rings, and, well, I just thought . . ."

"Oh. My. God. Athena. I *knew* you were spying
on me outside of the conference room! Is that why
Mom has been pestering me so much lately? Does
she think Bob and I are getting engaged?"

Bob lifted his collar with one finger and stretched

his chin uncomfortably. Poor Bob always did fluster easily.

"I was just admiring their ring!" Delphi continued frantically. "You have to tell Mama I'm not engaged."

"Delphi, relax," I said. "All she wants to know is why you're taking dance lessons."

"Don't tell Mama about the contest, Athena. She'll give me the third degree if I bring it up."

Bob put his arm around my sister's shoulders. "It'll be okay, Delph. Athena will handle it."

"When's the dance contest?" I asked.

"On the closing night of the fair," Bob answered.

"That sounds like fun," I said. "But why don't you want the family to know, Delph?"

"I don't want them to know yet," she insisted. "I'll tell them the day before the contest. That way Mama will leave me alone."

"I think you're worrying for nothing," I replied.

"For *nothing?*" Delphi cried. "Have you *met* our mother?"

"I get your point," I said. "If you're finished here, we can go find Niko and Case. Niko will be so excited to see you."

We exited the building and headed back toward the midway. As we drew near the giant pirate ship, Nicholas came rushing out of the gate followed by Case at a much slower pace.

"That was fun!" Nicholas cried, while Case took a seat on the empty bench and looked at me with a wan face.

"And that wasn't even a spinner," I said to Case. "Just wait."

"Thea Delphi!" Nicholas cried. He practically jumped into her arms. "Want to go on the Tilt-a-Whirl with me? I have tickets."

"After dinner, Niko," my sister said. "Thea Delphi needs some food."

After a few minutes of chatting, we all decided to head over to the food tent, where they were serving pulled pork and sweet, buttered corn on the cob. We loaded our plates with food, and then, as we sat at a picnic table and ate, the conversation shifted to the murder investigation.

"Detective Walters is watching me like a hawk," Bob said. "He knows I help you, and he hates it. Especially now, when he just wants this case closed."

"We have got to find out what kind of poison was used," I told Bob. "We have several suspects, but without that information, we'll have a hard time going much further."

"I don't know what to tell you," Bob said. "You could try calling the state lab. See if you can find someone willing to talk."

Case laughed. "I tried that already. Everyone seems insistent on keeping their jobs."

"Yeah," Bob said. "So do I."

"Enough murder talk," Delphi insisted. "Let's go win a goldfish."

"Tilt-a-Whirl," Nicholas exclaimed. "Then goldfish."

"No goldfish!" I said. "You have Oscar. That's enough."

"Come on!" Nicholas said to Case. "Before the crowd gets too big."

Case finished his last bite of corn and wiped the

butter from his mouth. "You and Delphi might have to take this one, Officer Maguire."

"Let's go, Niko," Bob said. "Luckily for you, I have an iron stomach."

We had just walked out of the big tent when I heard my name, then Case's. We turned to find Lila Talbot strutting through the crowd, waving her clutch purse at us. She was dressed in an off-white linen dress pulled tight at the waist by a dark blue belt, finished off by bright-red high heels. Her hair was tied back with a red polka-dot scarf. Resting above her left breast was a large, round red, white, and blue button with Mayor Sloan's smiling face on it.

"You're just in time," she said, threading her arm through Case's. "Come with me."

"Wait a minute," I said. "Just in time for what?"

"The speech," she said. "Mayor Sloan is giving a speech before the concert tonight. I'm on my way over to the bandstand right now."

Case politely pulled himself free from Lila's clutches and said to me quietly, "We might be able to talk to the mayor after his speech and pin him down on an interview time."

"Good idea." I turned to my sister and said, "Delphi, we're going to the bandstand to hear the mayor. Would you and Bob watch Niko for a while?"

"Sure," Delphi said. "We'll take Niko and catch up with you later."

Nicholas took a firm grip of her hand, then Bob's, and bounced up and down. "Come on! Let's go on the Tilt-a-Whirl."

"I don't do fast rides," Delphi said.

"You're in luck again, bud," Maguire told him, "because the Tilt-a-Whirl just happens to be my favorite. And your aunt promised that if I took dance lessons with her, she would go on rides with me. Remember that, Delphi?"

Delphi scowled. "Not that I can recall."

"Come on," Nicholas called. "Follow me."

"Thank you, both of you," I told them. "Let's meet up afterward, and I'll buy you all a cotton candy."

"Elephant ears!" Nicholas said.

"I'll take the cotton candy," Delphi said. And then, as Nicholas bounded ahead, she pointed her finger at me. "You owe me."


The grandstand was filled to the brim with revelers waving flags and voters holding signs that read *Vote for Mayor Sloan* and *Keep Sequoia Small*. Lila led us past the crowd through a side entrance protected by security. She flashed her plastic ID and was let into a fenced walkway that circled the stage. "This is so exciting," she said over the noisy crowd.

"Where are we going?" I asked.

"You can stand with me in the VIP section," she answered.

The roped-off area had a great side view of the stage and a firsthand view of the massive crowd. I was perfectly fine being away from the chaos and felt quite comfortable in our own private section. Up on the stage, the big-band musicians had already settled into position, each one tuning his instrument, preparing for the show. Front and center was a podium, complete with microphone, ready for the mayor's speech.

Case joined me next to Lila. "It looks like the mayor welcomed you into his inner circle," he said.

"With open arms," Lila answered. "I didn't even have to pressure him. Charles knew I would be an asset." She looked at me with a raised eyebrow. "And I didn't have to flirt, either."

"Have you learned anything yet?" Case asked. "Has he mentioned Carly or the fashion show?"

"He hasn't mentioned Carly's name, but I can tell you Carly was instrumental in running his campaign. Charles seems lost without her. He put me to work right away."

The lights on stage went dark, and the crowd grew silent in anticipation. From behind the stage a security guard headed our way. He was dressed in a black suit with dark hair trimmed close to the scalp. His head was on a swivel as he passed by our private area, his eyes scanning in all directions, pausing briefly on me, his stony expression sending shivers up my spine. He stopped at the stairs leading up to the stage and spoke into his cuff, his suit pulling taut across his broad chest and shoulders.

Lila leaned in closer. "Wait until you hear what I came up with for the speech. The crowd is going to go wild."

Charles Sloan came walking past us next with several people surrounding him, all talking, shuffling through papers and notecards. When he spotted me, he stopped and smiled, flashing bright white teeth and deep dimples, looking every bit like his campaign button. His thick hair was perfectly styled with a traditional part at the side, showing off a bit of gray above the ears—just enough aging to portray wisdom.

The smile, as well as his confident stride, seemed at odds with what Lila had said about him. He didn't seem lost without Carly. In fact, he seemed more self-assured than I'd ever seen him.

"Athena Spencer," he said confidently. He held out his arm. "Come! Join me on stage."

The thought of being on stage in front of the huge throng made my palms sweat instantly. "No, thank you," I said with a polite smile.

"Oh, come on! The people would love to hear from you."

"I'm not good in front of crowds. I'm fine right here, thanks."

Then the band started. The bass drum thrummed in the background as the trumpets began to play in harmony. More brass instruments joined in, playing a patriotic melody that swept through the crowd, bringing them to their feet, until the music reached a crescendo and the bright lights lit up the stage. The mayor made one last adjustment to the sleeves of his dark-blue pin-striped suit and trotted up the stairs, the crowd bursting with applause at the sight of him.

To say that Charles Sloan was well-liked seemed to be an extraordinary understatement at that moment. He moved from one side of the stage to the other, waving, pointing, and of course, flashing that brilliant smile. After taking his place behind the podium, he positioned the microphone and waited for the band to finish. The crowd quieted with the band.

"Good evening, ladies and gentlemen," the mayor started. "It's so great to see everyone here tonight. I can't tell you how grateful I am, and with your unceasing support, we will continue to make Sequoia the best small town in America."

More applause, which the mayor took in stride. "And when I say 'small town,' I'm not talking about size. Sequoia continues to grow. We continue to thrive. No, when I say 'small town,' I'm talking about community. I'm talking about the sense of ownership and pride that comes when the community stands together, when the community provides for one another.

"Look around you. Look at the faces of your neighbors and friends. These are the people that make Sequoia special. You won't find that same sense of pride from some big corporation. You won't see those same friendly faces when shopping at a mega-mall. Sure, you might save a few dollars in the short term, but I'm not thinking short term. We want to keep Sequoia thriving for years to come, and the only way to do that is to keep . . . Sequoia . . . small!"

He emphasized the last few words, pointing his hand at the crowd with each, and the crowd ate it up. They jumped to their feet and cheered.

The mayor continued. "I'd like to introduce

someone who knows what it means to keep Sequoia small. Lila Talbot, join me onstage."

Lila turned to us first, her palms together as though in prayer. "Wish me luck."

She trotted up the stairs in her red heels and joined the mayor on stage, receiving a smattering of applause. Thanks to her ex-husband, now in prison, most of the people in town knew the Talbot name, but not many knew the woman. I held Case's hand in mine, anxious about what she might say.

"Lila Talbot has been on a mission," Charles Sloan started. "First, she was instrumental in fending off the Talbot Company from demolishing our beloved Little Greece."

*She* was instrumental? That wasn't right.

"Then she was on the front lines in the fight against Pete Harmon, when he threatened to turn our sacred dune land into a parking lot."

*Lila* was on the front lines? That wasn't right, either. I looked at Case, who was shaking his head. Leave it to Lila to take all the credit. Sure, she did help save the dunes, and she did help us put her husband, Sonny Talbot, in prison, but instrumental? On the front lines? I wondered if that's what she came up with for the mayor's speech, why she thought the crowd would go wild.

But to my complete surprise, the crowd did go wild. Lila stood proudly in the spotlight, smiling and waving. I couldn't believe it.

Case turned to me and said, "You're squeezing my hand, sweetheart."

I apologized and let go.

"But that's only the beginning," Mayor Sloan continued. "Lila Talbot has also funded the creation of an organization dedicated to making sure these kinds of criminals will never get a foothold in our town. Speaking of which—" The mayor turned to face the VIP area.

I felt a cold chill wash over me as we locked eyes.

# CHAPTER ELEVEN

$M$y stomach dropped to my knees. *Please, don't do it. Please don't call my name.*

"I'd like to welcome the founding members of the Greene Street Detective Agency up on stage with us," the mayor said, "to take a bow for all their hard work in keeping Sequoia safe."

*Don't do it. Don't you dare do it.*

"Athena Spencer and Case Donnelly, come on up and join us."

The crowd applauded, but my heart was pounding so hard, the sound was just static in my ears. I tried to move but couldn't feel my legs. My worst fear was coming true, and my first instinct was to turn and run. I could see the mayor with his hand outstretched toward the stairs, waiting for our arrival. I felt Case's hand grab mine, but I still couldn't move.

Something I had never shared with Case was my utter and absolute fear of public speaking. Everyone knew that crowds rattled my nerves, but standing before a massive audience was petrifying. My legs quaked, and my hand was ice cold as Case pulled me forward.

"Come on, Goddess," he said.

Lila was smiling at us, clapping with the crowd, her expression expectant.

"I can't do this, Case. I can't go up there."

"What's wrong?"

"The crowd. All those people. I can't do it."

"Just take a bow. You'll be fine."

I breathed rapidly in and out, feeling faint as I followed Case up the stairs. The applause grew louder, and I found myself smiling instinctively as we approached Lila and the mayor. Case pulled my hand up with his, stretching it overhead, clearly enjoying the moment. I darted a glance at the audience, barely able to make out individual faces, and forced myself to wave.

*Okay,* I told myself. *This isn't so bad. All you have to do is stand here and smile.*

And then the mayor spoke into the microphone, sending chills to my very soul. "Athena, why don't you say a few words?"

I shook my head at him, forcing myself to smile but feeling faint again.

"What do you say, folks?" the mayor said. "Wouldn't you like to hear a few words from our very own Goddess of Greene Street?"

The crowd applauded relentlessly, everyone focusing solely on me. And then, as if my legs had a mind of their own, they began to shuttle me forward. Case's hand fell away from mine, and I suddenly found myself standing behind the podium.

The bright stage lights were blinding. The static in my ears was overwhelming. My mouth opened. And that was all I remembered.

From what Case told me afterward, I'd managed to thank the crowd for their support and then had sputtered to a stop until Case came to my rescue. He had spoken to the crowd about our mission for justice, and they'd loved him, of course. There was only one man I knew more handsome and charismatic than Charles Sloan, and that was my partner, Case Donnelly.

He held my hand in the VIP area and chuckled as I chugged a bottle of water. "I never imagined a person could turn as white as you did," he said. "You were really petrified up there."

"I was shaking so hard my teeth were actually clacking together. I'm surprised you didn't hear it."

"You were squeezing my hand so hard I'm surprised you didn't break it."

"I'm so embarrassed," I said. "And angry. I can't believe the mayor would just call us up on stage in front of all those people."

"You did fine," Case assured me. "The people got to see their goddess in person."

I finished the bottle of water, my embarrassment easing. "Thanks for coming to my rescue."

He raised my hand to his lips and kissed my fingers. "It's what I do. Now, let's see if we can catch the mayor and his security guard before they leave."

As the crowd began to exit the bandstand area, we found Charles Sloan behind the stage being briefed by his crew. We headed toward him, only to see him walk over to a group of supporters and begin to converse.

Case nodded toward the right. "There's the security guard. Let's have a word with him first."

The beefy guard had his arms folded across his massive chest while his eyes scanned the area. He gave us a scrutinizing stare as we walked up to him.

Case introduced himself first, to which he was given no reply. "And this is my partner, Athena Spencer. We're with the Greene Street Detective Agency."

The guard finally gave us a short nod and continued to sweep the area with his gaze.

"We'd like to talk to you about last Thursday evening at the fashion show," Case continued. "We understand you were there that night."

Without turning to look at us, he answered, "No comment."

"We just need to know whom you saw backstage," Case told him.

The guard pinned him with a hostile glare. "I don't talk to anyone unless Mr. Sloan tells me to."

"Okay," Case responded slowly. "We'll set something up with the mayor."

The guard glared for another few seconds, then went back to scanning the area.

The mayor walked over to us with a smile. "What did you think of my speech?"

"Honestly?" I blurted. I balled my fists at my sides, wishing I could muster the courage of Abby Knight and tell the man before me that his speech was pompous, his smile was plastic, and his impetuous invitation for us to come up to the stage was presumptuous at best. But instead, I smiled grace-fully and said, "The crowd seemed to enjoy it."

The mayor flashed his toothy grin. "They did, didn't they?"

"If you don't mind," Case said, "we'd like a few minutes of your time. We're working on the Carly Blackburn case and would like your insights on the night of the murder."

Charles Sloan glanced at his security guard, then quickly looked down at his watch. "I would absolutely love to help you right now, but you'll have to make it quick. I have hands to shake and friends to make."

Case wasted no time. He laid it all out quickly. "We've been informed that you were at the fashion show Thursday evening, and we understand that Carly was your campaign manager. Would you be able to offer your thoughts about what happened to her?"

The mayor rubbed his hand over his mouth, staring at the ground for a moment before looking straight at us. "Carly was a brilliant woman with a clear vision. Our team is scrambling without her. She will be sincerely missed."

I waited for more, but he was done. He looked at us with a seemingly well-rehearsed world-weary expression that I wasn't buying for a second.

"Is that all you have to say?" I asked.

The mayor pulled a business card from inside his jacket pocket. "Why don't you set up a time with my secretary to meet me at my headquarters? If you need anything else, you can contact my new campaign manager. And let me say that I can't thank you enough for what you've done for this town. I'm serious. Anything you need, you let Lila know."

"Lila?" I said in surprise.

"Did I just hear my name?"

I spun to find her walking toward us. "You're the new campaign manager?"

"In person."

"I have to dash," the mayor said, "so I'll leave you in Lila's capable hands."

"Before you go," Case said, "we'd also like to speak with your security guard."

"That's not a problem." He checked his watch again. "But I'm afraid we have to leave now. First thing in the morning, I'll give Ben and my entire staff permission to speak with you about anything you need. Lila, you see to it that they're well taken care of." He gave her shoulder a familiar squeeze and left.

"And there you have it," Lila said with a grin. "I told you I could get close."

"Maybe a little too close," I said. "What if Charles had something to do with Carly's death?"

Lila rolled her eyes. "Don't be so dramatic, Athena. Why don't you stop by campaign head-quarters tomorrow afternoon? I'll meet you there."

Before I could say more, Case put his arm around my shoulders. "Sounds like a plan."

As we walked away from the grandstand, Case asked how I was feeling.

"Tense," I told him. "And a little suspicious of Lila's new title."

"You're right. It does seem odd, but it could work in our favor to have an inside source."

"I can't even think about that right now," I said. "I just want to get out of here."

"I understand." He took my hand in his as we continued toward the midway. "Let's go find Niko and your sister, get some cotton candy, and call it a night."

I was definitely up for that.


Late that evening, I sat at my desk and opened my laptop to write my blog. It had been a long day, and I was still recovering from my onstage fright. Sitting still and silent in my peaceful bedroom, I thought back to my frantic state of mind and had to laugh at myself. After that, I felt better. And that gave me an idea for a topic.

### IT'S ALL GREEK TO ME
*Blog by Goddess Anon*

*Take Two Laughs and Call Me in the Morning*

*Is there anything better than a good belly laugh? The kind where you hold your sides, wipe your eyes, and rub the muscles in your face because they hurt? Seriously, when was the last time you did that? Did you know that doing so can help calm anxiety, boost your immune system, and reduce your risk of serious illness?*

*Boy, could I have used a good belly laugh this evening. My anxiety level was through the roof! And it all started when . . .*

\* \* \*

*Thursday*

"I believe in the power of laughter," my sister Maia was saying as Nicholas and I walked up to the booth at the diner the next morning. Yiayiá came out of the kitchen with a large glass of chocolate milk and a plate full of cheese-smothered *omelétta*.

"Niko," she called, "I have your favorite breakfast for you."

My son immediately did an about-face, scurried to the counter, and hopped onto a stool, leaving me alone in the booth across from Maia and my older sister, Selene. Delphi was nowhere to be seen.

Selene picked up a piece of crunchy bacon and continued the conversation. "Laughter is the best medicine." She rolled her eyes and took a bite. "Or so they say."

Obviously, they had read my blog.

"Anyway," Maia persisted, "I was at a yoga convention one time speaking in front of a crowd about Adho Mukha Svanasana when someone—"

Selene stopped chewing. "What is Addo Mucka Susanna?"

"Adho Mukha Svanasana," Maia corrected and sipped her coffee. "It's Downward Dog."

"Then why didn't you just say Downward Dog?" Selene snapped crossly.

Maia sat back with a scowl. "What's up with you today?"

Before Selene could fire back, I tried to redirect the conversation. "Maia, what happened at the speech?"

She leaned in. "I was really nervous. The speech wasn't going well. My throat was dry, and I was messing up my words, and then someone passed gas. Loudly. I was literally shaking with laughter."

"You don't need to say 'literally,' " Selene said.

"And why do you care?" Maia retorted.

"Girls," Mama said quietly, leaning over to refill their cups, "everyone can hear you."

I glanced around and spotted Mrs. Stella Galopodis sitting at the table across from us with her group of Red Hat ladies, unabashedly eavesdropping on our conversation.

The Red Hat Society was famous around town for their stylish dress and their old-fashioned manners. They were also well-known at the diner for feuding among themselves, an activity they actually seemed to enjoy.

Mama bumped me playfully with her hip. "Athena? Oatmeal again?"

"Yes, please," I said.

Maia leaned in closer and directed her attention toward me and Mama. "To finish my story, after the laughter calmed down, I ended my speech perfectly. And everyone seemed to enjoy it. So, I truly believe in the power of laughter." Looking at me, she said, "Did you read the blog this morning?"

"Not today," I told her. "But I get the point."

"I've never laughed at anyone at the hair salon," Selene said.

"I don't believe that for a second," Maia said. "Maybe if you'd take the stick out of your—"

Selene gave her a jab in the shoulder.

"I put your order in," Mama said, scooting Maia over so she could sit down. "Athena, what did you find out about Delphi and her dance lessons?"

"They're having fun," I said. "That's all."

Mama gave me a scrutinizing stare. "Are you sure? Are you sure there's not something more going on between Delphi and Bob?"

"If you don't believe me, ask her yourself," I said.

"I don't want to pry," she replied. "Now, Selene, why are you so crabby? Is it because you don't have a man in your life?"

"Mama!" Selene protested. "I just got up on the wrong side of the bed, that's all."

My mother did not look convinced. She rose with a sigh. "Okay. Fine. But there are all sorts of eligible Greek bachelors at the fair. Why don't you come down with me one evening, and I'll prove it to you?"

Selene gave her a scowl. "Can we change the subject, please?"

"What's wrong with the subject?" Mama asked.

"I don't need you to set me up," Selene insisted. "Please stop asking me about it."

I understood immediately why Selene was upset. When Mama decided it was time for one of her daughters to find a "good Greek man," she was relentless in completing her task, even when asked nicely (and sometimes not-so-nicely) to stop. Mama had done the same thing to me when I'd returned home from Chicago sans husband.

In order to help calm the situation, I decided to jump in. "Mama, how well do you know Eleni Sloan?"

"Eleni and I go way back," she answered, "before

she was the mayor's wife, before she was a Sloan, even. She's a smart businesswoman with a sharp wit and a Greek temper."

"How bad of a temper?" I asked.

Mama paused. Even though I had tried to act nonchalant, my mother knew too well when I was trying to get information out of her. Usually, it was the other way around.

"Why do you want to know?" she asked.

"Just curious," I said. "What about Eleni and her husband? Do they seem to get along?"

Mama studied me for a second. "What is this about, Athena?"

"I've heard some things about Mayor Sloan," I said. "A rumor of an affair that may have happened before I moved back to town. Do you know anything about that?"

"I've never heard any such rumor!" Mama said. "Where did you hear such a horrible thing?"

"From one of the models who was at the fashion show. I just wondered if you'd heard it, too."

"Charles Sloan is a good man and an upstanding citizen," Mama said indignantly. "I would question anyone's intentions in spreading such a lie." She huffed. "Enough of that talk. You girls eat your food, and I'll go see about your breakfast, Thenie."

As my mother walked away, Mrs. Galopodis cleared her throat. I glanced over at her, and she tilted her head toward me, then put a finger to her lips. I got up and stepped across the aisle, where she began to whisper, while the other ladies leaned in to hear, the feathers on their red hats meeting in the middle of the table.

# CHAPTER TWELVE

"You didn't hear it from me," Mrs. Galopodis said softly, "but there were rumblings about an alleged affair between Mayor Sloan and a young woman a few years ago."

I looked behind me to make sure Mama was not within ear's reach of the ladies' table, then I leaned in closer. "Rumblings?" I asked quietly.

"Oh, yes. It was quite the gossip. Everyone knew about it. Even poor Eleni. I felt so sorry for her." Mrs. Galopodis *tsk*ed. "Politicians! They're all the same."

"They're good liars," one of the women said.

"Dogs," another added. "Every one of them."

"The mayor must have used his influence to make sure the story fizzled out," Mrs. Galopodis continued, "and God knows what he told Eleni. She seems to have let it go, but we never forgot."

"I didn't vote for him," the woman sitting across from her commented.

"Neither did I," said another.

"Yet he keeps getting reelected," Mrs. Galopodis said. "Athena, I know someone who can tell you more. She used to work as a secretary at Mr. Sloan's law practice, but now she has a higher role inside his campaign headquarters. If you want to talk to her, I'll give her a heads-up that you might be stopping by."

"Thank you," I said. "That would be very helpful."

"Wonderful. Her name is Rosemary Dalsaurus. She's a very good friend of mine."

The woman across from her grumbled, "She was my friend first."

"I've known her since grade school," another said.

"Ladies, please." Mrs. Galopodis redirected their attention. "Rosemary is a brilliant woman. Did you know that Mayor Sloan's campaign wasn't gaining traction until they started using that slogan . . . Do you know what I'm talking about?"

" 'Keep Sequoia Small'?"

"That's the one," she replied. "My friend Rosemary was the one who came up with that slogan, but did she get the credit for it? Of course not. Just another reason to despise that man. I hope you get to the bottom of his deception."

I was saved from explaining to Maia and Selene what Mrs. Galopodis wanted by my mother's arrival with my food. My sisters were on to a new topic anyway, so I was able to eat in peace.

Nicholas and I arrived at the garden center at nine o'clock, where my dad was waiting with a project for Nicholas. I left the two conferring and headed back to the office to catch up on some accounting work that I was reluctant to let Delphi handle.

My sister came in for coffee a little while later, plunked down in a chair opposite the desk, and flipped through a magazine while her drink cooled. She was dressed that day in a magenta romper with a bright-pink, sheer scarf draped around her shoulders. Her dark, curly hair was pulled back in a scrunchie. She hummed cheerfully, blissfully unaware of my irritation.

I stared at her for a moment before clearing my throat, which finally caught her attention.

She looked up at me cluelessly. "Do you need something?"

"Yes, Delphi. You never told me about your reading with Abby and her mom."

She set the magazine in her lap and blew on her coffee.

"Well?" I asked. "What happened?"

Instead of responding like a normal human being, Delphi gave me a sly smile and sipped her drink.

"What?" I asked again.

"I may have seen something."

"Then why won't you tell me?"

"Because you don't believe in my abilities. What was it you said last week? I have a twenty-five percent success rate?"

"Delphi, will you please just tell me what you saw?"

"Yes. If you tell me that you believe in me."

I breathed in deeply and blew out a long sigh.

"No," she said. "No sighs. No eye-rolls."

"Okay, Delphi. Last week your visions helped me catch a killer and may have saved my life, and even though it may have been a coincidence, I'm inclined to believe you now."

"Thank you." Delphi touched her fingertips to her heart. "That really means a lot to me, and I'm glad my visions saved your life."

"*May* have saved my life," I corrected.

She moved the chair closer to my desk and leaned over. "I saw Abby being followed by someone," she told me. "There was a dark-blue aura attached to her while I did the reading, and in her coffee grounds I saw the letters *M* and *S*."

"What does that mean?" I asked.

"I have no idea."

"What did Abby say about it?"

Delphi leaned back. "I didn't tell Abby about it. That's what you told me to do. You specifically told me not to mention anything to Abby."

I huffed emphatically. "Then how are we supposed to know what those letters mean?"

"Why are you getting upset with me? I just followed your instructions. Jeesh."

"Wait a minute," I said. "*M* and *S*. Could that be Mayor Sloan?"

She shrugged. "I don't know."

"He was wearing a dark-blue suit yesterday at the fair. Could that be the dark-blue aura? Is Abby being followed by Mayor Sloan?"

"I don't know, Thenie. I've never met him, but if that's what you think it could mean, then trust your inner guide."

"Delphi," my dad said, sticking his head through the doorway, "I could use you up front."

"Be right there, Pops." Delphi pointed her finger at me. "Remember what I said. Trust your inner guide."

"Delphi, what does that even mean?"

She gave me a frown before slipping out the door.

There was a strange knot in my stomach as my sister left me alone in the office. Normally, I could chalk her visions and coffee-grounds readings up to coincidence, but Delphi's latest vision seemed too coincidental, and that worried me.

Case called right then, the sound of his voice calming my nerves. "Just checking in," he said. "Have you recovered from the fair?"

"I'm a little embarrassed, but feeling better."

"Will you be joining Abby and me at the office today?" he asked.

"I'll be able to leave Spencer's at noon."

"Perfect," Case said. "We can get some lunch together."

"Listen to this," I said. "I got a tip from someone at the diner. She said a friend of hers used to be the mayor's secretary and now works at his campaign headquarters. This woman might be able to tell us whether the mayor was having an affair with Carly. What do you think?"

"It's worth checking out. We need to set up a time to talk to the mayor anyway. Do you want to grab something to eat at the food trucks and then head over there?"

"Sounds like a plan to me. I'll contact Lila and let her know we're coming, then I'll meet you at the office at noon."

* * *

Shortly before noon, I told my dad I was leaving and headed down Greene Street to the detective agency. Upstairs, I found Abby working on my computer in my office.

"Hi!" she said brightly. "I was just doing a little internet sleuthing on Donald Blackburn."

"Learn anything interesting?"

"He's spent a boatload of money advertising his riverboat casino," Abby said. "He's all over social media, too, bragging about his son, Danny. There was no mention of Carly's death."

Case came into the doorway and leaned against the frame. "I've worked up a list of questions for him. That is, if we can catch him at the casino. Are we still on for eight o'clock?"

"I forgot to tell you, I have to close at the garden center. How about eight thirty?"

"Let's do it," Abby said.

Before Case and I left, I filled Abby in on Mrs. Galapodis's information and told her where we were headed. "We're having lunch first in the plaza across the street. Do you want to come along?"

"Thanks for the offer, but I'm going to do a video call with my staff," she said. "I'll grab something to eat later. You can fill me in this evening."

We left the office and headed across the street to the plaza, where several food trucks were parked. The sun was blazing in the sky, and I could see the heat waves rising from the food trucks. We decided to forego our regular slices of hot pizza for a couple of cold cut sandwiches and ice water from the deli just below our office.

We sat side by side on a park bench and ate our sandwiches, enjoying a lovely summer breeze under an awning of giant maple and oak trees around us. But even though it was peaceful without the summer tourists swarming the sidewalks, and Case's presence was comforting, I could still feel the knot in my stomach from Delphi's prediction. I contemplated telling Case about it, but I knew how he felt about my sister's abilities, so I left it alone.

"Did you talk to Lila?" Case asked.

"I did. She won't be at campaign headquarters, though, because she's working at the mayor's tent at the fair this afternoon. But she said Rosemary Dalsaurus would be expecting us."

We finished our sandwiches, drank our water, then headed north up Greene Street for three blocks until we came to the Thomas, Harper, and Sloan Law Offices building. We entered a short hallway with a door into the law office. There was another door to the back of the building, where the mayor's campaign headquarters were.

Opening the second door, we stepped into a room filled with people of all ages seated at long tables, some of them on the phone, some folding flyers, some stuffing envelopes. In the corner a television displayed the local news at a low volume. At the back of the room were several offices, the middle office being the largest and presumably Mayor Sloan's.

A woman who seemed to be overseeing the activity walked toward us. "Can I help you?"

"We're looking for Rosemary Dalsaurus," I said.

"I'm Rosemary." She appeared to be in her fifties, a plump woman with short wavy brown hair and a dimpled smile. She was wearing a pair of black pants with a white blouse that had a Mayor Sloan campaign button on it.

"I'm Athena Spencer," I said. "This is Case Donnelly. We're investigating Carly Blackburn's death. Mrs. Galopodis said you might be able to help us."

At the mention of Mrs. Galopodis, Rosemary glanced around, saw several workers watching curiously, and said, "I'm sorry, but I can't talk to you."

"Why not?" I asked in surprise.

She answered in a firm tone, loud enough for others to hear, "The mayor made it very clear that we were not to talk to you."

I glanced at Case in surprise. "That's not what he told us," I said to her.

She looked over her shoulder at the workers, then stepped in closer. She pointed to the door and said under her breath, "Meet me on the plaza in fifteen minutes."

We thanked her quietly and headed straight back to the plaza, where we took a seat on a park bench and waited. Five minutes later I spotted Rosemary on the opposite side of Greene. She crossed the street and walked up to a food vender, so we headed toward her.

She paid for an iced tea and moved away from the truck. "I can't stay long," she said and took a drink from the straw.

"That's okay," Case said. "We'll keep our questions brief."

"I hope you understand the reason for my actions at the office," Rosemary explained. "Before Charles left this morning, he made it very clear that we were not allowed to talk to any visitors."

"Do you know why?" I asked.

She shook her head. "I didn't know why at first, but when Stella Galopodis called, I figured it out. He doesn't want us talking to you."

"Then why did you agree to meet us?" I questioned further.

"Because I trust Stella, and I want to know what really happened to Carly Blackburn. But please, make it quick. I don't want anyone to suspect I came out here to meet with you."

"I understand." I took out my iPad and opened a new file. "We've heard that the mayor and Carly Blackburn were having an affair. Can you corroborate that?"

Rosemary glanced around, then said quietly, "I've never seen anything, And I want to be perfectly clear that I have never witnessed Charles and Carly being intimate, but I was working late one night, and I overheard Carly say she was going to expose him."

"Expose him of what?" Case asked. "An affair?"

"I don't know."

"Did she give a reason why she would do that?" I asked.

"No. I didn't stay long enough to hear the rest."

"Do you think Eleni suspected that anything was going on?" I asked.

"I have no idea."

"Do you know why Carly was hired as the campaign manager?" Case asked.

"I don't know for sure, but Carly did seem to

know a lot of people. And she was a good manager. But I don't think she was completely honest with Charles about what she was up to."

"What do you mean?" I asked.

"A few weeks before Carly's death," Rosemary replied, "she started receiving strange envelopes in the mail. Some were addressed to Carly with a return address from a Unified Construction Company. And some were sent to a CB Development Company, LLC, attention Carly."

Rosemary glanced around again, as though afraid someone was spying on her. "I'm embarrassed to say this, but I looked up the companies on the internet. I couldn't find anything on CB Development, but Unified Construction was the same company used by Samson Malls."

"Why is that important?" Case asked.

"Because Samson Malls is one of the companies that Mayor Sloan is campaigning against. He stopped their mega-mall from opening across the interstate. And right around that time is when the threats started against the mayor. That's when he hired security."

I typed it in and added a question: *Why was Carly receiving mail from a company the mayor had banned?*

Case waited until I had finished, then asked, "What made you think to investigate these companies?"

Rosemary shrugged. "I'm a curious person. Carly had never received anything at the office, not even a greeting card, so it made me wonder what she was up to."

"Did you find any connections to Carly in your research?" Case asked.

"No. Nothing." Rosemary's cell phone rang, and she pulled it out of her purse to answer it, turning away from us. She talked quietly into the phone, then slid it back into her purse. "I have to go. The mayor is back."

"Can I just ask one more thing before you go?" I asked.

Rosemary slid her purse over her shoulder and stood. "Go ahead."

"What do you think Carly was up to?"

"I'm not sure." She breathed in deeply, squinting up at the bright blue sky, then blew out and said, "But I have to say this. You can tell when a woman likes a man. You know what I'm saying? Like you and your partner. There's natural chemistry there."

I felt my cheeks turn pink. I wanted to ask her how she'd drawn that conclusion, but Case moved the conversation along. "What does that have to do with Carly?" he asked.

"It was obvious to me that she really didn't care for Charles," Rosemary answered. "She didn't show any signs that she was attracted to him, and yet the rumor about them persisted. And I'll leave you with that."

"Thank you for talking to us," I told her. "You've been a big help."

"Just keep my name out of your investigation," she whispered. "I like my job."

As she scurried away, I noticed Case watching her with a puzzled expression.

"What's wrong?" I asked.

"I'm just wondering why the mayor would tell us

he was giving us full access and then tell his employees they were not to talk to us."

"He's a politician," I said. "He tells people what they want to hear."

"I get that, but what is he afraid of?"

"Questions about his relationship with Carly?" I asked.

"All he has to do is deny any allegations," Case said. "Sloan's a lawyer. He should be able to handle our questions."

"Maybe he's nervous about the fact that he was backstage before the show."

"Then he could say he was there to see his wife." Case shook his head. "There's something suspicious about his behavior. If he has nothing to hide, why wouldn't he want to talk to us?"

"Somehow, we're going to have to get him to cooperate. Why don't we head back to the campaign headquarters right now and confront him?"

"Let's give Rosemary a chance to get back first."

We took our time returning to the law office, and once again we went through the second door into the big back room. But when we scanned the room, we saw neither the mayor nor his security guard.

I saw Rosemary and walked over to her. "Is the mayor in the building?"

"I'm afraid he just left," she said. "He had to go to a meeting."

"Is Lila here?" I asked.

"She went with Charles."

Case handed her a business card. "Would you give this to the mayor and tell him we'll be in contact?"

As we left the building and headed back down Greene Street, I said, "I have a strong hunch that Mayor Sloan is not going to take our call."

"I agree. What if I phone the mayor's office and set up an appointment with his secretary under a different name?"

"We tried that in our last case," I said. "It didn't go over well."

Case put his arm around me as we walked down the street. "How would Abby Knight handle it?"

I thought for a minute. "She'd catch him off guard."

"Exactly. What if we were to approach him as he left his office, say, at his car?"

"We'd have to do a stakeout," I said. "And that takes time."

"True."

"Maybe we could catch him at the fair, surrounded by people. He wouldn't be able to avoid us there."

Case removed his arm from my shoulder as we approached our building and opened the door to the stairwell. We stepped into our office and were met by a distraught Abby.

"Jillian is being charged with murder. The police just brought her back to town."

# CHAPTER THIRTEEN

"They're charging Jillian with murder?" I asked. "Based on what evidence?"

"I don't know," Abby said. "All I know is that they picked her up at her house an hour ago and are bringing her in. Her husband called me to ask for help. I tried calling her lawyer and had to leave a message with his secretary."

"I'll phone Bob Maguire," Case said. "He'll see to it that she's treated right."

As Case headed into his office to make the call, Abby said, "I want to be at the police station when they arrive. I want to let her know we're working on getting her out of there."

"Good thinking," I told her.

She checked her watch. "They should be here in half an hour."

Thirty minutes later, we stood at the police station's back door and watched as a squad car pulled up. A police officer got out and opened the back door. Jillian climbed out, pale and distraught, her hands behind her back in handcuffs. She caught sight of Abby and began to cry. "What's going to happen to me?" she sobbed.

"Don't worry," Abby said. "I've contacted your lawyer. He'll be here soon."

As the officer led Jillian away, she turned back to Abby. "You've got to help me, Abs! They can't believe I'm guilty!"

"I'm doing everything I can, Jill," Abby called back. "Hang in there."

As the officer took Jillian through the door, Abby turned to me. "I need to see Detective Walters."

We walked around to the front of the building, to the police station itself, and went in through the double glass doors. Abby marched up to the front desk, where a female officer by the name of Joyce Winters stood overseeing the entrance. "I need to see Detective Walters," Abby said.

"Your name?" Officer Winters asked.

"Abby Knight Salvare," she said. "Salvare Detective Agency."

"The detective is busy at the moment," the officer said. "Would you like to make an appointment?"

I knew Joyce because of how often I'd been at the station lately. She was kind and understanding, so I walked up beside Abby and said, "Hi, Joyce. I know he's busy, but it's important that we talk to Detective Walters right away."

The officer acknowledged me with a nod of her head. "Let me call upstairs and see if he's available." She picked up a telephone receiver and punched in a number on the phone. She turned her back on us to speak quietly into the phone, then hung up. "He says he'll give you five minutes."

"He'd better give us more than that," Abby muttered as we headed into the next room.

We went through security, then walked up the wide staircase to the second floor. I looked across the room and spotted Walters at his desk. "That's him," I said to Abby, pointing.

With fire in her eyes, Abby charged ahead of me, straight up to Walters, and said, "I want to know why you've arrested my cousin Jillian Osborne."

I walked up beside her. "This is Abby Salvare, from the Salvare Detective Agency in New Chapel, Indiana."

Walters gave us an exasperated look. He waved his hand toward wooden chairs beside his desk. "Have a seat." He had bags under his eyes, and he appeared unshaven.

We sat, Abby on the very edge of her seat, tension radiating throughout her body.

"You want to know why your cousin was arrested," Walters restated.

"Yes," Abby said. "What evidence do you have against her?"

"You want the whole list? Okay." He shuffled some papers around on his desk, uncovering a thick manila file folder. He searched around again for his glasses, and after securing the thick, brown frames against the bridge of his nose, he opened the folder and began. "She was behind the stage before the fashion show. She had access to the victim's dressing room before the victim arrived. She

provided and delivered the bottled water that held
the poison. She had motive. And"—he looked up
from the file to emphasize his final point—"Jillian's fingerprints were found on the water bottle
in question."

"Wait just a minute," Abby said angrily. "What
motive could she possibly have? Are you talking
about a falling-out the women had ten years ago?"

"Detective," I said, jumping in, "we have the
names of other people who were also backstage
before the show, who also had access to the victim's dressing room, and who had strong motives."

"Bring me hard evidence," he said. "I'd be
happy to take a look at it."

"We do have hard evidence," Abby said. "The
victim's ex-husband, Donald Blackburn, was caught
on security camera video leaving the backstage
area before the show started. We also have eyewit-
ness testimony to him being backstage."

"We've reviewed that video footage," Walters explained. "I talked to Mr. Blackburn personally and
subsequently cleared him. There is no evidence
pinning him to the murder."

"There are two more suspects with strong motives," Abby countered. "Have you cleared them, as
well?"

"Mrs. Salvare," Walters said with a heavy sigh, "I
suggest you drop this investigation and go on home
to Indiana. Without any further evidence, I'm
afraid you're just wasting our time. Now, if you'll
please excuse me," he said, sliding a pile of paper-
work across his messy desk, "I have a job to do."

That was the problem. Going by what Bob
Maguire had told us, Walters wasn't doing his job.

What he meant to say was, "Leave me alone so I can close this case and retire."

I looked at Abby and saw stony determination in her gaze. There was no way she was going to drop the investigation. We either had to bring Walters the evidence he needed or solve the case ourselves.

At eight thirty that evening, Case pulled into the riverboat's on-shore entrance and circled the enormous lot. After parking at the far end, the three of us got out of the Jeep. In front of us, across the water, stood the riverboat, which didn't seem all that large at first glance. It was sided in white, with an enormous neon sign in flashing blue letters above it: *BLACKBURN CASINO.*

The riverboat was docked in an inlet off Lake Michigan, just a few miles away from the fairgrounds. We crossed a wide bridge to get onto the boat, then walked in through ornate sliding-glass doors, stepping into a vast, low-ceilinged, dimly lit room filled with people, slot machines, gaming tables, and noise—lots of noise. I flexed my fingers and curled them at my sides. Crowds and noise. I was already feeling anxious.

"Let's head to the bar," Case said loudly. "It's at the back of the room."

He led the way through the packed room to a long, polished wood bar that ran across the end of the boat. For a weekday evening, the place seemed very crowded, but the bar was mostly empty. We took seats on padded red bar stools, Abby on one side of me and Case on the other. Case leaned in. "What would you ladies like to drink?"

"I'll have a glass of cabernet," Abby said. "I need to calm down."

"Make that two," I added.

Case motioned to the bartender and placed our orders. "Is Donald around this evening?" he asked the man.

"He's around here someplace," the bartender said, stretching his neck to look around the room. "Who wants to know?"

"Just a couple of old friends," Case answered casually.

The bartender, who seemed unconvinced, studied us as he uncorked the cabernet and filled our glasses.

We sipped our drinks and waited for a while but saw no sign of Donald. What I did notice was the bartender slipping away momentarily to the other side of the bar, where he picked up a telephone and had a short conversation. I suddenly had an eerie feeling of being watched, as if the multitude of cameras above our heads were all pointing directly at us.

We had only partially finished our drinks when Case spotted him and pointed him out to us. Donald Blackburn was a stocky man of medium height, with thick, short brown hair combed back off a high forehead. He wore a black T-shirt with the Blackburn Casino logo on the front and a pair of light denim blue jeans with black sneakers. He approached the casino bar with two burly men dressed in black T-shirts and baseball caps.

"You looking for me?" Donald asked bluntly.

"Mr. Blackburn, I'm Case Donnelly with the Greene Street Detective Agency. This is my partner, Athena Spencer, and this is Abby Salvare, also a private investigator."

"You're private eyes?" Donald's eyebrows pulled together. Then he turned to his bodyguards and made some kind of joke at our expense. The two men laughed heartily while Donald turned back to face us. "You don't look like detectives to me."

Ignoring his remark, Case continued, "We'd like to talk to you about Carly."

Donald's expression hardened, and his jaw pulsed with anger. "I have nothing to say about Carly. And just so you know, the police have already cleared me." He motioned to his two bodyguards, and they turned around to leave. Before Donald could follow them, Abby made her move.

"Do the police know about your argument with Carly on the night she died?" she asked.

Donald instantly turned his glare on her. "What argument?"

Abby showed him a narrow strip of paper. "This is a receipt from the Back to the Fuchsia flower shop for a bouquet of roses you purchased on the day of Carly's murder. Those same roses were found backstage in a garbage can. Would you like to explain what happened, or should we let the police know about the argument?"

Donald continued to glare at her, then he shifted his gaze to Case and then to me and finally back to Abby. "That's not bad detective work. Maybe I was wrong about you."

"Is there somewhere we can talk privately," Case asked, "or would you rather we ask our questions here?"

"Follow me."

We followed Donald through a door on one side of the bar and down a narrow hallway to a room paneled in dark wood, with a long dark wood table down the center. I turned to see the two body-guards take positions outside the door. Inside, the room was much quieter, allowing me to relax and focus.

The room was lined with long windows looking out onto Lake Michigan. The sunlight shining throughout the room was in stark contrast to the soft, gloomy yellow glow of the casino. We waited until Donald had taken a seat at the head of the table, then joined him. Case, Abby, and I took the seats to his left so our backs were against the sunlight. I took the iPad from my purse and opened the file marked *Donald*.

"I can explain," he began. He used two hands to smooth back his hair from his forehead, as though he was trying to compose himself. "First of all, the police know about the flowers. That's not new information. Like I said before, I've spoken with Detective Walters, and I've been cleared. But I can understand why you're not satisfied with the detective's investigation. I don't think the redhead did it, either, but I'm not going to cooperate with you if you treat me like a suspect."

Abby's tone was very matter-of-fact. "The redhead's name is Jillian. She's my cousin, and I'm going to treat everyone like a suspect until I find Carly's killer."

"You're looking in the wrong place, doll," Donald said. "You're wasting your time on me."

" 'Doll'?" Abby fired back.

Case jumped in. "Just let us ask our questions so we can get this over with."

Donald folded his arms across his broad chest and sat back. "Go ahead, hotshot."

Case lowered his eyebrows and gave Donald a piercing look, but Donald didn't seem to notice. I, on the other hand, took note of Case's beleaguered expression. I hadn't ever seen him anger so easily.

Abby used the awkward silence to flip through her notepad and then started the interview without hesitation. "I'd still like to hear your explanation," she said. "Why did you show up at the fashion show with flowers?"

"I brought them to the show because I needed to talk to Carly. It was important that I talk to her that day, so I brought the flowers to make things right between us."

"You wanted to make things right by giving her flowers," Abby restated.

"Why not? I'd tried everything else." Donald looked out one of the windows facing the water. "She kept ignoring me." He continued to stare, as if his answer was sufficient, but then rocked back in his chair, facing us again. "I figured she would appreciate a nice gift, a peace offering, so to speak."

"You made her angry, Donald," Abby said. "She threw the flowers in the trash."

He shrugged nonchalantly. "That's Carly for you."

"Is that really why you went there?" Case asked.

Donald tilted his head, his eyes narrowed at

Case. "Why do *you* think I was there? What's *your* conclusion, *detective?*"

"You were angry with her, weren't you?" Case asked. "Because she received the land in the divorce settlement. The land intended for your brand-new casino."

Donald chuckled at Case's conclusion as if it were amusing. "I gave Carly the land. That was all she asked for in the settlement. Guess again."

"But that's not all she wanted," Case continued. "She also filed for full custody of your son."

"You're right," he said quickly. "I was very angry about that. I'm a damn good father."

"Carly must not have thought so," I said.

"Forget about what Carly thought," he retorted. "You don't have the whole story."

"Then tell us the whole story," Case said. "Why was it so important to talk to Carly at the fashion show?"

"That's not where the story starts." Donald sat back, once again folding his arms across his chest. "What do you know about Ed and Hope Louvain?"

# CHAPTER FOURTEEN

Case didn't reply, and I could tell he was frustrated with Donald's evasive answers. I waited for someone to speak, my fingers poised over the iPad. Clearly, this interview wasn't going to be easy. Abby finally answered, and I was once again relieved to have her experience to guide us.

"We know about the bullying," Abby told him. "We know about the feud between Hope and Carly. We know that Hope smashed Carly's windshield and Ed Louvain covered it up."

Donald thrust his chin forward. "What do you know about the bullying?"

"We've heard conflicting stories," Abby answered vaguely.

Donald looked at her, his chilly gaze intensifying. "I'm sure you did, no doubt from Hope, who isn't the most reliable of sources, by the way." He reached deep into his front pocket and pulled out a cell phone. After pressing a few buttons with pudgy fingers, he turned the smudged screen our way. "This is what that Louvain kid did to my boy."

He thumbed through several photographs, each one worse than the last. Donald's son had a bruised cheek, a fat, bloody lip, and the last picture showed a deep purple circle under his eye. The pictures were heartbreaking. I could see a sheen of tears in the boy's eyes.

"This is not bullying," Donald said, tapping the last photo. "This is aggravated assault."

"What does that have to do with Carly's death?" Case asked.

Donald leaned back, taking his cell phone with him. "Why don't you tell me that, hotshot? Why don't you explain to me why you're looking at me as a suspect when, in fact, you *need* me to help solve the crime? Look at you. There's three of you. And you come in here saying that I'm a suspect because I brought Carly flowers? Come on. Three private detectives, and this is the best you've got?"

"We have reason to believe you were trying to hide your identity that night," Abby said. "Why?"

"Yeah, of course I was hiding my identity. Nobody wanted to see me there. Not the mayor, after what he's been saying about me; not Hope, for obvious reasons; and least of all not Carly, after what she did to me. So, big deal, I hid my identity. It wasn't like I was stalking her."

"But you were backstage before the show," Abby told him. "It sounds exactly like you were stalking her."

"Yeah, I was backstage long enough to get kicked out. What do you suppose I did to Carly in that short amount of time? With all three of you detective geniuses, you must have some sort of theory. Did I poison the flowers? Did I slip something to her? Secretly inject her with a syringe? In a crowded room, how am I supposed to have poisoned my wife? Check with Hope. She saw me talking to Carly. I never laid a hand on her."

I quickly typed a message into my notes about Donald's answer. Was he being coy? Was he trying to fool us, or did he really not know how Carly was poisoned?

"You still haven't told us why it was so important to talk to your ex-wife *that* night," Abby said.

Donald tapped his phone. "That's why," he insisted. "Those pictures are from the day of the fashion show. My kid was getting the crap beat out of him, and Carly wasn't doing a damn thing about it."

Abby interrupted his rant. "She got Chip Louvain expelled from school. That's something."

He laughed at her, but his tone was hostile. "That just made things worse. And you know what she told our son to do about it? She told him to fight back. That was her answer. That was Carly. She was a fighter. And guess where that got her? I wanted to keep my kid safe. She didn't deserve custody of him. She didn't even want it. She just wanted another win under her belt."

"And now you have custody of him," Case said. "Just what you wanted."

"Yes, I do. And I thank God for that. It's a tragedy what happened to Carly, but at least one good thing came out of it. I have my boy, and I have these photos, and we're going to make Ed and Hope and that horrible kid of theirs pay for what they've done."

"What are you going to do?" Case asked.

"Take them to court," Donald replied. "We have proof now. No one's going to cover up this crime. No one hurts my boy. Not while I'm around."

It seemed as though Donald's anger had worn off after getting his thoughts out. He stood up and looked out the window again. The window faced Lake Michigan, and the rhythmic lapping of the waves on the rocky shore seemed to calm him down.

He continued to stare out the window. "Carly tried to turn my son against me, you know. Told him he couldn't see me anymore."

"That must have really angered you," I said.

Donald turned to smile at me. "You know what he did? My boy? He came to see me anyway. He asked for my help, and I told him not to fight back. I told him to get pictures, videos, anything we could use, and that's exactly what he did."

"How does this relate to Carly's death?" Case asked.

Donald seemed irritated by the question. "You tell me."

Case glared at him. "Answer the question."

"Okay, private eye," Donald told him, "listen closely. Carly got the Louvain kid expelled, and that made things worse. My boy came to me for help. Now, what am I supposed to do when Carly won't talk to me? I wanted to show her the pictures. I wanted her to take this seriously, but she was more interested in fighting with Hope than helping my boy. So I guess she got what she deserved."

As I typed out his shocking response, Case tried his hand at asking Donald another question. "Are you saying Hope was the one who poisoned Carly?"

Donald shrugged his shoulders. "All I'm saying is that you don't mess with her kid and get away with it. Anyway, now you understand why I was at the fashion show. That was your initial question, wasn't it, hotshot?"

Case tensed the muscles in his jaw, breathing deeply and trying his best not to look aggravated. I put my hand on his, hoping to calm him down.

"Why did you leave through the backstage door?" Abby asked, pressing on.

"I didn't leave through the back," he told her. "I was kicked out, thrown out by that criminal Charles has working for him. Ben Logan, I think his name is."

"Do you know him?" Abby asked.

"Yeah, I fired him," Donald said. "He used to work security at the casino. That was years ago. Anyway, money started going missing from the vault. A little bit at first, then it escalated."

"Was Logan stealing money?" Case asked.

"No, if you can believe it, Logan *caught* the guy stealing money. And you know what he did? He blackmailed the thief and took the money for himself."

"Was he arrested?"

"You bet he was. I took him to court, got my money back. He spent a few years in prison. But guess who got him out early? Charles Sloan. The man who now claims that I'm sending him threatening letters. They're both criminals, as far as I'm concerned. If you need a fourth partner in this detective gig, let me know, because I'd be turning the screws on both those guys. If you want real suspects, go find that security guard and the man who hired him."

My fingers typed with purpose as this new information came out. Charles had helped his bodyguard get out of jail.

"Carly worked closely with Charles Sloan," Case said. "Why would he want to kill her?"

Donald gave Case a sly smile. "I didn't say he killed her. I think he had his henchman do it instead."

"You didn't answer my question," Case said. "Why would he want her dead?"

"That wasn't your question," Donald fired back with a smirk.

I looked up from my keypad to see Case's jaw twitching.

"I'll give you this one for free because maybe you didn't know Carly too well." Donald sat back again. "Carly wasn't a politician. She was a businesswoman. She was the one who convinced me to go ahead with the casino project, and Charles was the one who shut it down."

More new information. I couldn't be sure that Donald was telling the truth, but from what we'd already learned about Carly, it seemed possible. I typed it in.

"Now, you tell me," Donald continued, "why would

she go work for him? And more importantly, why would Charles hire her?"

"You tell us," Case said. "No more beating around the bush."

"Okay, then," Donald said. "My guess is that Carly told him the casino project was my idea, and that I was the one sending him threats. She made Charles believe that I was the enemy."

"So, you *didn't* want to build the new casino?" Abby asked.

"I wasn't *against* it," he answered. "But I wasn't interested in finding additional investors. Too much work. This little riverboat makes me some good money, just not enough to fund the kind of casino Carly wanted to build. She said she was going to take care of all that, so I let her. Then Charles blocked the deal, and a few months later Carly left me and started working for him."

"So, what was Carly up to?" Abby asked. "You clearly know more than you're letting on."

Donald smiled and touched his temple. "Carly was clever. Knowing her, she had a plan. You figure that out, and you'll catch her killer. That's what I told Detective Walters, but he doesn't care."

"What was Carly's plan?" Abby asked again.

"I don't know." Donald tapped his fingers on the table. "Ask Charles, who I'm sure is breathing down the detective's neck, wanting him to close the case quickly. That's why the redhead is in trouble. She's an easy target."

"Are you saying Carly is responsible for getting herself killed?" Case asked.

Donald gave an eerily unsympathetic look. "Maybe."

"It's easy to blame Carly now that she can't defend herself," Case said.

Donald sat forward and folded his hands on the tabletop. "It's easy for you to pin the murder on me, but here I am, free as a bird. No charges were ever brought against me. What does that tell you?"

"That you have enough money to hire a good lawyer," Case answered.

"Several lawyers, actually, and thank God for that, too. So let me say it again. Figure out what Carly was up to, whom it involved, and you'll solve your case."

Case rubbed his forehead, clearly still irritated. "Do you know anything about a company called CB Development Company?"

"Never heard of it."

"How about the Unified Construction Company?"

"Yeah," Donald replied. "That's the name of the outfit that was going to build the casino."

I wrote it down. Unified Construction was also contracted for the Samson Mall project that the mayor had shut down.

"Do you know why Carly would've received mail from Unified?" Case asked.

Donald rubbed his jaw. "When was this?"

"A few weeks ago."

"A few weeks ago?" he asked in surprise. "There you go. Now you're on to something. Why would they be communicating with Carly? Charles shut down our plans for the casino months ago."

Donald checked his watch and then stood. "Listen, I want you to find Carly's killer. I really do. Someone had the nerve to murder her in broad daylight, and that person should be put away for life. I'm rooting for you. Really." He walked to the door and held it open for us, stopping the interview without saying another word.

Case looked at me. "I guess that's it. Is there anything we missed?"

I looked over the notes and shook my head. "We got more than we asked for."

"Abby?" Case asked.

She stood. "I think we're done for now."

Donald handed Case his business card. "Next time, hotshot, give me a call first."

"I tried calling—many times," Case said.

"Well, next time, I'll answer."

As we walked out, Donald added, "You might not be the brightest detectives, but hey, at least you're trying."

"I wanted to punch him in the mouth," Case said as we exited the noisy riverboat into the muggy night. "I swear he was trying to get my goat."

"I think it worked," I joked. "But at least Donald seemed to be truthful."

Case shook his head, still clearly flustered. "I don't trust him."

"Let's focus on what can be verified," Abby said. "We know for certain that Donald was questioned by detectives and released. That was verified by Detective Walters himself."

"We also know that Donald's son was attacked on the day Carly was killed," I said as we wound our way through rows of cars. "The photos were time-stamped."

"Yes," Abby agreed. "Which gives validity to his reason for being at the fashion show. And I can check with the PTA and the school board, try to dig up some proof that Carly had Hope's son expelled."

"He gave us some important information, too," I said, "such as verifying that Hope Louvain was off-the-wall when it came to her son. And that she had seen Donald talking to Carly, which meant she could've entered Carly's dressing room while they were occupied."

"Another thing," Case said, "is that Donald's information coincides with what Rosemary Dalsaurus told us about Carly and her involvement with Unified Construction, which would suggest that Carly was confident the casino project would proceed regardless of what the mayor's policy was."

"Donald said Carly had a plan," I added. "If Carly's plan was to circumvent Mayor Sloan and build her casino, would that be a strong enough motive to kill her?"

"He is promising to keep Sequoia small," Case said. "So, let me float the theory Donald mentioned, that the security guard was in on the murder. He was backstage before the show. He could've had access to Carly's dressing room before she arrived."

"It's a possibility," Abby remarked. "I just don't see the mayor putting that much trust in a criminal."

"Don't forget, the mayor got Logan released from prison," I said. "Maybe it's a debt repaid."

"I still think Hope has the more realistic motive," Abby said. "And she had better access to

Carly's dressing room. Plus, Hope's husband is the chief of police, with a reputation of covering up his wife's crimes."

"If anyone had better access to Carly's dressing room, it was Eleni Sloan," I said. "We can't forget about her."

Case lifted the keys from his pocket and unlocked the doors as we approached his Jeep. "It sounds like the only thing we can all agree on is that Donald is the killer."

I smacked him playfully. "We can agree to disagree."

"I wish we knew what kind of poison was used," Abby said. "That could help us narrow it down even further. It would have to be someone who knew what kind of poison is invisible and tasteless."

"My friend on the force is trying to get the toxicology report for us," I told Abby. "But so far, he hasn't had any luck. I'll try reaching out to Bob Maguire again."

Abby huffed in frustration.

I opened the door so she could squeeze into the back seat. "I'm sorry."

"It's not you, Athena," she said. "We just have a whole list of suspects, and we're running out of time. Jillian is going to be arraigned soon. Her trial could start as early as next week."

"I understand," I told her. "I'll find a way to get that toxicology report. I promise."

"In the meantime," Abby said, "what else did you learn from Rosemary today?"

I sat down and buckled myself in tight. "Rosemary overheard Carly threatening Charles," I told her. "If they were having an affair, she could've been holding it over his head, threatening to expose him if he didn't let her proceed with the project."

"That changes things," Abby said. "That gives Charles a very strong motive."

"And to further the point," I added, "Rosemary also said she saw no real chemistry between the two and, in fact, doesn't think Carly was attracted to Mayor Sloan at all."

Case reversed out of his parking spot and drove us out of the lot. "She was blackmailing him."

"Wait a minute," Abby said, leaning between the seats. "Say that again about Carly not being attracted to the mayor."

"Rosemary said there was no chemistry between the two," I told her.

"That's it!" Abby said. "Chemistry! We haven't considered the chemistry angle."

"I don't understand," I said.

"Who would know more about poisonous chemicals than a chemist?" Abby asked. "Or a chemistry *teacher*?"

I looked at Abby through the rearview mirror. "Hope Louvain."

# CHAPTER FIFTEEN

"**H**ow are we going to approach Hope?" I asked Abby. "I'm sure she'll be on her guard after our last encounter."

"Why don't you call her? Tell her we had a falling-out. Make it seem like juicy gossip. Maybe she'll be more willing to talk."

"I can do that."

Case pointed to his phone on the dashboard. "I have her number saved."

I looked up her number as Case pulled onto the state road leading back to town. The warm summer wind started to rush through the doorless Jeep, blowing my hair in all directions, making it impossible to see. "How am I supposed to call her now?"

He pulled off at a side road and the let engine idle.

I turned around, apologizing for the wind, but

Abby's hair was pulled up tightly behind her head. She smiled. "I'm always prepared."

In a moment, Hope answered. I put my phone on speaker mode so everyone in the Jeep could hear. "Hi, Hope, this is Athena Spencer."

"Oh, hi," she said with reluctance. "What can I do for you?"

"I want to apologize for the way we left things."

"Is that all?" she asked curtly.

"Well," I said, trying to think of something gossipy to say about Abby while she was sitting right behind me. "I'm sorry that Abby came on so strong. She and I haven't really been seeing eye to eye lately."

"Is that so?"

I could immediately hear a change in Hope's voice, so I continued. "Yes, we had a bad fight, and she left, so now I'm trying to pick up the pieces."

"What was the fight about?" Hope asked eagerly.

"It was about you, actually. I don't think you had anything to do with Carly's death, and Abby was just adamant."

"Can you believe her?" Hope agreed. "And what's with that horribly gaudy convertible she drives? Yellow is *definitely* not her color."

At that, Abby shot forward, reaching for the phone. I pulled it away just before she could grab it. "Also," I said, "I have a few more questions I'd like to ask you. Is it okay if I drop by after school tomorrow?"

There was a pause. "Just you?"

"Yes," I answered. "Just me."

It sounded like she put her hand over her phone

to talk to someone in the background. Then she said, "Why don't I come down to your office after school?"

"That would be fine," I said. "Five thirty-five Greene Street, upstairs."

"I'll see you then," she said and ended the call.

I looked at Abby in the rearview. "Well, that was easy."

"You did a good job," Abby said. "I just hope you can get some information out of her."

"Won't you be there?"

She shook her head. "I'll go down to the plaza or something. I doubt she'll talk if I'm there. You and Case can handle that one."

"Um," Case said slowly, "I might've forgotten to mention that I'm working in Saugatuck all day tomorrow. I won't be around."

"Well, that's not good," I said to Case, trying to hide my disappointment. "I don't feel comfortable talking to Hope alone."

"I'll stay out of sight in Case's office," Abby said. "I don't think you should talk to her alone, either."

"Then it's settled," Case said as he pulled back onto the road. "Good luck tomorrow, ladies, and good work tonight."


Later that night, I thought about what Donald Blackburn had said about Hope's retaliations, remembering that Eleni Sloan had also brought it up. Clearly, any mention of Hope's son ignited her temper, but why? Could it be she was afraid the stories about the boy were true?

And that got me to thinking about tempers, so I did some research and came up with a blog topic. Anger.

### IT'S ALL GREEK TO ME
*Blog by Goddess Anon*

*Time to Put Out the Fire*

*I recently had a confrontation with a neighbor over her teenage son, who was bullying someone close to me. Rather than being concerned that the bullying was true, this neighbor's temper flared to such a degree that she became a bully, too. Why did she have such an extreme reaction? Was she being overprotective, or did she fear the accusation was true? And what could I have done about it?*

*According to the website Reachout.com, "Anger usually occurs when there's something going on in life that makes you feel upset, frustrated, hurt, or bored. Sometimes anger is an immediate response to a specific event, while at other times it builds up over time. Whatever the reason, feeling angry or seeing someone else become angry should alert you that something isn't right."*

*Oh, boy, did that hit the nail on the head. But now, what to do about it? Any suggestions?*

*This is Goddess Anon bidding you* Antio Sas.

*Friday*

"Thenie doesn't have a temper problem," Maia said as Nicholas and I joined my sisters at our booth at the diner the next morning. "She's always in control."

"Unlike some people we could mention," Selene said, casting her gaze toward our mother, who was pouring coffee for the Red Hat ladies across the aisle.

"What are you talking about?" I asked.

"Goddess Anon's blog this morning," Maia explained. "It was about anger, a subject we all know too well."

"Dealing with anger is easy," Selene bragged. "Just count to ten."

Maia shook her head. "I've tried it. Doesn't work."

"My mom stands me in the corner when I have a temper tantrum," Nicholas said.

"Sweet little Niko?" Selene asked. "I've never seen you have a tantrum."

Nicholas shrugged. "I'm all grown up now."

"I've learned how to deal with anger," Maia said. "I go to my zen place."

Selene rolled her eyes and looked at Nicholas. "Little Maia is all grown up, too."

"Oh, please. You don't even know what a zen place is," Maia countered.

"Coffee?" my mother asked me even as she proceeded to pour. She glanced at Selene. "Why are you counting?"

"Counting is my zen place," Selene answered dryly.

"It's what Selene does when she gets angry," I added.

"Oh, just do what I do," Mama said. "Smile. It makes all your troubles melt away. I don't even remember the last time I was angry."

The three of us looked at each other and burst out laughing. "Mama," Maia said, "you have a terrible temper!"

My mother started to disagree, then thought better of it. Instead, she gave Maia a forced smile. She held her hand out for Nicholas. "Come with me, *glykó mou agóri*." My sweet boy. "Your yiayiá has a special treat for you in the kitchen."

After they'd left, Selene leaned toward me. "Athena, Mama is driving me crazy! She's trying to set me up with someone, and she won't let up."

"You can't fight her," I said. "Just go out once and tell Mama it didn't work out."

"I just can't do it," Selene said. She glanced around to be sure no one else was listening, then said in a hushed voice, "He's a *pig* farmer, Athena. From Kalamazoo! And he's coming to the Greek tent at the fair this evening to meet me! And Mama will be there. You have to come, Thenie. You have to help me out."

"Help out with what?" my mother asked, joining us again.

"With the baklava," Maia said quickly, covering for Selene.

"I was just going to ask you, Athena," Mama said. "Your sisters and I are working the St. Jacob's tent at the fair tonight. Why don't you stop by and have some dessert? Bring Niko and Case. Make a night of it. Have some fun."

"I can't," I said. "I'm doing investigative work this evening."

"More work," Mama huffed. "Look at those bags under your eyes. You need a break from work. I'm surprised you even have time for breakfast."

"I'll take a break when the case is over," I reminded her.

"Well, it's a shame. You won't have a chance to meet Thomas Pappas," Mama said. "Tom's a nice Greek boy who wants to meet Selene."

"He's not a boy," Selene said, "and I'm not interested."

"You haven't even met him," Mama said. "At least give him a chance."

Selene put her head in her hands. "Okay."

Mama patted her on the shoulder. "That's my girl."

When our overbearing mother had stepped away, Maia reached her arm around Selene to comfort her. She leaned in close to say, "Just count to ten."

Sitting at the computer at the garden center later that morning, I received a text message from Abby stating that she was going to head down to our office to do some research. Since my morning work was finished, I decided to join her there.

The sun was hot and the sky cloudless as I headed down Greene Street. Dodging tourists on the sidewalk, I passed an ice cream shop and breathed in the aroma of freshly baked waffle cones. I adjusted the strap of my purse over the shoulder of my short-sleeved blue shirt, glad I'd chosen to wear a pair of white capri pants instead of long pants.

As I approached the Greene Street building, I stopped to wave at Gracie, the owner of the deli, through the window. Having just opened our detective office on the floor above the deli, I hadn't had a chance to get to know Gracie personally, but we'd ordered enough food recently to be preferred customers. Next to the deli was the door to our stairwell.

As I reached for the handle, the door was flung open violently, slamming my hand into my chest and knocking me backward off my feet and onto the cement sidewalk. I sat up, stunned, already feeling a throbbing bruise forming on my backside and pain radiating from my wrist. I watched as the door to our stairwell closed slowly, revealing a large man in a black trench coat and black baseball cap lumbering swiftly in the opposite direction. Before I could make out any identification, the owner of the deli came rushing out.

Gracie held out her hands to help me up. "What happened, hon?"

"I don't know," I replied, easing my way to my feet.

"One minute you're giving me a wave and the next minute you're falling backward onto your rear end. Are you hurt?"

"No, I'm okay, Gracie. Really. Just a bit confused. Thank you for helping me."

I kept my eyes on the corner of Greene Street, wondering who could've been so inconsiderate as to knock me down and rush away. Surely, the man would've known that he'd opened the door on someone. Could it have been one of the apartment residents?

"You might want to get that hand looked at," Gracie said, eyeing the nasty scratches on my right palm. "You might have a fracture."

I opened and closed my hand, flinching slightly. "I think it'll be okay."

"Listen, you come back at lunchtime, and I'll have a sandwich ready for you. On the house."

I thanked her and opened the stairwell door. Up the stairs on the right was our office, followed by several apartments down both sides of the hallway.

I could see the glass pane of our door as I climbed and noticed the light inside was off. Abby hadn't yet arrived. I slowly unlocked the office door and stepped inside, almost missing the piece of yellow paper on the floor. I picked it up and opened it. Inside, printed in block letters it read: *Leave the investigation to the police.*

# CHAPTER SIXTEEN

My mind instantly flashed to the man in the black coat and hat. There was no reason for him to wear a trench coat on a hot day unless he was trying to hide his identity. I went straight to my desk and pulled out my phone, hitting the redial button for Case's number. It rang four times and went to voice mail, so I left a message for him to call me ASAP.

"Athena?" I heard Abby call.

"I'm in here."

She stuck her head in my office doorway. "Is everything okay? The front door was open."

"I forgot to close it." I stood up and held out the piece of paper. "This was on the floor inside."

She took the paper, reading it aloud. " 'Leave the investigation to the police.' Wow. We must be on to something. Someone is getting nervous to leave a threat like this."

"The note isn't *exactly* a threat, is it?"

"The threat is implied," Abby said. "Do what it says or face unknown consequences."

"What do we do?"

"Be cautious. Make sure we keep the doors locked. Make sure we're not being followed. Stay alert. It's happened to me before."

*Followed.* Suddenly the words of my pseudo-psychic sister sprang forth. *Abby is being followed by a blue aura. The letters M and S. Follow your inner guide.* Delphi's visions were becoming harder to ignore.

"Have you noticed anyone following you lately?" I asked Abby.

"No," she said thoughtfully. "Why?

I flexed my fingers again, this time feeling a tightness where a bruise was forming at the base of my palm. "A man opened the stairwell door right into me and knocked me down." I pointed at the note. "I think it was the same man who left that."

"Did you get a look at him?"

I shook my head. "Not really. He was moving fast. Tall, burly, wearing a black trench coat and hat."

"How tall?"

A nervous laugh escaped my lips. "He looked pretty tall from my vantage point. I was practically on my back."

"Could it have been Donald?"

I thought about it for a second and shook my head. "I don't know. He seemed taller than Donald."

"Charles Sloan?"

"No, heftier."

"The security guard?"

I remembered the big, broad-shouldered man

in the suit trailing closely behind the mayor at his last rally. He fit the description perfectly. "If it was him, then the note is most likely from Charles Sloan."

"You're right," Abby said. "It would also mean that the security guard isn't just the mayor's bodyguard but, as we suspected, also his lackey, doing whatever the mayor needs him to do."

"Like poisoning Carly."

"And to play it out," Abby said, "if the mayor is behind Carly's death, then he intends for Jillian to take the fall for it. Hence the wording on the note—leave the investigation to the police—who've already decided on her guilt."

I took another look at the note on my desk. "If the message is a threat, why leave it so ambiguous?"

Abby studied it for a moment. "An actual threat would be illegal."

I massaged my bruised wrist, checking to see if it was swelling. Luckily it didn't feel broken. "You're right. Charles was a lawyer. He would've known to leave the note vague. I think he sent it."

Abby huffed impatiently. "Which is why he's been avoiding us. Somehow we have to get him to talk."

I eased myself down at my desk, still stunned by it all. "What do we do about the threat?"

"Use it to our advantage," Abby said. "The note is handwritten, which is extremely careless if it was written by the same person who murdered Carly."

"Good point, but would the mayor be so careless?"

"I wouldn't think so. Unless it was rushed, or he

had his bodyguard send it. We need a handwriting sample from both the mayor and his bodyguard, just to be certain." Abby sat down across from me and studied the threatening note in her hand. "But how can we get a sample without raising suspicion?"

"I think I have an idea." I picked up my phone and punched in Lila's number. After three rings, she answered, "Hey, Athena! How's the investigation going?"

"Going well, thank you. That's why I'm calling, actually, to see how *your* investigation is going."

"My investigation?"

"Yes, Lila. Your undercover investigation?"

"Oh, right. It's going very well! The mayor hasn't tried to sleep with me or murder me, so I'd say he is clean."

"Well," I said, "it might be a little too soon to rule out the mayor completely. We should probably interview him first. Would you be able to get me an appointment with him sometime soon?"

There was a pause, and then she came back on the line. "He's got meetings all afternoon, but if you could come by his tent at the fairgrounds this evening. . . . Say around six? That's usually a quiet time. People are eating."

I put my hand over the phone and said to Abby, "How about six o'clock this evening at the fair?"

"I can be there," she said.

"Okay, Lila. We'll be there at six. In the meantime, we're going to need a sample of his handwriting. Can you get that for me?"

"What kind of writing?" Lila asked.

"His *hand*writing."

"Of what?"

"Of anything," I said. "You work in his campaign office. I'm sure there is something there with his handwriting on it."

She paused, then said reluctantly, "I'll try."

"Oh, and don't tell him that we're coming to the fair tonight. Okay?"

"Why?"

"Because," I explained gently, "it feels like he's avoiding us, so I'd like to catch him off guard."

"Athena, I can't do that."

"Why not?"

"Because I've earned his trust. I'm part of his inner circle now. I can't let him be ambushed."

"Hold on, Lila. Do you remember *why* you were trying to earn his trust?" I paused to wait for an answer but heard nothing. "To help our investigation?"

"Yes, I remember."

"Then help us with the investigation," I pleaded. "Make sure Charles is at the booth at six o'clock tonight and do *not* let him know we're coming."

"Okay," Lila said slowly, "I won't say a word. But you have to act like you just happened to be there. I don't want him to know I set him up."

"Will do. Thank you." I ended the call and turned to Abby, "We're all set."

Abby checked the time and stood. "I want to get over to the jail and talk to Jillian, so I'll see you back here at three o'clock to meet with Hope."

"See you then."

I limped back to the garden center with my bruised backside and scraped-up wrist, continuously glancing around for the man in the black trench coat. I couldn't shake the feeling that it wasn't the mayor who'd sent that note. It seemed too rushed and careless. But it could've been his bodyguard, possibly acting alone in his boss's interests.

On the other hand, it very well could've been Donald Blackburn who'd written the note. He'd already confirmed his reputation for hiding in plain sight, and he also had big, burly bodyguards who fit the description of the man who'd knocked me down.

I entered Spencer's to find everything humming along nicely, albeit much darker since we had to rely on the generator for power. I noted that Abby's mom's garden stakes, which were on display at the base of the statue of Athena, were selling well and made a mental note to let Abby know.

I stopped at our kitchenette to take some ibuprofen for the pain in my hip, then continued to the office, where I sat down at the desk to call Case. This time he picked up.

"Hey, Goddess, sorry I haven't called you back. I just finished an interview and had to grab a bite of lunch. How are things going? You sounded stressed in your voice mail."

I filled him in on my run-in with the burly stranger and the threatening note, letting him know what we suspected.

"The main thing," Case said, "is that you're okay."

"A little bruised. A little unnerved. Otherwise, all right. Abby advised us to make sure we keep the doors locked and to be cautious."

"That's a good idea," Case said. "What's our next move?"

"We need to go back to the fairgrounds this evening to talk to Mayor Sloan. Lila said to stop by his tent about six o'clock to catch him. Want to join Abby and me?"

"I'm not sure I'll be back in time. I have several more interviews to conduct. I'll let you know if I can make it."

My phone beeped. I checked the screen to see an incoming call from Bob Maguire.

"Hey, Bob is calling, and I need to take this."

"Okay, I'll be in touch later."

I ended Case's call and clicked over to Bob. "Hello, Officer Maguire. What's up?"

"I found out what kind of poison was used," he said.

"You did?"

"It wasn't easy, but I got it."

"You're amazing, Bob. What was it?"

"It's a chemical called tetrahydrozoline."

I grabbed a pen. "Would you spell that for me?"

He spelled it out and then said, "In large doses it causes severe nausea and vomiting, rapid pulse, high blood pressure, and will stop the heart within fifteen minutes to half an hour of ingesting. And here's the most interesting part. It's the main ingredient in over-the-counter eye drops."

"Seriously? So, someone emptied a bottle of eye drops into Carly's water bottle?"

"You got it. It's tasteless, colorless, and odorless. It slows the respiratory system and causes heart failure."

"How would someone know to use eye drops?" I asked.

"There was a murder case a few years ago that aired on television that brought national attention to the product. I'm wondering if Carly's killer expected the drug to go unnoticed. Medical examiners only recently started testing for it."

"Interesting," I said. "This is great information, Bob. I don't know how to thank you."

"You can solve this case and send Walters packing. The sooner he retires, the better."

"I'll do my best. Thanks again."

I hung up and sat back in my chair. Eye drops. Anyone could have purchased them. Anyone could have seen the television show about them. But which one of the people backstage would have been angry enough to use them?

My head was starting to pound from all the information I'd taken in, and my backside was starting to throb from sitting on my bruised tailbone. I called Case and left a detailed message about the poison, then left the office and went out back to see what Nicholas was up to. If anyone could take my mind off the case, it was my son.

At ten minutes before three o'clock, Abby and I sat down in my office at the detective agency and went over our questions for Hope. I had already filled Abby in on Bob Maguire's information on the eye drops, which had surprised her. She'd come across one case where the poison ricin was used, but never anything involving eye drops.

"There was something else I found interesting," I told Abby. "Tetrahydrozoline only takes about fifteen minutes to start working."

"Fifteen minutes," Abby repeated. "That's quick. I can't imagine a whole lot of people know that eye drops can poison someone, which once again brings me back to the chemistry teacher." Before she could say more, there was a knock on the outside door.

"That must be Hope now," I said, talking quietly. "Make sure you stay in Case's office."

"I'll stay out of sight," Abby whispered. "Do you have all the questions?"

I patted my iPad. "Got them right here." I walked through the reception area, unlocked the front door, and opened it.

But to my surprise, it wasn't Hope. It was her husband, Chief of Police Ed Louvain. And he did not look happy.

# CHAPTER SEVENTEEN

"**C**hief!" I said in surprise. I looked past him. "Is Hope with you?"

"She won't be joining us." He gave me a cold once-over, then said in a no-nonsense voice, "How about you and me having a talk instead?"

I swallowed, feeling suddenly unnerved. Ed Louvain was a big, imposing man, tall and broad-shouldered with a hawkish face, buzz-cut light-brown hair, and hard, cold green eyes that were now laser-focused on me. It didn't help that he had on his navy police uniform, his badge shining on his chest, his gun strapped to his thick, black belt.

And then from behind me I heard, "Why don't we all have a talk?" Abby walked past me with her hand outstretched. "Chief Louvain, I'm Abby Knight Salvare. I'm a private detective working on the Carly Blackburn case. It's very thoughtful of you to take your wife's spot for this interview."

Ed Louvain looked a little nonplussed as he shook Abby's hand. Clearly, he thought his presence would be intimidating, but as he towered over Abby, who was smiling brightly, it was obvious who had the upper hand.

Abby indicated my office. "Let's go in there and talk."

I walked around the desk and sat down, still in awe of what I'd just witnessed. While Abby and the chief took seats across from me, I opened my iPad, ready to take notes.

"We hope your wife is okay," Abby began.

"She's fine. Just busy." Ed adjusted his big body in the chair. "What can I answer for you?"

I looked at the list of questions we'd written down for Hope and didn't know where to begin. They weren't intended for her husband. As I scrolled through the list, my iPad went dark. I sat in front of the blank screen as the realization hit home. I'd forgotten to charge it. And instantly my mind went blank, as well.

Fortunately, Abby took the lead. "We understand there have been problems between Carly Blackburn's son and your son, resulting in your son's expulsion. We also understand it caused tension between Hope and Carly, resulting in a heated argument before the fashion show."

"I don't know anything about an argument," Ed said, shifting again in the chair. "But I can tell you my son has been vilified by the Blackburns."

"Did you know Hope was angry with Carly over your son?" Abby asked.

"We were both angry," he said.

"Was Hope angry enough to smash Carly's windshield?"

The chief said nothing.

"Your wife seems to have quite a temper," Abby prodded.

"I see where you're going with this," he said, "but Hope would never hurt anyone intentionally."

"Carly was in her car at the time Hope smashed her windshield," Abby said. "She could've easily been hurt."

"Stop right there," he said angrily. "My wife didn't kill anybody."

"Why was she never charged with anything?" Abby asked. "Like aggravated assault?"

"Because Carly never filed a report," he retorted, then added cannily, "unless you have proof to the contrary."

And because Carly was dead, all we had was a third-person account. He had us there.

"Does Hope ever use eye drops?" I asked.

He gave me a puzzled look. "I don't know. Why?"

"Because that was the poison used on Carly," I said.

He sat there looking stunned for a moment, then said, "Anyone could've bought eye drops."

"But only a few people would know the chemical composition of eye drops, and even fewer people had access to Carly's water bottle," Abby said, "your wife being one of them."

Ed ran one hand through his hair. Finally, he said, "I know my wife better than anybody, and I

mean it when I say she wouldn't kill anyone. She's
kindhearted. She's a good mother."

"Mothers are ferocious when it comes to de-
fending their children," Abby said.

He sat there for a moment thinking about what
she'd said. Then he leaned forward. "You're looking at the wrong person. If you want to know
whom you should be investigating, let me give you
a tip—off the record."

"Okay," Abby said.

He talked low and steadily, as if each word held
its own importance. "I happen to know that Detective Walters was investigating Mayor Sloan's security guard."

"He *was* investigating?" Abby asked. "But he's
not now?"

"Walters dropped it," Ed explained. "But here's
the inside scoop. The security guard, Ben something, tried to get on the police force and was re-
jected, so he went to work at the Blackburn Casino
instead. And guess what? He stole money and was
sent to prison."

"How is that relevant?" Abby asked.

"When the mayor first reported these supposed
threats," the chief explained, "I offered him the
names of several good men to work as security. Instead, he hired a man with a criminal record."

"Why would he do that?" Abby asked.

Ed cleared his throat. "Let's just say this Ben
character might not play by the rules."

"And that suits the mayor?" I asked.

Ed shrugged. "Maybe it suits him just fine.
Here's the thing. Mayor Sloan claims to have been

threatened, but he's never shared any evidence with the police. No letters. No emails. No evidence at all."

"Then why did he hire a security guard?" I asked.

"My guess is that Charles Sloan needed a favor, and he recruited a criminal to help him out. The threats were just a cover."

"Is it possible Mayor Sloan could've put pressure on Detective Walters to drop the investigation?" I asked.

Ed rubbed his nose. "Are we done here?"

"Don't be coy," Abby insisted. "Are you saying that the mayor hired the security guard to kill Carly?"

Ed held up both hands. "Whoa, whoa, whoa. I'm not saying that. I'm only telling you what I know. Detective Walters was looking at the security guard as a suspect. Now he's not. Let's leave it at that." He stood up and adjusted his belt. "Now, we're done here."

"One more thing," I said. "I'd like a sample of your handwriting."

He balked at my request. "Why?"

"Why not?"

"Fine. You leave my wife alone, and I'll give you a sample."

Before I could oppose, Abby agreed to his deal. "Write this out. 'Leave the investigation to the police.'"

"What does that mean?" he asked.

"If you're not guilty, then it doesn't matter, does it?"

He stood up, glaring at Abby. "Forget it. No deal. You stay away from my wife. I'm keeping my eye on you—both of you."

I showed him out of the office and came back to find Abby making notes in her notebook. "What did I tell you about that iPad?" she joked. "I'm telling you, pen and paper is the way to go."

"Thanks for taking over," I said. After retrieving a charging cord from my desk drawer, I plugged in the dead device and said, "What do you think about Ed Louvain?"

"He didn't convince me of his wife's innocence, that's for sure. He was clearly trying to guide us in a new direction, But he did bring us some interesting information about the security guard." Abby put her pen down. "I think we really need to dig into this guy. And I'm very curious as to why Walters dropped the investigation. Maybe the mayor did put pressure on him." She flipped the notebook closed. "With some careful questioning, we may find out tonight."

Shortly before six o'clock, after making sure Delphi was closing the store that night, I went out front and waited for Abby to pick me up. It was a warm evening with a light southwesterly breeze, a perfect night for a ride in a convertible. I felt bad that I wasn't taking Nicholas with me to the fair, but I didn't plan on staying long.

Abby pulled up a few minutes later in her shiny yellow Corvette. She was dressed casually in tan capri pants and an orange and tan plaid shirt, the orange setting off her bright red hair. She smiled as I got in. "You came prepared. And I love your outfit."

I turned my head, making my ponytail swing. "I did come prepared. And thank you." I arranged the skirt of my light green sundress beneath me and fastened the seat belt. "How did your visit with Jillian go?"

"She's very depressed," Abby said. "Her arraignment hearing is still two days away, and she's frantic to get back to her little girl."

"What are her chances of being released on bond?"

"Slim," Abby replied. "The evidence is stacked against her." She heaved a sigh. "We've got to get this investigation moving."

She drove us across town and turned into the fairground entrance, where she made her way across the lumpy field to the rows of parked cars. Then we walked across the grassy terrain, this time free of mud, and paid our entrance fees at the gate.

We headed up the big blacktop walkway, passing carnival games and fried-food stands. And right before the St. Jacob's food tent stood a bright blue tent with a big sign in black letters across the top that said, *Meet and Greet with Mayor Sloan*.

"Here we are," I said.

Inside the tent, Lila and two other women were standing behind a table that ran across the front. The table was loaded with free giveaways—cup cozies, pens, buttons with the slogan *Keep Sequoia Small* across the front, coffee mugs, and bottle openers. But contrary to what Lila had predicted, there was a line of people waiting to talk to the mayor.

"Athena, Abby, good to see you," Lila said as she walked over to us. "Charles had to slip out for a bathroom break. He'll be back any second."

"Were you able to get a writing sample?" I asked.

"I didn't feel comfortable taking something off his desk," Lila replied. "Sorry."

I glanced around at the buttons and bumper stickers and campaign posters with the mayor's smiling face on them, and I had an idea. "Can I have a poster?"

Lila handed me the poster. Then her eyes grew wide. "This dress!" She reached for my hand and spun me awkwardly. "It's beautiful. You look good in blue."

I looked down at the patterned dress. "It's green."

"More like a blue-green. And your hair looks so full and bouncy. I see you're learning a lot from our new friend, Abby."

To my utter humiliation, Lila leaned over to whisper a conspicuous thank-you to Abby. "I didn't think Athena had anything to wear other than beige and white, like she's always on a safari."

I had to bite my tongue to keep from retorting, *And you always dress like a drunk yoga instructor.* But I remembered my mother's advice and forced a smile. *Find your zen place,* I told myself.

We chatted with Lila about the campaign, and a few minutes later the security guard walked in through a flap at the back of the tent, glanced around, eyed me for a moment, then held the flap open for the mayor. Sloan came striding inside, his brown hair neatly side-parted and combed back, looking sharp in a light gray suit and a gray, white, and red–striped tie over a white shirt. He spotted us, smiled his winning smile, and came right over.

"Athena Spencer!" He held out his hand, and I shook it. "Good to see you. Thanks for stopping by."

"This is my friend and associate, Abby Salvare," I said. "Abby is a private detective, too."

"A pleasure to meet you, Abby," Sloan said, turning on the charm.

"Could we talk for a minute?" I asked.

His smile grew forced. "Sure. I have a few minutes. Why don't we step over here?"

We moved to the opposite side of the tent, where we couldn't be easily heard. He faced us, arms folded across his suit coat. "How can I help you?"

"First of all," I began, "my mother is a big supporter. I'm sure she would love a signed copy of your poster."

"Well then," Charles smiled, his chest fairly puffing with pride, "whom can I make it out to?"

"How about, 'To the best mother in town. Leave your troubles behind.' "

Charles looked up from the poster in confusion. "You want me to write that?"

"Sure. It's something my mother always says. She'll get a kick out of it."

From his pocket he pulled a bright blue pen with the words *Vote for Sloan* across the side. After a few scribbles, he handed the poster back to me. "Is that all I can do for you?"

I quickly checked the autograph and noticed the handwriting was completely different from that of the threatening note, so I rolled up the poster and stuck it in my purse.

"We also have a few questions about the night of Carly's murder," Abby told him, as she pulled out her notepad.

Charles glanced over our shoulders with consternation at the line of people waiting.

"It won't take much time," Abby assured him, "and then we'll be out of your hair."

"Go ahead, then," he said.

She retrieved the pen from her purse and said, "I hope you don't mind if I take notes."

He waved his hand. "Be my guest."

Abby readied her notebook while I began. "We were told you were backstage at the fashion show the night Carly was killed. Is that true?"

He looked up at the ceiling, his fingers pressed against his lips, thinking. "I believe I stepped backstage briefly to wish my wife good luck. That was right before I went out and introduced the show. There are many witnesses who can attest to that." He smiled confidently.

I watched Abby write down his response, fearing that Sloan would try to charm his way through our interview, treating Abby and me as though we were starstruck supporters hanging on to his every word. Hopefully our questions would shake things up a bit.

Speaking of which, I noticed Abby's arm shaking next to me. I looked over at her, and she smiled at me, encouraging me to proceed.

"Where was your security guard during the show?" I asked.

"I believe he was securing the premises," he said with a smile. "That's his job, after all."

"Are you aware that your security guard worked for Donald Blackburn before working for you?"

"Yes, I did know that," Sloan answered. "Why?"

"We're just checking up on everyone who was backstage," I said.

Once again, Abby shook her arm briskly and then placed her pen against the paper, cursing under her breath.

Charles cleared his throat. "Is something wrong?"

She looked at me. "You're never going to believe this."

"Out of ink?"

Abby's cheeks flushed red, and before I could pull my fully charged iPad from my purse, Mayor Sloan reached his hand out. "Please," he said. "Have mine."

Abby reluctantly took the cheap campaign-sloganed ink pen and motioned for me to continue.

"Are you aware the police were investigating your security guard?" I asked.

"You must be mistaken," Sloan assured. "I would've been alerted if that were the case."

"We have a confidential source who says otherwise," I said.

After a brief flash of indignation, the mayor calmed himself and leveled out his expression. "Let me assure you," Sloan responded smoothly, "that I have every confidence in Ben. He made a few mistakes in the past, but now he's an upstanding citizen. Are there any other questions I can help you with?"

Abby finished writing down his response, then said, "We understand you stopped Unified Construction Company from building a shopping mall on the other side of the highway."

"It was going to be a mega-mall," the mayor said, "and yes, I did. As you're aware, my goal is to keep out big businesses." He smiled his campaign smile. "I'm all for the little guy."

"Would there be any reason why Carly would've been in communication with Unified on your behalf?" I asked.

"On *my* behalf?" The mayor pursed his lips. "Not that I can think of."

"What about CB Development Company?" I asked. "Have you ever heard of them?"

At that, the mayor's polished veneer seemed to crack. "Excuse me?"

"CB Development," I repeated. "Does that mean anything to you?"

"I'm not familiar with the name." In a low voice, he asked, "Should I have heard of this company?"

"We want to know the correlation between the two companies," I said.

"Having never heard of them," he replied coolly, "I really couldn't say."

I was hoping Abby was picking up on the mayor's transformation. He no longer stood with his shoulders back, and his smile no longer seemed charming. Instead, his shoulders had stiffened, and his hands, which had been relaxed at his sides, came up to adjust his tie. His eyebrows lowered, and his gaze grew chilly as he once again threw the question back to me. "What do you know about this CB corporation?"

For some reason, the question came across as threatening, and I found my own shoulders tensing. "We know very little except that Carly received mail from Unified Construction and also CB Development Company," I answered. "That's why we're asking you if they're connected."

Sloan glanced around at the increasing crowd and frowned, clearly growing impatient. "I don't have any more information for you, and quite honestly, Carly's death is still hard to discuss. Perhaps we can continue at a later date." He motioned for his security guard to join him, no doubt to have us escorted out, but Abby wasn't buying his act.

"We're trying to find answers in the death of your campaign manager," she said loudly. She half-turned toward the crowd, speaking more to them than to Charles. "You want answers, don't you?"

"Of course," he snapped, giving her a chilly glance. Then he straightened his lapel and put his smile back into place. He put his hand out, shepherding us farther back into the tent, away from the crowd.

I glanced over at Lila, who was standing behind the table, trying her best to placate the ever-growing line of fans. She turned to give me a desperate look, but all I could do was hold up my finger and hope she could buy us some more time.

"Let's talk about the threats you received," Abby said. "Do you know who sent any of them?"

"No," he replied sharply. "They were all anonymous."

"Were they handwritten?" Abby asked.

"No, typed out."

"Did you suspect any were from Unified?" I asked.

"They were certainly one possibility." He gave me a curious glance. "Are you trying to tie Carly to the threats?"

"We just find it odd that she would receive mail from Unified at your campaign headquarters," I said. "And that would be especially true if Unified had threatened you."

"If we could take a look at the threats you've received, it might help us," Abby said.

"Do you still have those letters?"

His jaw pulsed with tension. "No."

"Do the police have them?"

"I'll tell you what the police have," he answered crossly. "They have Carly's murderer in jail right now."

Abby didn't back down. "Let me rephrase the question."

"Yes," he replied, "why don't you do that?"

"What happened to the letters?" she asked.

"I destroyed them, that's what happened to them," he snarled.

If they'd ever actually existed.

Lila interrupted our intensifying interrogation to announce that some of the people in line were starting to leave. At that, Mayor Sloan ended the interview.

"One more thing," Abby said. "We'd like your permission to ask your security guard a few questions—"

Sloan had been on the verge of saying no, but

then Abby added, "Unless you don't feel comfortable with us talking to him."

"There's no reason for me to feel uncomfortable. Of course, you may talk to him." He motioned to the guard. "Ben, come over here."

As the beefy guard ambled over, a scowl on his face, I noticed he wouldn't look at me. He had on navy shoes and a dark-blue suit, the jacket stretched taut over his muscular chest and shoulders.

"Ben Logan, this is Athena Spencer and Abby Salvare. They're private detectives, and they'd like to talk to you."

Logan gave a nod to his boss, who then strode away. The guard folded his arms across his massive chest and looked straight at Abby, once again avoiding my gaze. He said nothing.

"I understand you did a sweep of the backstage area before and after the fashion show," Abby said.

"Correct."

"When you did your initial sweep," Abby asked, "did you stop at any of the dressing rooms?"

He narrowed his eyes at her. It almost looked as though Ben had something to say, but he merely looked away and said, "No."

"Are you aware that someone tampered with the victim's bottle of water?" Abby asked.

He looked around as though scanning the area. "I heard that, yeah. What's that got to do with me?"

"Did you see anyone tamper with the water?" she asked.

"No."

"Did you handle the bottled water at all?" Abby pressed.

"Now, why would I do that?"

"Maybe because your boss instructed you to," Abby countered.

"Lady, you're crazy." He folded his arms over his chest. "I'm done answering your stupid questions."

"Then *I* have a question for you," I said. "Did you leave a note under my office door?"

Logan's ears turned bright red as he finally faced me, his eyes cold slits. "I don't know anything about any note, and I don't know what office you're talking about."

"Someone who looked a lot like you knocked me down while leaving my office building today," I said.

"I don't know what you're talking about."

"Where were you today about two thirty?" I asked.

"With the mayor," he said.

"We can check with the mayor's secretary, Mr. Logan," Abby said. "Are you sure you want to stick by your answer?"

"Look," he said, getting louder, "if the mayor is in a meeting, I wait outside until he goes somewhere. But I swear I was nowhere near Greene Street."

I paused, wondering whether Ben had realized his mistake. How had he known our office was on Greene Street? "Would you like to prove that you didn't write the note?"

"How?"

"Give us a sample of your handwriting," I told him. "You can use the back of this poster."

"I'm not doing anything unless the mayor tells me to."

"Did the mayor tell you to write that note?"

Logan simply stared at her, opening and closing his fists anxiously.

"Ben?" the mayor called. "I need you to secure the area."

"Yes, sir." With a flicker of a smile, the hefty guard sauntered away.

As I watched him disappear into the crowd, I said to Abby, "I have a feeling the mayor called him away on purpose."

"I think you're right."

"And the guard was lying about being with the mayor this afternoon."

"You're right about that, too," Abby said. "We never told him your office was on Greene Street."

"Exactly."

My phone beeped with an incoming text. It was from Selene: *Can you come to St. Jacob's tent? I need you to stop me from killing Mama.*

Oh, boy.

# CHAPTER EIGHTEEN

"Would you like to sample some homemade baklava?" I asked Abby.

"Love to," she said.

"Then let's head over to St. Jacob's tent," I told her. "The Greek Orthodox women are selling it."

We headed back up the midway and turned down the blacktop path that led past all the food tents, stopping at a small green tent with a big sign over the entrance that said, *Homemade Baklava!* Selene and one other woman were standing inside tables that formed a U-shape, all three tables filled with trays of the homemade pastry. There was no sign of my mother.

Abby looked over the trays. "What'll you have? I'm buying."

"Absolutely not," I said. "My treat."

As Abby pointed out the slice she wanted, Selene waved me over to the side. "Mama just left, thank God. She's driving me crazy, Athena!"

"Has your Greek guy shown up?"

"No sign of him," Selene said. "Thank God for that, too."

"Okay," I said, "when the man shows up, just remember my advice. Tell him you're not looking for a relationship."

Selene twisted her fingers together. "But Mama told him I *am* looking for a relationship. She beat me to the punch."

"Then just tell him the truth. Tell him Mama is crazy, and she doesn't know what she's talking about."

Selene laughed. "I can do that."

Abby walked over and handed me a paper plate with a slice of baklava on it. She had already taken a bite of hers and was chewing, her mouth full of the rich pastry. She swallowed and said, "Don't look behind you, but I think the security guard is tailing us."

"Where is he?"

"Straight across the path, by the elephant ear stand."

Without turning, I said, "Do you see him, Selene? Big guy in a navy suit."

My sister looked over my shoulder, her eyes searching until she spotted him. "What's going on?" she asked. "Who is he?"

I didn't want to trouble my sister about the threatening note, nor did I want to tell her that the man who was now following us could've been the one to leave it. And that he could possibly be a killer for hire. I could only imagine what would happen if that gossip spread around the diner.

Mama would never let me leave the house again. "He works for the mayor."

"And he's following you why?" she asked.

"Good question," I said.

Selene sighed. "What have you gotten yourself into now, Athena?"

Abby finished another bite. "It's nothing to worry about."

I was thankful Abby hadn't gone into detail, but Selene wouldn't let it drop. "Are you in trouble?" she asked.

Just then a man in his late thirties approached the tent. He was tall and incredibly fit, wearing a pair of worn overalls over a sage-green T-shirt. His eyes glimmered a bright blue beneath shaggy brown hair, and his smile was wide as he stood in front of my sister.

He held out his hand to her. "You must be Selene. I'm Tom Pappas."

To my surprise, Selene blushed and reached for his outstretched hand, seeming to melt at his touch. "It's a pleasure to meet you, Tom." And by the look in her eyes, she meant it. "Come have a piece of baklava."

He smiled into her eyes. "I'd love to."

I took a deep breath and let it out. My work here was done. In fact, it hadn't been necessary at all. But at least Abby and I had gotten to enjoy the baklava.

I turned back to Abby, who was scanning the crowd for the security guard. "Looks like he slid back into the shadows."

"Why do you think he was following us?"

"I don't know. Intimidation perhaps."

I shivered, remembering how I'd been knocked to the sidewalk. "Let's get out of here."

"How about one more slice?" Abby replied, pulling out her wallet. "My treat this time."

When we finally headed for the exit, the fairway was jammed with people, and the thumping music was deafening, setting my already-taut nerves on high alert. I couldn't help but keep my head on a swivel, wondering if we were still being tailed. Abby, too, was constantly looking over her shoulder.

At one point, I turned to look behind me and ran into a group of people, who then parted to let me through. I started forward again and came to a sudden halt when a young mother with a wide stroller stopped directly in front of me. Abby continued around the stroller and was instantly swallowed up by the crowd.

I stood on tiptoe, searching for Abby, and felt a hand brush against my shoulder. I pulled the straps of my purse closer to my body and darted around the stroller, continuing toward the front gates. I felt a hand again, this time firm on my shoulder. My heart started to pump faster, and I picked up the pace, almost tripping over a couple in front of me when I heard my name.

"Athena, stop!"

I swung around, startled to see my partner standing behind me. "Case, what on earth are you doing here?"

"I came to find you. I just saw Selene, and she pointed me in your direction. Are you done with the interviews?"

I had my hand over my heart, trying to calm myself. "Yes, we were just leaving."

"Are you okay?"

"Yes," I told him. "Just a little freaked out."

"Where's Abby?"

"I don't know. I lost her in the crowd." I grabbed Case's hand so we wouldn't get separated, and together we headed for the gate. And there was Abby standing calmly next to the exit sign scrolling through her phone. "I thought I'd lost you," I told her.

"Not that easily," she said with a laugh.

We headed back to her car, the sounds of the fairgrounds diminishing as we made our way across the vast parking lot. Still feeling eyes on my back, I turned to look over my shoulder. Several people were walking casually behind us, chatting and laughing, nothing suspicious. When I turned back around, I noticed Abby scanning our surroundings.

Case finally broke the silence. "Did I miss something? Are we being followed? What's going on?"

"I don't think so," I answered. "Not anymore."

"The mayor's security guard was keeping tabs on us," Abby said. "But he won't follow us out here, not while he's on detail."

"Sounds like there's more to this story," Case said. "Why don't we grab some food somewhere, and you can fill me in?"

"How about having dinner at my hotel?" Abby asked. "That's close, and it's always empty. It'll be nice and relaxing."

"That works for me," I said.

"Athena, if you want to go with Case and fill him

in on our possible stalker, I'll meet you both at the Waterfront."

We waited until Abby had safely pulled out of her parking spot before Case led me a few rows down to his Jeep. On the way to the hotel, I filled him in on our interviews with the mayor and his security guard.

"Are you sure the security guard was the same guy who knocked you down?" Case asked.

"Not one hundred percent sure, but he certainly fits the description. And he knew where our office was without being told."

Case didn't answer right away. He shifted in his seat, his eyes darting between the rearview and driver's side mirrors. "Okay," he said, "then one of our stronger theories is that the security guard worked as a hired killer for Charles Sloan."

"Right. The only problem is that we haven't figured out what the mayor's motive is. But we can discuss that with Abby over dinner. There's her car right in front of us."

Once again, Case seemed more focused on the rearview mirror.

"Is something wrong?" I asked.

"You know that feeling you get all the time, like you're being followed?"

"It's not *all* the time."

"Well, I think it's contagious. Don't turn around."

His last few words were unnerving. "Don't turn around? Why? Are we being followed?"

He nodded slowly, his eyes still darting between mirrors. "Since the highway exit. I think we'll know for sure once we get to the Waterfront."

I watched as Abby changed lanes in front of us.

As Case did the same, I sat in nerve-racking silence, trying to subdue the urge to turn around. I couldn't see anything but bright headlights in the passenger side mirror, but I did notice the car behind us had also changed lanes.

We followed Abby into the Waterfront hotel's parking lot. The car behind us did the same. "What should we do?" I asked.

"Nothing yet," Case said.

Abby pulled her car into an empty space near the rear of the lot. There were several other parking spaces closer, but the spot she chose was directly under a floodlight. Smart move. Case drove past her parking spot and circled around, the car behind us following even closer then.

"It's a guy, but I can't see his face," Case said.

I had my phone at the ready. "Should I call the police?" I asked.

"Hold off a minute." Case arrived back at Abby's car and pulled into an empty space near hers, the bright yellow convertible now clearly visible in my sideview mirror. Abby was still in her car gathering her belongings. I dialed her number to alert her and waited for her to pick up.

As her phone rang, the car that had been following us pulled into the spot directly behind ours and right beside Abby's, its headlights shining brightly through our back window. In the sideview mirror, I could still see Abby in her car.

My call went to voice mail. "Case, she's not picking up."

At that moment Abby exited her car, and as she did, the headlights behind us went dark. Before I could see who was driving, the car door opened, a man got out and immediately approached Abby, wrapping his arms around her as though to incapacitate her.

Before I knew what was happening, Case was outside the car rushing toward the man. I jumped out and ran to help, not even knowing what I could possibly do. As I approached, Case grabbed the man from behind.

I heard Abby shouting, and the next thing I knew, Case was down on the ground with his hands forced behind his back.

"Marco," Abby shouted, "stop! I know him."

Marco held out his hand to help Case up. "Sorry about that, man."

As Case brushed off his clothing, Abby said, "Case, meet my husband, Marco Salvare. Marco is an ex–Army Ranger. He has very quick reactions."

"Yes, I can see that," Case said. "It's a pleasure to meet you."

Marco shook his hand. "Same here." He was dressed in a black T-shirt with the logo *Down the Hatch* on it, a pair of slim-fitting blue jeans, and scuffed black boots. His hair was dark brown, as were his eyes, and with a five o'clock shadow on his jaw, he was an extremely handsome man. He and Abby made an attractive pair.

"This is my partner, Athena Spencer," Case said, and I shook Marco's hand.

"I've been hearing a lot of good things about you, Athena," Marco said with a charming smile.

"What a coincidence," I said. "I've heard a lot about you, too." And suddenly my sister's predic-

tion popped into my mind. Abby had indeed been
followed by an *M.S.* Marco Salvare. Could that be a
coincidence, too?

Case rubbed his shoulder. "You're going to have
to teach me that move."

"I'd be happy to," Marco said. "You never know
when you'll need it."

"Sorry I couldn't answer your call, Athena," Abby
said. "I was on the phone with my mom. She's watching our pets."

"Is there a problem?" Marco asked her.

"Nope. She just wanted me to know she fed
them and took Seedy out for her walk."

Marco rolled his eyes.

"Let's go have some dinner," Abby said. "I'm
starving."

As we walked across the parking lot, my phone
rang. I stopped to answer it and heard, "Athena?
This is Rosemary Dalsaurus. I'm sorry to be calling
so late, but I just got home."

"That's okay, Rosemary. How can I help you?"

"I wanted you to know that an envelope from
the CB Development Company came for Carly
today. I showed Mayor Sloan and asked if I should
find out where to forward it. He said he'd handle
it and took it into his office. His door was open so
I could see what he was doing. He opened Carly's
mail, Athena. And then he put it into a folder in
his filing cabinet." She paused, then said, "It doesn't
feel right to me. What do you make of it?"

"I'm not sure what to make of it, Rosemary. I'll
have to run it past my partner and see what he
thinks. At any rate, I appreciate your letting me

know. If you see anything else unusual, give me a call."

We reached the hotel's front entrance, and Case opened one of the double doors for me. "What was that about?"

"I'll fill you in over dinner."

In the Waterfront's dining room, the four of us were shown to a table near one of the big windows that looked out onto the lake and their swimming pool. Marco took in the white tablecloths, the silver-edged china, the beautiful chandeliers, and nodded in approval.

"Very nice," he said. "Very classy."

Abby opened her menu. "The food here is excellent, too."

"Let's start with a bottle of champagne," Case said, summoning the waiter.

Once Case had ordered the bottle and glasses for all, Marco said, "Bring me up to speed. The last I heard was that you were going to try to interview the mayor."

"We did that," Abby replied. "He didn't give up any useful information, so there's still the question of whether he had a sexual relationship with Carly. We've had three people tell us it was true, just with no positive proof. Only rumor."

"Motive?" Marco asked.

"We haven't locked in his motive," Abby said.

"However, we don't think the mayor would have poisoned Carly himself," I added. "He wasn't back-stage long enough. But his security guard was back-stage before the models got there, which would've given him access to Carly's dressing room."

"Is the security guard loyal enough to kill for the mayor?" Marco asked.

"We don't know," Abby said. "We do know that the guard owes the mayor for getting him released from prison."

"So only with the help of his security guard did the mayor have the means and opportunity," Marco said. "And you have only a possible motive. He sounds like your weakest suspect."

"There's also a question about what Carly was involved in," Case added, "and whether that could have caused her death. We know she received mail at the mayor's campaign headquarters from a construction company called Unified, the same company she and her ex-husband had contacted about building their land-based casino. It's also the company whose plans for a mega-mall were shut down by the mayor, which leaves the question about what she was planning and whether someone found out about it."

"That someone being the mayor," I said, "who is against big businesses building in town."

"Carly also received mail in care of a CB Development Company," Abby said, "which we know nothing about."

"Well, then," Marco said, rubbing the dark stubble on his chin. "That looks like your next lead. That's what I'd be focused on."

"And here's an update," I said. "Just before we walked into the hotel, I got a call from Mayor Sloan's campaign secretary, who said Carly received a letter just today in care of CB Development Company. The mayor took the letter, opened it, then filed it away."

"Why would he open Carly's mail?" Abby pondered. "And why would he keep it—unless he was involved somehow?"

"It sounds like you need to dig up information on CB Development," Marco said.

"Normally, I'd take care of that end of the investigation," Case told him. "But I've had my hands full with another job."

"Then why don't you let me look into it?" Marco asked. "I have to go back to New Chapel tomorrow, but I can work from there."

Abby reached over and threaded her fingers through Marco's. "That would be great, sweetheart. Thank you."

He smiled into her eyes. "No problem, sunshine."

I had to sigh at the obvious love they shared. I glanced at Case and saw him smiling at them, too. Then we glanced at each other, and Case reached for my hand. Not being one for public displays, I patted his hand playfully and picked up my menu.

Our waiter appeared with the bottle of champagne, ending the awkward moment. After he'd filled our glasses, he said, "May I take your orders now?"

After a nice, relaxing meal, I glanced at Abby. "I wish we could get a look at the letter Carly received today. I can't help but wonder why the mayor kept it."

"Where's the mayor's office?" Marco asked.

"In a small, three-story building on Greene Street," I answered.

"A small building." Marco rubbed his hands together. "Maybe it can be breached. I'm free this evening."

"In this case, sweetheart," Abby said to him, "I think we have another means of gaining entry. Athena, didn't Eleni say she has a key to her husband's office?"

"What are you suggesting?" I asked.

"What if we enlisted Eleni's help in finding that letter?" Abby replied with a twinkle in her eye.

"Enlist the help of a suspect?"

"Why not?" she replied.

"Do you really think Eleni would help us?"

"If she knew Charles had kept a letter sent to Carly, wouldn't you think she'd be very interested in what that letter was about?"

Marco patted Abby on the back. "It's worth a try."

"Okay," I said. "I'll phone Eleni right now and set something up." I stepped away from the table to make the call.

When she answered, I said, "Eleni, this is Athena Spencer. I have a favor to ask of you."

"Well, hello, Athena. How can I help?"

"A piece of mail arrived at your husband's campaign headquarters yesterday, a piece of mail for Carly Blackburn that may be instrumental in helping us with her case. Unfortunately"—I paused, unsure of how to explain it—"your husband kept the letter."

"I'm sure he's planning to forward it to Carly's estate," Eleni said.

"The thing is," I said, "he opened it and then filed it away."

Silence. Then very skeptically, Eleni responded, "How did you learn about this?"

"I'm not at liberty to say," I replied, "but it's important for us to know what the letter is about."

"Us?"

"Abby Salvare and me."

"I was under the impression that reading someone else's mail is illegal," Eleni replied coldly.

"Your husband has already opened it and read it," I replied. "We wouldn't be asking if this wasn't important."

Eleni didn't sound happy. "What exactly do you want me to do?"

"Help us get into his office," I said.

More silence.

"You have a key, right?"

"Yes," she said. "I'm just not sure it's the right thing."

"Aren't you a little curious as to why your husband kept Carly's letter?" I asked.

Eleni was silent again for a long moment, then she sighed, as though she'd resolved her own doubts. "I am curious."

"Do you know what time his headquarters closes?" I asked.

"Five o'clock," Eleni replied.

"Are you available to go tomorrow after five?"

"No, I'm not," she replied. "If you want my help, we'll have to go this evening. It's the only time I'm free."

I glanced at my watch. It was already eight o'clock. "How about eight thirty?"

Sounding very reluctant, she agreed. "Charles gets home at ten. I'll have to be back by then." She paused, then added, "We'll have to meet in the alley behind the building. I don't want anyone to see me."

"Great," I said. "We'll see you there."

I stepped back to the table and told everyone about the plan. "We're going to have to leave now to make it there by eight thirty. She wants to meet in the back alley, so she's not seen by anyone."

Abby turned to Marco with a sad smile. "Sorry, sweetheart. Looks like I'm going to be working tonight."

"It goes with the territory," he said. "Just one thing, though. Athena, how well do you know this Eleni?"

"I've known her casually for several years," I answered, "but my mom has known her for a long time. Why?"

Marco took Abby's hand in his. "I just don't want you two walking into a trap."

"How about if we accompany them?" Case said to Marco.

"Eleni isn't expecting more people," I said. "She might get spooked."

"Then Case and I will wait in the car," Marco said. With a wink, he added, "You won't even know we're there."

Abby squeezed his hand, then turned to me and said eagerly, "Okay. Let's go find out what Carly was up to."

# CHAPTER NINETEEN

Despite Abby's eagerness, as we headed back to town I was feeling on edge, nervous about what would happen if the mayor decided to stop by his campaign headquarters. How would we explain ourselves?

At eight thirty, Case, Marco, Abby, and I stepped into the alley that ran behind the shops on Greene and saw Eleni far down the block, standing at the back of the brick building that housed the mayor's campaign headquarters. Case and Marco immediately stepped back out of sight.

"We'll wait in the car around front," Marco said.

"Call if you're in trouble," Case added.

Abby glanced at me. "Ready?"

We headed up the alley and saw Eleni check the time on her watch.

"Thanks for helping us," I said to her.

Eleni inserted her key into the lock, then looked

back at us. "My husband can't find out about this. He gave me this key for emergencies."

"Agreed," I said.

Eleni opened the heavy steel door and held it for us to enter. She closed it behind us, then, using the flashlight on her phone, led the way up a hallway and into the main room.

Guided by our phone flashlights, we made our way through the long rows of tables to a door marked *Private*, which Eleni opened. She looked around, then motioned for us to follow.

I shone my light around the room and saw a gray metal desk, a door that led to another office, and three large gray metal filing cabinets. I looked at the filing cabinets in dismay. "Where do we begin?"

"We'll each take a cabinet," Abby said, setting down her shoulder bag. "We can start by looking for a letter or a file with Carly's name on it."

"And don't touch anything else," Eleni instructed.

I put my purse on the desk and walked to the first cabinet. I pulled out the top drawer and, holding my phone in one hand, began perusing the files, flipping through folder after folder, realizing the search was going to be more time-consuming than I had imagined. I rifled through the entire top drawer but saw nothing with Carly's name on it.

Eleni, who was standing beside the third cabinet, shut the top drawer with a bang. "Nothing here."

We continued looking. After going through the second drawer, I checked the time on my phone and said, "It's after nine o'clock."

"We'd better hurry," Eleni said.

I started on the bottom drawer, sifting through the files until I reached the back of the drawer. "Nothing here."

Eleni shut the bottom drawer. "Here, either."

"I found something," Abby exclaimed and pulled out a file from the bottom drawer. "It's marked *CB Company*." She took the file over to the desk and opened it. Inside we found half a dozen letters addressed to Carly at CB Development Company, LLC. The letter on top was from Unified Construction Company.

Abby took out the letter to read it aloud. "Carly," she read, "this is to confirm that you still plan to proceed as outlined in our last correspondence. We have drawn up the necessary legal documents and can forward same to your attention as soon as we get the initial payment. Please let us know at your earliest convenience."

"What in the world does that mean?" Eleni asked.

"Carly must be a part of the CB Development Company," I said.

"Carly Blackburn Development Company," Abby put together. "Marco should be able to dig up more information about the company with this information." She put the letter on the desk and took a photo of it with her phone.

The next letter in the file was also from Unified Construction. It included a detailed list of specific building requirements. Beneath it, folded in thirds, was a blueprint. Written at the top was: *Proposed Casino*.

"Then Carly was planning to build the casino

after all," I said, as Abby took photos of both the letter and the blueprint.

"That can't be right," Eleni said. "My husband stopped the project."

"Maybe Carly was planning on going behind your husband's back," I said.

"No," Eleni insisted. "He would've stopped her, too."

"Did he have the legal power to stop her?" Abby asked.

"He could've gone to the city council and requested they deny Carly a building permit," Eleni said.

"What I'd like to know is why the mayor has this file," I said.

Eleni crossed her arms over her chest. "I'm wondering that, too."

Suddenly, we heard voices coming from a distance and then the sound of a door closing. We quickly shut off our flashlights. I glanced around for a place to hide, but there was only the desk. I motioned to Abby, and we both ducked behind it while Eleni slid behind the open door.

I heard the mayor's voice, indistinct at first and then clearer. "—and then the crowd went wild, Lila."

I nearly gasped aloud. *Lila?*

"I know," came a familiar voice. "I was there."

"The speech you helped me with for the opening night was excellent," Charles Sloan said. "We need to do that again."

"I think I can make that happen," Lila replied.

"If anyone can," Charles Sloan said in a low, almost sexy pitch, "it's you."

"We need to get out of here," Abby whispered. "Let's go through the other door."

"Quiet!" Eleni whispered back.

I crawled over to the door and quietly turned the handle, but the door was locked. I motioned to Abby and pointed to Eleni. "That's our only way out."

"We can be sure there's going to be a big crowd for closing night," Lila said, "so it's got to be a powerful speech."

"We'll have to work closely on this one," Charles said. "That might mean some long hours alone." He paused, then said in that same low pitch, "Does that bother you?"

As the situation became clearer, Eleni looked across the room at me. She was wedged behind the open door, but I could see her entire body tense in anger.

"I'll clear my schedule," Lila said in a no-nonsense fashion, "so we'll put in however many hours it takes. This may be our last opportunity to get in front of a big crowd."

"Then we'll have to make the most of it." There was another pause, then Charles said, "Speaking of making the most of it, we might not have another chance to be alone like this."

"You know what?" Lila said. "It's late. I think we should call it a night."

"The night doesn't have to end now, you know."

There was the sound of indistinct movement and then a slap.

"If you ever try that again," Lila said in a terse voice, "I will walk out and never come back. Do you understand me? What would your wife say?"

"It's okay," he said. "We have an arrangement—"

"I don't want to hear about it," Lila said firmly.

Another pause. And then Charles said, "I apologize. I overstepped my bounds."

"I'm going to call it a night," Lila said. "We can work on your speech tomorrow afternoon."

"Lila, please forgive me," Charles said in a pleading voice.

A few moments later, the light went out and then a door shut.

None of us moved. We waited, listening, but heard nothing. Finally, Abby rose. "Let's go," she said. "We have what we came for."

Still standing behind the open door, Eleni broke into sobs. She covered her face with her hands. Her shoulders shook.

I walked over to her and put my arm around her. "I'm so sorry."

I guided Eleni to Charles's desk, where she sat down in his chair. She laid her head on her arms on the desk, still crying. "How could he do this to me *again*?"

I glanced at Abby, who raised her eyebrows at me.

"Again?" I asked.

Eleni lifted her head to look at us, her mascara running down her cheeks. "Charles promised it would never happen again. He was so afraid I'd divorce him and ruin his good name."

"Then he *did* have an affair with Carly?" I asked.

Eleni shook her head. "I couldn't prove it. I only heard the rumors."

"Then why do you say he's doing it to you again?"

"Three years ago," she sobbed, "with one of his secretaries." She gestured toward the door. "And now he's at it again."

"You don't have to worry about Lila Talbot," I said. "She won't let anything happen."

Eleni looked at me with sorrowful eyes. "What if I was wrong about Carly? What if they did have an affair like everyone kept saying?"

"I'm sorry, Eleni." I rubbed her shoulders, not knowing what else to say.

"Why are you still with him?" Abby asked.

Eleni gently swiped under her eyes with her finger. "That's a good question."

Abby closed the file and returned it to the filing cabinet. "It's late. I think we should leave."

We made our way out of the building, and Eleni closed the back door quietly. We walked up the alley to the cross street and said our good-byes.

"Please don't say anything to Lila about what happened here tonight," Eleni said.

"Don't worry," I replied. "She won't know you were here."

"Thank you for helping us," Abby said. "I'm sorry for the way it turned out."

Eleni sighed. "You know the old saying, forewarned is forearmed. I'm not sure I'll ever fully trust Charles again."

We parted ways in the alley, heading in separate directions. "Well, that was enlightening," I said. "Now we know that the rumors are true about Charles's past affairs."

We walked up the side street to where Marco's Prius was parked, but no one was there. Abby pulled out her phone. "I'll text Marco."

She typed in her message, and we waited a few minutes, then I slid my phone out of my purse and texted Case: *Where are you? We're at the car.*

Five minutes later, both of our phones dinged with incoming messages. Mine said, *Be right there.*

A few minutes later, both men turned the corner and came striding toward us.

"Where were you?" Abby asked her husband.

"In the yard beside the library," Marco replied, unlocking the car doors with his key fob. "I was showing Case the takedown move."

"How did it go?" I asked.

"A little too well," Case replied. "I think my shoulder popped out of my socket."

As he started the motor, Marco said, "Tell us what happened. Did you learn anything?"

Abby gave him the rundown as we headed back to the Waterfront. But the information we'd learned had only filled me with new questions. "If the mayor is so against building the casino, why keep the blueprint? Carly's gone. What's the point?"

"It seems pretty clear to me," Case said, "that the mayor was involved in the project."

"Would the mayor really be that stupid?" I asked. "Would he hire a woman who had fundamentally different ideas about the future of this town?"

As Marco pulled up in front of the hotel, Abby said, "What's important is that now we have something concrete to tell Detective Walters that should convince him to take a hard look at Charles Sloan. I'm going to go see him in the morning. And then I need to head to the jail to talk to Jillian. So have a good night, you two. I'll stop by the office tomorrow afternoon to discuss our next move."

Marco turned to us, sitting behind him. "I'll be heading back home in the morning. It was good working with you, Case, Athena. I'm sure we'll see each other again."

We got out of the Prius and watched them drive away. "They're good people," Case said.

"I just wish we were doing a better job helping them," I replied. "I don't want to let Abby down."

"We're getting close to finding the murderer," Case told me.

"Case, we haven't even crossed anyone off our suspect list yet. For all we know, Fran could be the killer."

"She doesn't have a motive."

"But you get the point, right? Abby thinks the mayor is involved, you think Donald killed Carly, and, to tell you the truth, I can't get rid of this feeling that Eleni is hiding something."

"I've changed my mind about Donald. I think the mayor is behind Carly's death."

"See?" I told him. "We can't even agree on a top suspect."

"Athena, don't get so worked up. We'll solve the case, I promise."

"Okay," I said with a resigned sigh. "Should we meet at the office tomorrow afternoon?"

"I'm going to Saugatuck tomorrow, remember? I have to finish the job."

"I wish we could focus on one case at a time."

"You'll be fine without me for one more day."

"Abby's coming to the office tomorrow to discuss our next steps, and I have no idea what to do."

"You don't have to have all the answers. Abby asked for your help, and that's exactly what you're doing. Helping. Imagine where she'd be right now without you."

"I guess you're right."

He put his arm around my shoulders. "I know I'm right. You just need to reenergize for tomorrow. I'll be in Saugatuck most of the day, but I'll have my phone on me if you need anything."

I stretched up to give him a kiss. "Thanks for the pep talk."

"Anytime, Goddess."

The next morning seemed to fly by. I'd rushed to write my blog, and I was afraid it would read that way, but my mom and sisters seemed to enjoy it all the same. Back at Spencer's, my dad had the day off, so it was just me, Delphi, Drew, and Nicholas at the store all morning.

Midday I was sitting in my office, filling out an order for fall plantings, when I heard the sharp squeaks of Nicholas's sneakers against the tile floor as he ran up the hallway. He showed up at the office door, red in the face, out of breath, with Oscar's yellow rattle in his hand.

"What's wrong?" I asked, standing.

He pressed his hand into his side, panting. "There's a man."

"What man?"

"A man. In the alley. A big man. Watching me. I ran as fast as I could."

I rounded the desk, dashed past my son and out the door. I made my way down the center aisle of the big barn and wound through the rows of patio furniture, pushing my way out through the back door, squinting in the bright sunlight. Nicholas came out after me, but I stopped him. "Stay inside. Go tell Aunt Delphi to call the police."

"I'm scared, Mom. Don't go back there."

"Do what I told you, Niko. "

I ran to the metal cabinet, picked up a sturdy garden rake leaning against it, and took off down the pathway toward the locked gate at the back of the property. I unlocked the gate and stepped into the alley. With the garden rake in hand, I walked up the alley, calling out, "Ben! I know it's you! Show yourself."

Nothing.

"Did the mayor send you?" I called.

Still nothing. No movement, no sound.

"The police are on their way. You'd better come out."

I proceeded all the way to the end of the alley, turned around, and headed back. Whoever had been there was gone.

As I walked in through the back gate, I noticed the sprinkler head was still stuck open and the jets were soaking the pathway.

Delphi came running toward me, her phone in her hand. "Bobby's on his way. What's wrong?"

"Niko saw a man standing back here watching him. I tried to find him with no luck."

"A man was back here?"

I didn't have the patience to explain it, so I pointed to the water spraying from the broken sprinkler head instead. "You said you would take care of that last week."

"I know. I'm sorry. I'll fix it. Don't worry."

I pressed my lips together before I said something in anger. I should've known better than to trust my bubble-brained sister to fix anything. "Tell Bob to meet me back here," I finally said. "I'll be trying to fix the sprinkler while I wait."

"No, Athena. I promised you and Dad I would take care of it, and I will. Right now."

I left Delphi wading through the mud and went back up the flagstone path to wait for Bob. As I passed by the hydrangeas, my sweet little boy sprang out of the bushes with Oscar's yellow rattle in his hand, looking like he was ready for battle.

"Did you see the man?" Nicholas asked.

"I didn't see anyone. Can you tell me what he looked like?"

Nicholas described a tall, bulky man with short, dark hair wearing a gray shirt and sunglasses. It sounded close enough to the description of Ben Logan to make me believe he'd been scoping the place.

"I want you to stay inside today," I told him.

"What about Oscar?"

"Where is Oscar?" I asked.

"He got spooked by something and took off. I went to look for him, and that's when I saw the man. "

"Then Oscar is safe. I'm sure he's just hiding somewhere." I put my arm around my son. "Why don't you go see Drew at the register? I'm sure he'll have something for you to do. "

We entered through the back door and walked down the center aisle of the big barn. Nicholas stopped short at the sight of a man in a gray shirt. He was waiting by my office door with his back turned. I knew at once it wasn't Ben Logan. "May I help you?"

Nicholas shifted his body behind mine, just as the man turned around. On his shirt were the words *Sequoia Electric.*

"I'm Dave," the man said. "I'm here to work on the electrical panel. The gentleman I spoke with said you were having a problem with the electricity going off. The young man at the desk told me to wait back here."

Nicholas tugged on my arm and said quietly, "That's the man I saw in the alley, Mom."

Dave knelt down to talk to him. "Sorry if I scared you, little guy. I had to park down the alley a little way."

"It's okay, Niko," I told him. "Go talk to Drew."

Nicholas kept his eye on the man as he shuffled around the corner.

"Come with me," I told Dave. "I'll show you where the electrical panel is."

After I had shown Dave where to start working, I returned to my office and had just sat down at the desk when Bob Maguire stopped by. "What's going on?" he asked.

"I thought I was being followed, but it turned out just to be a repairman. Sorry to bother you. Ever since my run-in with a stranger at the detective agency, I've been on edge."

"Understandable," he said. "Are you closing the store tonight?"

"Yes, my dad's off today."

"Delphi and I have our final dance lesson this evening, so I'll be tied up, but I'll make sure a squad car is on patrol. If you have any doubts about your safety, there'll be a car in the area. "

"That's good to know, Bob. Thank you." I got up and came around the desk. "Where are you parked? I'll walk you out."

"I'm around back, in the alley."

We headed through the store and out the back door, down the path that ran between the rows of shrubs, heading toward the gate. As we drew near the gate, I saw Delphi standing in the grass, staring at the water spraying from the sprinkler head.

A call came in on Bob's radio. He spoke into his shoulder receiver, then said to me, "I have to go." He winked at Delphi. "See you later, Delph."

"Bye, Bobby," she called. Then she put her hands on her hips and turned her attention back to the sprinkler head.

"Delphi, all you have to do is turn the water off to this section and call the sprinkler company. I showed you where I keep the list of repair people. Remember?"

"I'll get on it," she said.

"I'm leaving for a while," I told her. "Pops is out, so you're in charge while I'm gone."

"You don't have to worry about me," she replied.

How I wished that were true.

Still feeling spooked, I decided to drive the several blocks to the detective agency. I found a parking spot near the plaza and made my way through the food trucks and picnic tables scattered throughout the area. I had that same feeling of being followed, putting my nerves on high alert.

As I passed the deli, I waved to Gracie through the window, then had a sudden flashback to the door being flung open, sending me sprawling back onto the sidewalk. I approached the door carefully and made my way up the stairs to the office. I used my key to get in and made sure to lock the door behind me. I found Case's office door open.

He glanced over the top of his monitor. "Hey, Goddess."

"I'm surprised to see you here," I said. "I thought you'd be in Saugatuck."

"I'm just about ready to wrap up here and take off," he said. "One more trip should do it. How's your day going?"

"Not that great," I replied, taking a seat across from him. "I feel like I'm being followed again."

"Why? Is Marco back?"

"Very funny. No, I'm serious. Nicholas saw someone in the alley, and I assumed it was Ben Logan, but it was just a repairman my dad had called a few days ago."

"I'm glad it was a false alarm."

"I'd just feel a whole lot better if you were around."

Case rose from his chair and motioned for me to come closer. He wrapped his arms around me. "I'm sorry. I have to finish the job today."

"I know. I just wish we could both focus on *this* job."

He held me at arm's length. "This is a business. We can't turn down work."

"It's a new business, a growing business with amateur detectives. I think we should focus on one case at a time until we are both comfortable taking on more jobs."

"Do you want me to stay?" Case asked. "Would that make you feel better?"

"No. Finish your job. Abby and I can handle things today."

Case pulled me in for another hug. "There's my confident Athena."

Abby stuck her head in the doorway. "Hello. I don't mean to interrupt, but I have good news."

I unwrapped from my partner's embrace, curious to what she had to say, but a loud bang at the outer office door nearly startled me out of my skin.

# CHAPTER TWENTY

Case put his finger to his lips. "Stay here."
He walked quietly out of the office, then I heard him chuckle as he turned the lock.

"Are we bolting the door during the day now?" I heard Lila ask angrily.

Abby and I walked out to find her with her hands on her hips. "How are clients supposed to get in?"

"Sorry," I said. "I had a run-in with a stranger and thought I was being followed."

"We're taking precautions," Case said.

"I suppose that's okay, then." Lila put her shoulder bag on the reception desk and sat down behind it. She was wearing a slim-fitting white skirt with a bright blue blouse and matching heels. Her long blond hair lay loose around her shoulders. "How's the investigation going?"

"Slowly," I replied. "What are you up to?"

"I'm on my way to the mayor's campaign headquarters," she said. "I just thought I'd stop in and see how things are going."

Case, Abby, and I stood in the reception area waiting for her to continue. Over the past several months, I'd come to know Lila Talbot very well. I didn't expect her to come right out and say she was wrong about Charles, but at the very least, I expected her to come clean about it.

"So, no problems with the mayor?" I asked.

She tapped her French-tipped nails on her purse strap. "No. No problems at all. We're going to work on his speech for Sunday night."

"And he hasn't tried any funny stuff?" I asked.

"No. He's been a perfect gentleman. I told you I'd have no problems with him."

"Really? Because I was at the mayor's office last night," I admitted. "I saw what happened."

Her fingertips halted, and she looked up at me with wide eyes. "You were there?"

"Yes, Abby and I were both there."

She looked away quickly and resumed her nervous tapping. "Then you know that I handled it. He won't try it again."

"Why would you keep information from us?" I asked. "This is the very reason you went to work for him."

She lowered her head slowly. "It's embarrassing."

Feeling sorry for her, I put my hand on her shoulder. "It's not your fault."

"I thought he really needed me," she said. "I thought I was finally needed somewhere."

"You are," Case replied. "You're needed here. You might've been wrong about Charles, but your mission was successful. Now we know for certain that he's capable of cheating on his wife."

"More than capable," Lila told us. "I have no doubt the rumors about him are true."

"You don't have to stay on as campaign manager," I told her. "Your job is done."

"I can't just leave. I made a commitment."

"Would you be willing to continue your undercover work?" Abby asked.

Lila looked up at her, her eyes brightening. "Sure."

"While we were investigating," Abby explained, "we found several letters Carly had received about building a proposed casino. Do you think you might be able to work some talk about the casino into your next conversation with the mayor?"

Lila nodded confidently. "No problem."

"What is Charles doing tonight?" Case asked.

She thought a moment. "He'll be at the office until three. We have to work on his speech for tomorrow. Then we have dinner with the county commissioner, so that should go till about seven thirty. Then he's doing another meet-and-greet at the fairgrounds. That usually lasts till around nine."

"Try to get that info tonight," Case told her. "We're running out of time."

Lila rubbed her hands together with a smile. "I'll do my best."

"And, Abby," Case continued, "you were about to tell us some good news."

"Yes, Marco is going to start researching CB Development Company later today. He's working at Down the Hatch all day, but he'll have a chance to do his internet sleuthing this evening."

Lila looked confused. "Who is Marco?"

"My husband," Abby answered. "He's a private investigator."

"And what is Down the Hatch?" Lila asked.

"It's a bar he owns."

Lila shook her head as though she understood, but the look of confusion lingered.

"Okay, I'm running late," Case said. He reached inside his pocket for his key ring. "I'll try to finish up in Saugatuck quickly and be back before dark. Don't forget to lock the door when I leave."

Case gave me a hug and walked out the door, but before closing it, he turned around. "And by the way, Lila," he said, "good work."

I locked the door when he left and turned to find Lila dabbing her eyes. "Case just give me a compliment."

Back at Spencer's, Delphi told me the electrical repairman would have to come back on Monday to finish repairing the wiring. In the meantime, Delphi explained, we needed to keep the generator gassed up. I knew my dad wasn't going to be happy about that. Running Spencer's on the generator meant that just the big barn, cash register, and office, with its computer, stayed on. No lights in the conference room, kitchenette, storage room, or the hanging lanterns around the patio. Luckily, there were hardly any customers all day.

At six o'clock, my dad took Nicholas home for dinner, and shortly afterward Abby called to say Marco had uncovered some startling information about the CB Development Company. Since I had to stay at the garden center that evening, I suggested we meet there. Abby said she hadn't eaten, so we decided to order food from the Blue Moon Café, and she'd pick it up.

At seven o'clock, she arrived carrying a large white paper sack filled with two containers of food. I apologized for having to eat in the office, explaining about the generator.

I cleared off my desk to make room for Abby to sit across from me. She pulled up one of the chairs that faced the desk and removed the food. We ate in companionable silence for a few minutes, then Abby began to fill me in on Marco's information.

"We were right," Abby said. "Carly was the brains behind CB Development. She's listed as the company CEO and treasurer. And you'll never guess who her business partner is."

"Donald," I guessed.

"Nope. Charles Sloan."

"The mayor!" I said in surprise. "Her *business* partner?"

Abby nodded. "A silent partner."

"I can't believe it."

"But the file he has makes sense now, doesn't it?" Abby asked. "Carly handled the correspondence, and Charles kept everything in his office, which is why he made no attempt to forward Carly's mail to her estate."

"But that means he was aware of the plan to build the casino, going against everything his campaign stands for."

"Ah, but here's how he was going to get around it," Abby explained. "The land they were intending to use is actually outside the city limits, so technically, Charles could still say he was going to keep Sequoia small."

I shook my head. "He can't campaign against big business and then build a casino. It doesn't matter where he builds it."

Abby held up her index finger. "Here's where it gets interesting. Charles pulled his investment two weeks before Carly was killed. Without the money, Carly couldn't move forward with the deal." Abby pulled up the photo app on her phone. "Look at this. The latest correspondence Carly received was from Unified Construction. They were ready to start the project. All they needed was the initial payment."

"That fits the timeline," I told her. "Rosemary heard them arguing about two weeks before the fashion show. Carly must've found out that Charles pulled his investment and threatened to expose the affair if he didn't follow through."

"That would give him a strong motive to kill her," Abby said. "If Carly exposed him as a fraud, he'd be ruined. It's possible Charles hired the bodyguard to dispose of his problem. Ben could've been on the lookout for an easy opportunity to get rid of Carly, and what better way to do it than while the mayor has a whole audience as an alibi?"

"So, what do we do?"

Abby thought for a moment. "All I can think of is to confront Charles directly."

"Wouldn't that be dangerous?"

"Not if we catch him at the fair, where there are people around. I'll set my phone to record and see if we can get him to confess."

"That won't be easy."

Abby shrugged. "It's the best we can do. I can't see Detective Walters going after the mayor unless we have some kind of confession."

"You're right about that."

"Great," Abby said. "We can try to talk to Charles tonight. I think his meet-and-greet is over at nine."

I looked at the clock. It was almost time to close the store. "Okay, give me twenty minutes and I'm ready to go."

"I'll go freshen up," Abby said. "Are the lights working in the bathroom?"

"No, sorry. You'll have to use the flashlight on your phone."

At eight o'clock, Drew closed the register and headed home. I locked the front doors and returned to the office to complete my final report on the computer. I was just about finished when my phone rang. Case's name popped up on the screen.

"Hey, Goddess. What's going on?"

"Listen to this," I told him. "Marco dug up some information on CB Development company. Guess who Carly's silent business partner was."

Without pause, Case answered, "Charles Sloan."

The pause came from my end. I did not expect him to guess correctly.

"Am I right?" he asked.

"How did you know?"

"Easy," Case explained. "Because you said *silent* business partner. Charles wouldn't have wanted anyone to know that he was building a casino, which makes me wonder if the silent business partner didn't silence his business partner."

"Good detective work, hotshot," I teased.

"Funny. But that still leaves me with one big question. Why would Charles get involved in this scheme to begin with?"

"I don't know, but maybe Abby and I will ask him that tonight."

"Ask who what?" Abby said as she entered the room.

"I'm on the phone with Case. He wants to know why Charles got involved with Carly in the first place."

"That's a very good question," Abby responded cheerfully. "Maybe we'll lead with that one."

"Now, hold on a minute," Case said. "I don't want you getting yourself into a dangerous position while I'm out of town."

"We won't be in any danger," I told him. "We're going to confront him at the fairgrounds."

"I don't like it," he said. "Not with Ben around. I think you should wait until I get there."

"Where are you now?"

"I'm about twenty-five minutes outside of town. Just do me a favor and wait until I get to the garden center."

"You'd better hurry," I said.

"You'd better wait," he responded.

No sooner had I ended the call than I heard a sharp knock on the front door. Abby and I locked eyes immediately.

"Are you expecting someone?" Abby asked.

I racked my brain. No one in my family was expected to return that evening. I checked my phone but hadn't received any calls. "Officer Maguire mentioned the police would be on patrol in the neighborhood," I told her. "Maybe it's them."

"And if it's not?"

I paused to consider her question, but my curiosity won out. "I'm going to take a look outside. You can stay in the office."

"No way." Abby stood up. "I'm coming with you."

"Then stay behind me and keep your phone at the ready. If anything happens, lock yourself in the office and call the police."

The ceiling lights from the office crept through the slats in the blinds, giving me just enough light to see my way down the hallway. Abby followed closely behind. As luck would have it, the power being off worked in our favor, keeping us safely encased in shadows as we passed the register.

Just then I heard another knock on the front door. "Athena," I heard. "Are you in there? It's Eleni Sloan."

"What in the world is she doing here?" Abby whispered.

"That's what I'd like to know."

I approached the door slowly, peering out through the window as I drew nearer. At another loud bang, I shot back into Abby, who lost her balance and fell backward into the base of the statue of Athena, causing her mother's mushroom garden stakes to fall over. She tried to grab them, but they scattered loudly across the floor.

"Athena," Eleni called again. "I know you're in there. Open up. I've got something exciting to tell you."

I glanced at Abby, who apologized and said, "If you want to let her in, I still have my phone at the ready."

I stood with my hand near the door lock, contemplating my decision.

"It's about Charles," Eleni added.

I unlocked the front door and let her in.

Eleni entered the garden center carrying a large tote bag and wearing a wide smile. In a buoyant voice, she said, "Hello, girls. Have I got news for you!" Without even waiting for our answer, she pulled a bottle of champagne out of her tote. "I hope you have glasses."

Her black hair was pulled back in a loose bun, and the deep hues of her makeup shadowed her eyes. The bottle she held glinted in the bright glow of the overheard emergency lighting as she swung it happily back and forth. "Well," she said, "are you ready for my news?"

I led the ladies back through the dimly lit garden center and into my office, where I offered Eleni a seat in front of my desk. Abby declined to sit, preferring to stand in the doorway, her phone still at the ready.

"How did you know I was here?" I asked Eleni.

"I spoke with your mother."

Her eyes were red and swollen, as if she'd been crying, but her smile was in complete contrast. I remembered what Abby had said about her inner radar, and mine was buzzing like an alarm clock.

"Why didn't you call?" I asked her.

"I don't have your number."

"But my mother has my number."

"Athena," Eleni said in exasperation, "I wanted to surprise you. Both of you. Do you want to hear my news or not?"

"Why us?" Abby asked.

Eleni turned in her seat to look at her. "You've opened my eyes. You kept asking why I stayed with Charles, and honestly, I didn't have an answer. Come, have a seat, Abby. This is a time to celebrate. Now, where are those glasses?"

My suspicions were aroused, but so was my curiosity. I walked over to the cabinet the coffeemaker sat on and looked inside. "All I have are paper cups."

"That'll do," she said as she peeled back the foil around the cork.

I glanced around at Abby as I set the cups on the desk. She gave me a look that told me she was suspicious, as well.

Eleni popped the cork on the champagne.

"Maybe we should go to the diner," I offered. "It's just a few blocks away. We can get some nice glasses and toast properly."

"Not necessary," Eleni said. She began to fill the paper cups. "You know, I didn't want to believe it. In fact, I forced myself to think Charles would never cheat on me again. Clearly, I was wrong. And I must thank you for that, too. If we hadn't gone to his office, I'd have never known about Lila."

As Eleni finished pouring the champagne, she spied the dusty copy of *The Crucible* lying on the desktop. "I see you kept the book I gave you." She picked it up and flipped through it. "Are you reading it?"

"Not yet," I replied. "I haven't had a chance."

Eleni put the book down and covered a sneeze.

And then I thought of the bookstore, of the dust floating through the air, of my own allergies kicking up, causing my eyes to itch and water. I glanced at Eleni and again noticed her red, swollen eyes, just like Fran had reported seeing the night of the murder.

And suddenly everything became clear.

Lifting her paper cup, Eleni said, "Girls, please, have some champagne while I make a toast."

# CHAPTER TWENTY-ONE

I gave Eleni a hard stare. "We're not drinking the champagne."

Her eyebrows drew together. "What's wrong?"

"I think you should take a drink first," I replied.

Eleni looked at me in complete bafflement. "Why?"

"Because you poisoned it."

Her mouth dropped open. "Poisoned it! You're being ridiculous."

"Your allergies gave you away, Eleni," I said. "You poisoned Carly's water with your eye drops, and now you're about to do the same to us."

Eleni set her cup down hard on the desk and looked at me in shock. "Are you accusing me of killing Carly?"

"I am."

"Do you remember what I told you about accusations?"

"I do. You said accusations can be damning and gave me the book as an example. But I couldn't read the book because I'm allergic to the dust. Just like you are." I smiled, proud that I'd finally solved the case. "You sealed your own fate when you gave me that book."

Eleni shook her head sadly, as though I had lost my mind. "You've known me for how many years now, Athena? Your mother and I practically started the GMA together. You really think I would poison someone, and in the middle of a fashion show, no less?"

"On the night Carly was murdered," I said, "you came straight from the bookstore. Your eyes were red. It looked like you'd been crying, but it was allergies."

"Dust makes me sneeze, Athena. That's not a crime."

"You showed up early the first night. You saw Jillian setting out the water. You knew it would take about thirty minutes for the poison to work, so you had to show up early the second night, too."

"Athena," Eleni replied, "let me explain."

"You were the first person to help Carly as she lay dying," I continued, thinking aloud as I pieced together the rest of the puzzle. "The first person to call for help. It was the perfect alibi. Who would suspect the mayor's wife?"

Eleni stood abruptly. "I've had enough of this. I came here to celebrate with you. I didn't poison Carly, and I'm not trying to poison you. If you would just stop for two seconds and let me explain."

"There's no need to explain," I told her.

"Then let me prove it to you." She picked up her paper cup and completely drained it. Banging it down on my desk, she said, "Satisfied? Or do you think I'm poisoning myself, too?"

She reached across for Abby's drink and finished it in several long gulps. "How about now?"

"Eleni," I asked fervently, "what are you doing?"

She pushed the cup aside and picked up the champagne bottle. "I've been saving this for a special occasion, and I couldn't think of a better way to thank you both than to share it with a toast." She reached for my cup and held it up, saying sardonically, "Here's to the end of a long chapter, and to those who helped me turn the page."

Abby and I stood in shocked silence as Eleni finished my champagne. I'd been so certain that Eleni was the killer, that she'd come to poison us. How had I gotten it so wrong?

Eleni sat down, letting the straps of her tote bag slip from her shoulder. She covered a hiccup and made a show of checking her watch. "We can sit here all night if you'd like me to finish off the bottle," she said dryly, "or you can let me explain about Charles."

She waited for us to respond, but we both stood there dumbfounded.

"Okay, then maybe this will open your eyes," she said. "I have information about my husband that may help you solve the murder."

She'd barely gotten the words out when the room went completely dark.

"What's happening?" Eleni asked in a startled voice.

At first, the sudden darkness startled me, too, but then I realized I'd made another embarrassing mistake. "It's the generator," I admitted. "It must've run out of gas."

I grabbed my phone and turned on the flashlight, as Abby did the same. "I have to refill the generator," I explained to Abby. "Will you be okay in here?"

"She'll be just fine," Eleni insisted. "The champagne is getting warm anyway."

Abby nodded. "I'll be fine."

I hurried through the big, dark barn, knowing the way to the back door instinctively.

I pushed open the door and made my way down the flagstone path, between rows of ornamental shrubs and saplings. I cursed myself as I carefully made my way in the dark. I had been so sure that Eleni was the killer—the book, the allergies, the eye drops—it all added up. I asked myself again, how could I have gotten it so wrong?

As I neared the alley, streetlamps from the side street cast a faint glow on the storage shed. Behind the shed I found the gas cans and picked one up. That was when I noticed water coming from the corner of the lot. I stepped closer and saw that the sprinkler head was still broken, spraying a steady stream into the muddy yard and onto the pathway. "Way to go, Delph," I muttered angrily.

I heard a noise coming from the shed and spotted a small white nose with a black tip poking out of a homemade doggie door. Oscar jumped out and scurried over to me, dropping his yellow rattle at my feet.

"Not now, Oscar," I told him.

He grabbed the toy and scampered up the path ahead of me into the darkness. As I approached, I could see him faintly, standing on hind legs, waiting for me. When I drew near, he dropped the rattle at my feet.

"Oscar, sweetie, I can't play now."

I shined my light onto the ground to find the rattle. As I did, I noticed a large muddy footprint on the path beside me. I shined the light ahead and saw more footprints. They appeared to be fresh, and they were heading up the path toward the back door.

Quietly, I set the gas can down and covered the light from my phone, hardly daring to breathe. I listened intently, but the only sounds came from the side street a few buildings down and the occasional breeze that swept through, causing the leaves and branches to rustle gently.

Very quietly, I moved past the hydrangeas with Oscar scampering by my side. I stopped as a twig snapped in the darkness. Oscar immediately darted away. I waited in silence, standing as still as the statue of Athena. From where I stood, the back door to the barn was just twenty feet away. All I had to do was make my way across the patio and lock myself inside. I took a deep, steadying breath and started across the open patio.

Suddenly Oscar leapt out of the bushes. I gasped aloud as he dropped the rattle at my feet once again. I heard another twig snap, and Oscar turned his head toward the back door, staring at something I couldn't see. I quickly swept the light across the door but saw nothing. As I approached the barn, I moved the beam onto the generator near the building and still saw nothing.

At another rustling noise, Oscar darted away into the nearby shrubs. My fingers trembled as I held up the light. "Who's there?" I called in a shaky voice.

A large figure stepped out of the shadows. I dropped my phone and stumbled backward, landing on my already bruised tailbone. I pushed myself back as the hulking figure towered over me. I recognized Ben at once.

"What do you want?" I asked in a shaky voice.

"Shut up," he growled. "Get to your feet."

My fingers touched something soft on the ground behind me. It was Oscar's rattle, and it gave me an idea. I picked up the toy and rattled it.

"I said, get up!" Ben commanded.

I rattled it again, harder this time. Ben stepped backward, clearly confused. "What the hell are you doing?"

I rattled the toy one more time and called out as loud as I could, "Oscar! Fetch!" Then I threw the toy at Ben's chest.

As he put out his hands out to catch it, I could hear the scraping of claws on the pavement as Oscar darted out of concealment. The raccoon lunged after the rattle, leaping up at Ben, then snatching the toy and pushing off into the bushes. Ben stumbled backward into the hydrangeas, giving me time to spring to my feet and dart past him. I pulled open the door, slammed it closed behind me, and held it closed as I fumbled to turn the lock.

Before the lock could latch, Ben was at the door. He pulled the door so hard I thought it had come off the frame. The door swung open violently. My grip loosened, sending me backward off my feet. I caught myself with my wrists but still landed hard on my tailbone again, the pain radiating down my legs. I crawled under a patio table, and then another, using the darkness to my advantage. Trying not to make a sound, I crawled under yet another, putting as much distance between us as I could.

I heard Ben's heavy breathing as he searched the area. In one swift movement, he scattered the chairs away from the first table. Then another crash came as the table was upended and the glass tabletop shattered against the ground.

I inched back until I came to a wall. Ben moved closer, pushing more chairs out of his way. The table in front of me lifted and came crashing down. I looked for a way to escape, but I had backed myself into a corner.

Then I saw a light shining down one of the aisles and heard Abby call, "Athena, what's going on? Are you all right?"

"Abby, run!" I yelled. "It's Ben!"

I heard loud footsteps as the big man took off toward the light. Then the office door slammed closed, and I could hear Ben pounding against the frame. It would only be a matter of seconds before Ben broke down the flimsy office door. I had to do something.

I scooted out from beneath the table, my eyes adjusting to the darkness, and ran down the center aisle, where we kept the garden tools. I grabbed a heavy shovel off the rack and headed through the barn. I crept up behind Ben at the office door and raised the shovel high above my head. I brought it down with all the force I could muster, and Ben dropped to the ground instantly.

"Abby," I cried between gasps for breath, "call the police. I dropped my phone outside."

The door opened, and in the faint moonlight shining through the window behind them, I could see Eleni and Abby peering out at the man lying prone before them.

Eleni held up her phone. "I just called them. They should be here any minute." She held the light from her phone over Ben's body. "Is he dead?"

"I don't know," I answered. "I hit him pretty hard."

She reached down to check his pulse. I had a sinking feeling as Eleni pressed her fingers into his neck. "Please tell me he's not dead."

"He's alive," she said.

I let out a sigh of relief.

Abby shined her phone's flashlight on Ben. "Let's go wait outside for the police before he wakes up."

Instead of turning to go, Eleni nudged him with her foot.

"What are you doing?" Abby asked in alarm, shining her light on Eleni.

"Eleni," I said, "we have to go."

She bent over him, patting down the sides of his shirt and along his waist as though searching for something.

"Eleni," I said again, "we need to get out before he comes to."

She rose and turned to face us. I stepped back with a gasp at the sight of a small pistol in her hands. Abby stood stock-still.

Eleni pointed the gun at Abby. "Turn off that light. We're not going anywhere."

# CHAPTER TWENTY-TWO

I didn't know what else to do but raise my hands. "Eleni, what's going on?"

She smiled at me. "I must give you credit, Athena. You almost had me figured out. You were so close."

"Eleni, think about what you're doing," Abby said in a calm voice, switching off her flashlight.

Eleni nudged Ben's leg with her foot, trying to rouse him. When he didn't move, she said, "Back in the office, girls. Have a seat. And in case you haven't guessed it, the police aren't coming."

My heart began to race. I glanced at Abby, expecting her to be as shaken as I was, but she appeared calm.

"What do you intend to do?" Abby asked as we backed up. "Shoot us? Your fingerprints are all over the office. Don't you think the police will figure it out?"

"Shut up and go sit down," Eleni demanded, gesturing toward the desk.

Abby and I sat in the seats facing my desk. I turned to see Eleni standing in the doorway, just enough light coming from the window to make out her silhouette and the revolver still aimed in our direction.

"Eleni," I said. "You don't have to do this."

"Unfortunately, Athena, you've given me no choice."

She held the gun shakily in one hand, the other clutching the purse strap around her shoulder, a tiny crack in Eleni's brave façade. She kicked Ben's leg and ordered him to get up, but he didn't respond.

"Put the gun down and let's talk," Abby said slowly.

Eleni leveled the gun at Abby as she moved past us, through the office, taking a seat behind the desk. She set her phone facedown with the flashlight on, giving off just enough light to see. "I'm really, *really* not in the mood for a chat," she said sarcastically.

Out of the corner of my eye, I noticed Abby sliding her phone out of her pants pocket. She hit buttons with her thumb, then placed the phone between her legs. "What's your plan, Eleni? You can't kill us and drag us out of here yourself. You need Ben, but he's out cold."

Eleni glanced nervously at the prone figure just outside the door. "Then we wait until he comes to."

"How long will that be?" Abby pressed. "What if it's hours? Do you really think no one will check on us when we don't show up?"

"Shut up and let me think," Eleni snapped.

Abby ignored her order. "So, tell us," she said, "why did you kill Carly?"

Eleni glared at her. "You want a confession?"

"Why not?" Abby replied. "We've got nothing better to do."

"Fine, I'll tell you." She rested her arm on the desk, keeping the gun barrel focused on Abby. "You must think I'm a monster. But I'm not." She shook her head, her pupils dark and large. "I'm a protector," she continued. "Carly was the monster. I killed her to protect my husband."

"Protect him from Carly?" Abby asked.

"She could've ruined everything we'd worked for."

"So, all that talk about you leaving him because he had an affair was a lie?" I asked.

"I had to tell you something to get in the door," she replied. "I know Charles isn't faithful. But he is ambitious. And so am I. The only difference is that Charles wants money, and I want power."

"And Carly was a threat to your ambition," Abby said.

"When Carly came to Charles with the casino proposal, I told him it was a bad idea, but he didn't listen. Carly promised to make him rich, and that's all he's ever cared about. She promised that no one would ever find out about his involvement, but I didn't believe her. And it turned out I was right.

"I tried to fix things," Eleni continued. "I sent Charles the anonymous threats—and it almost worked. Charles agreed to pull out of the deal, but that was when Carly put her plan into action. She threatened to expose his interests, to ruin him if he didn't follow through."

"So you killed her," Abby said.

Eleni shrugged. "I had to."

"Ben worked with you to kill Carly, didn't he?" I asked.

She laughed. "Oh, heavens no. Ben is just as bad as Carly was, both using blackmail to get what they wanted."

"Then Ben must've caught you poisoning Carly's water," Abby said. "He caught you and threatened to go to the police if you didn't pay."

"He's a money-hungry lout. Ben, get up!" Eleni shouted. But he still didn't move. She rubbed her forehead, as though trying to decide what to do. Finally, she looked up at me and motioned with her gun. "Go ahead, Athena. I can see you have more questions."

I knew she was stalling for time. I gripped the bottom of my seat, wondering how long it'd been since I'd talked to Case. Wondering if he would get here in time. Because as soon as Ben came to, our lives were over.

"Why is Ben helping you now?" Abby asked.

"He wanted his money, so I told him he would get his money as long as he helped me dispose of you two."

"Then what?" Abby asked. "You think Ben is going to accept the hush money and then leave you alone? What if he demands more to keep quiet?"

Eleni gnawed on her lip. "Ben, get up!"

"I don't understand something," I said. "Why did you let us into your husband's office if you knew Charles was involved with the casino? Why give us more evidence?"

"So I could buy myself more time," Eleni explained. "You were getting too close. I needed to shift the narrative. Luckily, Lila walked in and gave me the perfect story."

"Does Charles know what you've done?" I asked.

"He doesn't need to know. As long as he smiles and waves and says his lines and gets himself reelected, that's all that matters." She half-rose from her chair. "Ben, wake up!"

As if on cue, Ben groaned. Almost immediately, I heard a loud bang somewhere in the garden center. Eleni rose at once. "What was that?"

I was wondering that myself. "It sounds like a garden tool fell off a rack," I told her.

Another loud bang startled her out of the chair. She moved around the desk, the pistol still aimed our direction, and stopped at the door. I turned in my chair to watch as she nudged Ben's leg with her foot. "Ben, for God's sake, wake up!"

When he didn't respond, Eleni bent down to shake him. At once Abby sprang from her chair and rushed Eleni. Before she could raise the gun, Abby grabbed her arm and bent it behind her back. Eleni cried out in pain and struggled to pull her arm free, but in one move Abby twisted her wrist backward, causing her to cry out again.

I ran over to help, wrestling the gun out of her

grasp as Abby pushed her to her knees. "Get some rope!" she cried.

And suddenly Case appeared in the doorway, wrapping his arms around Eleni to pin both of her arms down. "Are you okay?" he asked us, as Eleni struggled. He pushed her onto her stomach on the floor and knelt over her, holding both arms behind her back.

Abby sagged in relief.

I stared at Eleni lying on her stomach and shook my head in disbelief. "What just happened?"

Abby threw her arms around me and gave me a big hug. "You solved the case."

I hugged her back. "You need to teach me that move."

Minutes later, a whole contingency of police officers arrived, including Bob Maguire. Abby and I gave him a quick rundown of our situation, then an EMT checked out my bruised tailbone and scratched-up wrists while a pair of EMTs loaded up Ben's limp form and carried him out to a waiting ambulance. Then, as a team of forensics moved in and out of the garden center, Case, Abby, and I went outside to talk.

"How did you find us?" I asked him.

"You didn't answer your phone," he explained. "That's not like you. When I arrived at the garden center, the front door was locked, but I saw both your cars out front. I went around back and found the door busted open. I guessed Ben was behind it. I never thought Eleni would be involved."

"Athena figured it out," Abby said, patting my shoulder. "She suspected Eleni right away."

"And you have Eleni's entire confession recorded on your phone," I said. "I saw you slide your phone out of your pocket."

"Actually, I dialed 911," Abby explained. "I put the phone on mute so Eleni wouldn't hear the dispatch operator. I knew the police would listen to the phone call, and I knew our location would be pinged, so I had to get Eleni talking while we waited for the police to arrive."

Case shook his head with a smile. "You two make quite a team."

Abby smiled at me. "We do, don't we?"

A dark sedan squealed to a halt in the street before us, and Detective Walters stepped out of the car. In his scuffed brown shoes and wrinkled button-down, he casually walked over to us. "You ladies all right?" he asked gruffly.

"We're fine," I answered.

"We solved the case," Abby said.

Walters placed his hands on his hips and lifted his belt, his mustache twitching as he said, "I kinda figured you would."

*Sunday*

Under my father's orders, I took the day off. Wanting something to do, I offered to help Mama prepare for the family dinner, but she ordered me to relax on the sofa. I turned the TV to a travel channel and tried to slow my thoughts, but the previous day's events kept replaying in my mind.

Shortly before the relatives were to arrive, Nicholas came into the living room and sat down beside me, talking excitedly about how Oscar had helped save me.

"Yes, Oscar's a hero," I told him, "but you're my hero, too, Niko. You're the one who taught Oscar to fetch." I put my arm around him and hugged him close. "What do you say we turn that old shed into a nice home for our little hero?"

Nicholas looked at me in surprise. "Really?"

"As long as your grandfather gives us the okay," I said. "And as soon as my tailbone heals."

Nicholas leapt up from the sofa. "I'll go get you some ice."

Because we were now open at Spencer's until two on Sundays, our family dinners didn't start until three o'clock. And right on the dot of three, Uncle Giannis, Aunt Rachel and their sons, Aunt Talia, Uncle Konstantine, Yiayia and Pappoús, along with the six of us, plus Bob Maguire and Case, gathered.

On the patio behind our house, Mama had filled a long table with food and set up enough card tables and chairs for everyone. There was grilled lamb on a spit; *pastitsio* (Greek lasagna); whole chickens roasted with crispy, lemony potatoes; a cucumber, feta cheese, Kalamata olives, and tomato salad; and *spanakopita* (tiny spinach and feta triangle-shaped pastries).

Case and I were seated at one of the card tables with Delphi and Bob, who were chattering happily to us about their dance lessons. Nicholas sat at the next table with Maia and Selene.

"*Kalispera,* everyone," my mother said, standing in front of the food table. "Come up and get your food."

We all got in line at the big buffet table and took full plates back to our tables, the backyard filled with the sounds of silverware clinking against plates and happy voices. As the meal drew to an end, Delphi rose and tapped her knife against her glass.

"I have an announcement," she said, glancing around at everyone. "Bobby and I are entered into the County Fair Dance Contest, which is tonight, and you're all invited."

That set off a round of happy chatter. "We'll be there!" Mama cried, which was echoed by everyone else.

"That's why you were taking dance lessons?" Selene asked.

"We will all be rooting for you tonight, Delphi, my dear."

"Thank you, Mama," Delphi said.

"Hello," I heard someone call. I turned around to see Abby followed by her cousin Jillian walking around the side of the house. "We don't mean to interrupt."

"Abby," I said. "Join us." I stood and welcomed them onto the porch, facilitating quick introductions around the table. Abby was beaming, but Jillian was the true sight to behold. The color had returned to her lightly freckled cheeks, her long, silky copper-colored hair flowed freely down her shoulders, and there was an obvious sense of relief radiating all around her.

After the introductions were finished, Jillian turned to me and wrapped me in a fierce embrace. We were almost the same height, so she could whisper in my ear easily. "Thank you for saving me."

I tried to pull away to respond, but she held me harder. "My little Harper thanks you, too."

When our embrace ended, Abby joined us and said, "It's all about helping innocent people stand up for themselves, right, Athena?"

I gave her a knowing smile. "It's what we do."

"Girls," my mother said, "sit, eat, there's plenty to go around."

"I think Jillian wants to get home to her little girl," Abby said. "We just stopped by to say thank you."

"Can you believe it's Eleni Sloan?" my aunt Rachel asked, which started everyone talking about Eleni.

"Give us an update, Bob," my dad said. "Real quick while everyone's here. What's happening to Eleni now?"

Bob's ears reddened as he was put on the spot, and everyone turned to listen. He finished his bite, then cleared his throat. "Eleni isn't admitting to anything," he told us. "But it doesn't matter because we have most of her confession recorded through Abby's 911 call. And the mayor's security guard, Ben Logan, has told detectives everything. Let's just say he was very talkative after the DA told him he could be tried as an accessory to murder."

"So Mayor Sloan wasn't involved?" Uncle Konstantine asked.

"Not in the murder," I explained. "But he was involved in a scheme to build a giant casino on the outskirts of town."

I explained about the mayor's plan, after which Uncle Giannis said, "It's a shame the citizens of this town don't know what a liar their mayor is."

"To be fair," Case said, "he was backing out of the deal."

"But only when it became too risky," I added. "He didn't want to do anything to hurt his chances for reelection."

"It's a shame," Mama said. "Charles Sloan has done great things for this town, but he won't be getting my vote this time."

Her sentiment was echoed by everyone.

"Tell us how you solved the case, Athena!" Aunt Rachel called.

I gave them a rundown on how the pieces of the puzzle came together, and Abby explained Carly's plan to blackmail Charles, which had everyone shaking their heads in wonder.

"Abby's husband, Marco, was a big help," I replied. "And Case was right there with me, helping me figure things out."

Case rose to stand beside me. "My only regret is not getting there sooner when Athena and Abby were in danger." He put his arms around me and looked into my eyes. "I'll make sure that never happens again. One case at a time, as you said."

Abby and Jillian were understandably excited to get home, but my mother, of course, insisted they stay.

"We need to be going," Abby countered politely. Then she spied the table of desserts. "But I will take a piece of baklava to go."

We said our good-byes and sent Abby and Jillian home with enough desserts for both of their families. The dinner resumed after they'd left, leaving Case and me to resume our conversation.

"One case at a time, huh?" I asked playfully.

He pulled me closer. "You got it, Goddess."

I leaned toward him to say quietly, "Then I think we should turn to our next case."

"Which is what?" Case asked.

"The case of the missing love life," I whispered.

Case took me in his arms and kissed me right there in front of my family. To my surprise, everyone began to clink their knives against their glasses until we kissed again.

Mama stood and lifted her glass. "Everyone, raise your glasses. Once again, I will toast my daughter. Three cheers to the Goddess of—"

My phone rang, making her pause. "Sorry," I said, pulling my phone from my pocket. I silenced it and gave her an apologetic look.

"Let's try it again," she said. "Three cheers to the—"

Case's phone rang. He muted it and showed me Lila Talbot's name on the screen.

"One more time," Mama said. "Three cheers to the Goddess of—Oh, for heaven's sake!"

Both of our phones had dinged at the same

time. We pulled them out to see what was going on and saw a group text from Lila: *SOS I NEED YOUR HELP NOW! CALL ME AT ONCE.*

"Can I finish my toast now?" my mother cried. And without waiting for my answer, she hoisted her glass once again. "Here's to the Goddess of Greene Street!"

Everyone joined in her cheer. I thanked them, then Case and I excused ourselves and went inside to call Lila.

"What's wrong?" I asked, putting her on speakerphone. "Case is here with me."

"Charles hasn't shown up to run through his speech, and he's not answering his phone. I drove to his house, but no one answered the door. His speech is in a few hours. What should I do?"

I explained to her about Eleni and told her the mayor would certainly cancel his appearance because of it. "He's not going to stand in front of an audience fielding questions about his wife."

"His supporters don't know anything about that, Athena. It hasn't hit the news yet. We're expecting a packed house tonight, and *they* will be expecting their hero to show up. If he doesn't show, I don't know what to do. I can't let all those people down."

"They're going to find out tomorrow what happened," I said.

"But what about tonight? What am I going to do *tonight*? Please, Athena. This isn't just about Charles. There's a whole group of people who worked very hard to get to this point. I can't abandon them now."

"Then just tell the crowd what happened. You can let them down easily."

"Will you and Case come to the fair?" she asked. "I need your support."

I could hear the desperation in her voice. Even though every bone in my body was begging me to decline, I couldn't. Lila had come through for us on more than one occasion. I wasn't about to let her down now.

I breathed in deeply and let it out, asking, "What time should we be there?"

# CHAPTER TWENTY-THREE

Two hours later, we found Lila backstage at the grandstand, where an enormous crowd had gathered. Lila saw us and came hurrying over. "Athena, he resigned! Charles has resigned as mayor! His secretary called a few minutes ago. What am I going to tell the crowd now?"

"Just read your speech. Or speak from the heart. You can do this, Lila."

She grabbed a set of notecards from her purse and flipped through them, barely reading a word on them. "I can't do it, Athena. I can't go out there. I'm a nervous wreck."

"Lila," I asked, "what's wrong?"

The crowd began to chant, "Mayor Sloan! Mayor Sloan!"

Lila looked around in terror. Her hands shook as she held the notecards. "I can't do it. I can't go out there."

"Someone has to tell them the mayor isn't

here," Case said. "We can't just leave them hanging."

Lila steadied herself on Case's shoulder. "I'm sorry. I just can't do it."

I listened to the crowd chanting and closed my eyes. I thought of myself frozen on the stage earlier and clenched my fists. I remembered Charles Sloan's chiding smile as he forced me up on that stage, and I inhaled deeply.

"Mayor Sloan, Mayor Sloan," the crowd chanted, louder now, clapping along.

I opened my eyes, held out my hand, and let my breath out. "Give me the cards," I said firmly. "I'll do it."

Case and Lila stared at me, and I felt an icy shiver sprint up my spine. I took the notecards from Lila and turned to face the stage. "Someone has to tell them who the mayor *really* is."

"Hold on just a minute," Case said. "Are you sure you want to do this?"

As I listened to the crowd chant, my nerves pulsed. "I have to do this."

The band started their triumphant entrance march, and the lights on stage lit up in vibrant red, white, and blue lights.

My stomach was queasy at the thought of facing all those people, but one look at Lila's hopeful face, her hands in prayer form, one glance into Case's encouraging eyes, one vision of my son's proud face, and I knew the time had come to conquer my fear.

I took a few deep breaths and tried to still my racing heart, then I walked onstage with legs shaking so hard I thought they would buckle, with palms so damp I feared the ink on the notecards would smear. It seemed to take forever to walk over to where a microphone waited on its stand. As I approached it, the band finished their introduction, and the crowd quieted.

I wet my lips. I cleared my throat. And with trembling hands, I lowered the microphone stand to my level. Then I began to speak.

"Hello—" "I cleared my raspy throat and started again. "Hello, everyone. My name is Athena Spencer—"

"The Goddess of Greene Street," a man called loudly, which started everyone clapping.

I looked at the notecards in my hand, at the speech Lila had so carefully crafted, took a deep breath, and started to speak. "I know you were all expecting to hear from Charles Sloan tonight—"

At the mention of his name, the crowd clapped even louder.

"—but I'm sorry to inform you that he has resigned from his position as mayor."

There was a loud gasp from the audience. The cheers and clapping quieted immediately, leaving me alone onstage in front of a stunned crowd. All eyes were on me.

*You can do this, Athena.*

"I know this comes as a shock to you," I began, "and I'm sorry to be the one to tell you that your mayor is—"

The words *liar* and *cheater* formed on my lips. "Mayor Charles Sloan is not the man . . ."

I paused and looked out at all the disappointed faces. I looked over at Lila, who stood at the edge of the stage with her hands clasped together expectantly. I looked at Case, who held a look of reservation. Then I thought back to the inspiring speech I'd heard Charles Sloan give on this very stage, and I had a sudden rush of inspiration. A sense of calm washed over me.

"Over the next few days," I began, hearing my voice boom and echo throughout the crowd, "you will learn why Mayor Sloan has resigned from his position. Some of you will be shocked or saddened, and some might be angry, but I can assure you that no matter what happens, Sequoia will persevere. Charles Sloan may be gone, but his message of community and prosperity remains.

"Mayor Sloan worked very hard for this town," I continued, "but he wasn't the only one. There is a whole team of talented people behind the scenes who helped Charles Sloan craft his policies."

I waited to hear a response but received nothing more than a few awkward claps.

"For example," I continued, "'Keep Sequoia Small' was an idea thought up by Rosemary Dalsaurus, a very smart and very brave woman who worked for his campaign. She came up with the slogan. And what a slogan it is."

I repeated the slogan and then asked the crowd to repeat it with me. "Keep. Sequoia. Small!" To my surprise, the crowd continued the chant, growing louder with each refrain.

"And do you remember the speech you heard last week? That was written by his campaign manager, Lila Talbot. Lila, will you come out here, please?"

I looked out but couldn't see her. I could only hope she was willing to join me.

"Lila wrote the incredible speech you heard last week. She also wrote the speech Charles was supposed to give tonight. I think we should hear it. What do you say?"

With that I heard the smattering of applause grow louder. Lila walked out from the shadows, and upon seeing her, the applause grew and grew until she was standing next to me, waving at the cheering crowd. She leaned in so I could hear her and said, "Thank you, Athena."

She stood at the podium and thanked the crowd, and suddenly my job was done. Lila had the stage presence of a professional, and she took the limelight with incredible grace, her voice smooth and silky over the loudspeakers.

"We will do everything we can to keep Sequoia small," Lila began. "We, the citizens of Sequoia, will do everything in our power to keep our wonderful town thriving. And whomever we elect to take Mayor Sloan's place will share our vision."

I walked offstage with legs that were still shaking, a throat that was still dry, and a heart still running a race in my chest. But I had conquered my fear, and for that I was proud.

Once I was offstage, Case hugged me. "You did it," he said with a wide smile. "How does it feel?"

"Like I need a big glass of wine," I told him.

"I can make that happen." Case put his arm around my shoulders. "What do you say we go share your success with your family?"

I glanced at my watch and gasped. "Case, we're missing the dance contest!"

As Lila continued her rousing speech, Case and

I hustled down the pathway, out of the fenced arena, and down to the big brick building at the end of the fairway. We entered in time to see ten couples standing at the front of the dance floor, while an emcee stood at a microphone, and three judges sat at a long table behind him. Spectators sat at round tables that circled the wide dance floor, and a trio of musicians sat off to one side.

As Case and I made our way around the tables, I caught sight of Niko waving at me from the other side, seated with my yiayiá and pappoús. The entire Karras clan sat at nearby tables.

"And last but not least," the emcee announced, "our first-place prize goes to Sarah and Mike Gillen!"

As the happy couple strode forward to accept their gilded trophy amid a round of applause, I saw Delphi and Bob clapping, looking surprisingly pleased. Case and I took our seats next to Niko and my grandparents. My mom and dad were seated across from us, my mother checking her watch and shaking her head at me.

As soon as the presentation was over, Delphi came running over to us, with Bob right behind. "We took third place!" Delphi announced triumphantly.

"Congratulations, you two," Case said and shook Bob's hand.

I gave Delphi a hug. "You did good, sis."

Delphi was animated. "I know third place isn't great, but here's the cool part. Remember when I did the coffee grounds reading for myself?"

"Um, no," I replied.

"Sure you do. I saw the number three. As in *third place*? See, O ye of little faith? I got it right!"

And then I did remember her vision. She had not only predicted that the number three would come into play, but she had also seen water and danger and the letters *BL*—the water leak, the muddy footprints, and Ben Logan. I wrapped her in a big hug. "You *were* right, Delph. I should've trusted your vision."

She pushed me back, holding me at arm's length. "What do you mean?"

"You didn't fix the water leak," I explained. "You saved me."

She let go and smacked her forehead. "The water leak! I completely forgot."

I gave her a long look. "Are you kidding?"

"About what?"

Delphi saw me roll my eyes and shake my head. "About what?" she asked again.

"Never mind, Delph. Congrats on third place."

"Okay, everyone," the emcee announced, "the dance floor is open, and our trio has some great music for you. Come up and dance the night away!"

Nicholas jumped up to greet me and wrapped his arms around my waist. "You missed it, Mom. Thea Delphi did so good!" He took my hand and led me away from our table. "Can we go dance now?"

"In a bit," I told him. "I want to say hi to the rest of the family."

"Come on, Niko," my sister Maia called. She stood up and held out her hand. "Dance with me."

"Will you make sure she comes, Case?" Nicholas asked.

Case laughed and ruffled Nicholas's hair. "I'll do my best to get your mom onto the dance floor."

Nicholas took my sister's hand and disappeared onto the crowded floor.

My mom stood up for a hug. "I'm glad you made it, Athena. You, too, Case." She pointed toward the dancing couples, where I could see Delphi and Bob arm in arm, laughing and enjoying themselves. "Look at Delphi out there," Mama said. "She didn't win the contest, but you'd never know it by looking at her."

To my surprise, I also saw my sister Selene on the dance floor, smiling and twirling with her date, Thomas Pappas. "Selene seems to be happy," I told her.

"Because she took my advice," Mama said. She shrugged indifferently. "If only all my daughters did the same."

"What do you mean by that?" I asked.

"You promised that once this case was over, you would have some fun."

"And I will."

"Now is a good time to start."

"Oh, yeah?" I teased. "I'll dance when you do."

Mama huffed, but then she turned toward my dad and held out her arm. My dad stood and took my mom's hand, then leaned close to say quietly to me, "Checkmate."

I laughed as he and my mom slipped in among the dancing couples.

"Well," Case said to me, "shall we join Niko?"

"I don't want to leave my grandparents alone," I told him.

Hearing that, my yiayiá rose, grabbed my pappoús, and motioned for us to join them. My aunts and uncles were on the floor dancing, too. Which left Case and me, all by ourselves.

Case offered his hand. "Let's go have some fun, Athena. You've earned it."

So I danced with Case. I danced with my son. I danced with my sisters. I danced with my grandparents and my mom and my dad.

And I had fun.

*Keep reading for a special excerpt!*

**BIG TROUBLE IN LITTLE GREEK TOWN**
**A Goddess of Greene Street Mystery**
**By**
**Kate Collins**

In a tourist town on Lake Michigan, Athena Spencer keeps busy raising a son (and a pet raccoon named Oscar) while working at her family's garden center. But sometimes she also has to get the dirt on a murderer, in the new series by the *New York Times* best-selling author of the Flower Shop Mysteries . . .

Athena has invited Case Donnelly, recently relocated from Pittsburgh and awaiting his PI license, to accompany her to a Save Our Dunes fundraiser and art festival. And her date proves helpful when the body of a disgraced photographer turns up during a nature walk.

The crime—and the photos taken by the dead man—raise a lot of questions about local politics, environmental battles, and the victim's womanizing ways. As Athena's endearing Greek American family strives to solve a mystery of their own (uncovering the identity of Athena's anonymous blog), she and Case try to find the tangled roots of this murder and make sure there's no sanctuary for a killer . . .

***Look for* BIG TROUBLE IN LITTLE GREEK TOWN,** *on sale now!*

# CHAPTER ONE

*Saturday, 10 a.m.*

"**P**opcorn. Get your caramel-coated popcorn right here."

"Let's stop," I said to Case, pushing up the strap of my sundress. "It smells delicious."

"Athena, fifteen minutes ago you told me not to let you ruin your lunch."

"I forgot about the popcorn." I gave him a sheepish smile. "Just one bag and I'll behave. It'll be my treat."

We stopped at the popcorn stand, bought a bag of the sweet/salty stuff, and took stock of our surroundings: arts and crafts booths, food booths, a lovely woodland area, sand dunes, a view of Lake Michigan, and happy people enjoying a perfectly sunny Saturday morning. It had been so long since I'd taken a Saturday off, I'd almost forgotten how enjoyable my little tourist town could be.

The June sun was streaming down in beams through the voluminous puffy clouds, raising the temperature above 80 degrees, making sundresses and shorts a necessity. I had my long brown hair up in a ponytail and had on an aqua-colored sundress, a flowy style just perfect for a warm day. Case was wearing sandals, khaki shorts, and a dark green T-shirt that brought out the green flecks in his light brown eyes. He'd met me at the pier where his houseboat was docked, and even though I'd promised he'd find the art festival interesting, I'd had to practically drag him there.

Sequoia, Michigan was well-known for its weekend festivities, drawing people from all over the western side of the state as well as from northern Indiana and Chicago. I was glad to see the festival had already attracted a huge number of locals as well as tourists.

Entitled Art for the Park, the festival was well underway by the time we arrived.

The rambling, old Victorian mansion that hosted the event sat at the southern end of Greene Street, a corner lot on a wide expanse of land that had been all but forgotten until the historic home had been repurposed. From the porch hung a large sign that read *The Studios of Sequoia* and listed the services they offered: painting lessons, private art rooms, art sales, and studios for rent. This was the first time the Studios of Sequoia had sponsored a festival, and so far, it looked like a huge success.

A woman was standing on the wraparound porch giving a tour to a small group. Case and I passed by the house and wandered through the crowd into the backyard, a magnificent expanse of land with a perfect view of Lake Michigan. The back of the house had a large cement patio big enough to host painting classes or entertain guests.

"Shall we look around?" I asked Case as he munched on a handful of the sweet-smelling caramel corn.

Behind the mansion's property was a large tract of dune fronting Lake Michigan, as well as a forested area with hiking trails. The land had once been a beautiful public park, but time and lack of funds had turned it into an eyesore.

Case pointed to one of the banners strung across the yard. "Save Our Dunes," he read. "Save them from what?"

"The dunes have been off-limits because of erosion." I picked up a pamphlet sitting on a nearby booth. "'Art for the Park,'" I read aloud. "'All profits will go to help save our dunes from destruction.' Save Our Dunes—we call it SOD—was started to raise awareness and education about Sequoia's treasured strip of natural dune land."

Case grabbed a second handful of popcorn. With his dark, handsome good looks and athletic build, I wasn't sure which looked yummier, him or the popcorn. "Looks like they have a lot of support."

We passed more booths and tables set up in a wide square on the expansive back lawn, people selling jewelry, hooked rugs, brightly colored pottery, drawings, even sculptures. Anything considered art was fair game at this festival.

I flipped through a selection of vintage movie posters as Case continued to eat the popcorn. "So, this is what you call interesting?" he asked.

I snatched the bag from him. "You just lost popcorn privileges."

A deep voice to my left caught my attention. "Hello, Goddess of Greene Street."

I swung around and came face-to-face with Hugo Lukan, the photographer who'd taken my picture with the now-famous *Treasure of Athena* statue that graced the entrance to my father's business, Spencer's Garden Center. The *Treasure of Athena* and I had made quite a splash in the newspaper after I'd helped solve a double homicide that centered around the six-foot-tall statue of the goddess Athena. That investigation had earned me the title the *Goddess of Greene Street.*

"Hello, Hugo."

Hugo was a lean, nervous, forty-something man who was always on the move. With prematurely white hair, he took photographs for the daily newspaper and also sold his photos to magazines and advertisers. Now on his third divorce, Hugo was known around town for his penchant for flirting and his scandalous lack of scruples.

He shook my hand and then Case's. "You're a hard man to reach, Donnelly."

"I've been busy," Case said. He eyed the professional camera hanging around Hugo's neck. "Are you here on official business?"

Hugo did a quick sweep of the crowd. "I guess you could say that. Let's have you two stand closer and smile for me."

We did as he suggested, and he took our photograph. "It's always nice to see a celebrity mingling with the common folk," he teased.

"You're lucky I'm in a good mood," I teased back.

"You get your private eye business up and running yet?" he asked Case.

"Still working on it," Case replied.

Hugo glanced around again as though checking for someone. "You'd better hurry," he said, suddenly serious. "You and I have a lot to discuss."

"What do you two have to discuss?" I asked, feeling suspiciously left out of the loop.

He lowered his voice. "I can't talk about it here, but I do need Case's expertise. Watch your mail."

"Are you selling any of your photography today?" Case asked, changing the subject.

"Are you kidding?" Hugo rolled his eyes. "This festival is a waste of time. The Save Our Dunes group wanted me to donate some of my photos for the park renovation project, but what I'm working on now will help their cause more than any donation could. Just wait and see."

"Wait for what?" I asked.

As though he hadn't heard me, Hugo glanced around again. "There's Pearson Reed. If you'll excuse me, I need to speak with him, so I'll let you get on with your day. Enjoy the festival." Hugo turned and practically trotted away.

"A celebrity, are you?" Case asked, putting an arm around my shoulders.

"No autographs, please. This celebrity is officially off-duty. Now, if you'll do me the honor of filling me in."

"Don't mind Hugo," Case said. "I met him last week at a bar. He was going on about some conspiracy within the city council and asked for my help. I told him it'd have to wait until I got my private investigator's license. He wasn't too happy about that."

"I don't trust him, Case. He does exceptional photography, but otherwise doesn't have a very good reputation."

"That's why I've been avoiding him."

"He sounded very serious."

"He said wait and see. I guess that's all we can do."

We kept walking down the aisles of booths, my eyes focused on Hugo as he followed Pearson through the crowd. "Pearson Reed is on the city council," I told Case. "His wife is a friend of mine. Maybe we should look into this conspiracy Hugo mentioned."

"Not until I get my P.I. license. I don't want to jeopardize my career before it starts."

We passed by a beverage booth sponsored by Sequoia Savings and Loan, where I waved to my friend Darlene, a senior vice president at the bank. We saw a face-painting booth for kids, a booth selling artisan cheeses, and another selling goat milk soaps and lotions. We stopped at one called Jewel's Jewels, explored a booth selling watercolor art, and browsed a long table of homemade desserts sponsored by the Women of St. Jacob's Greek Orthodox Church. They had baklava, *kourabiedes*, and my favorite, *galaktobourekos*, among others. To go with it they were offering Greek coffee, a sweet, strong, pressed coffee that was dessert in itself.

"We have to stop here," I said. "I want you to try the *galaktobourekos*."

"I can't even pronounce it. Why would I want to try it?"

"Do you like custard? Because these are heavenly little squares of custard pie with honey drizzled on top."

Case motioned toward the empty bag of popcorn in my hand. "I promised to keep you from ruining your lunch."

"And I promised you this art fair would be interesting."

"Touché."

"Buy one for me!" I heard and glanced down to the next booth to see my youngest sister, Delphi, sitting behind the table. With her dark, curly hair pulled back in a ponytail, she had on a deep teal T-shirt and tie-dyed harem pants in teal and gold with her ever-present flip-flops, those also in gold.

"What are you doing here?" I asked, moving down to stand in front of her.

"Raising money." She smiled up at me. "Check out our sign."

I glanced up and saw a sign that read: *Mind, Body, Spirit.* And in smaller letters underneath: *Reiki Healer, Psychic Medium, Massage Therapist, Tea Leaf Reader.*

"Delphi, you don't do tea leaf readings." And her coffee ground readings were iffy at best.

"Go away, then," she said with a pout. "You'll ruin business."

"Athena, are you causing trouble?" I heard, and turned to my left to see my mother standing inside the Greek church's booth, arms crossed, shaking her head, an amused look on her face. Next to her stood my older sister Selene, my younger sister Maia, and my ten-year-old son, Nicholas.

"Look at that," Case whispered in my ear. "It's a family affair."

"Hi, Mom," said Nicholas, or Niko, as he preferred to be called now. "Can I have a piece of custard, too?"

"Not now, honey," I said. "You'll ruin your lunch."

"There's the pot calling the kettle black," Case said quietly, earning him another poke in the shoulder.

I came from a big, zany, half-Greek, half-English family of two parents, four sisters, a Greek grandmother and grandfather, and lots of aunts, uncles, and cousins. Like my sisters Maia and Selene, I was named after a Greek goddess. Delphi was named after the Oracle of Delphi, which she assumed made her an oracle, too. Unlike my sisters, however, I took after my father in looks, while my three sisters took after my mother, with long, dark, curly hair, rounder faces, olive complexions, and sturdier bodies than our willowy, fair-haired, English relatives.

"Athena," my mom said, snapping her fingers beneath my chin, causing the gold bracelets on her arm to clatter.

"Sorry, I was just thinking."

"Leave Delphi alone," Mom said. "She's making money for SOD."

In lieu of sticking out her tongue, Delphi wrinkled her nose at me. I wrinkled my nose back and turned away. I usually tried to monitor her coffee ground readings when she did them for customers at Spencer's. Amazingly, although she often put her foot in her mouth, now and then she actually got her readings right. She claimed a 75 percent success rate, which I highly doubted.

"Nice to see you, Case," my mom said. "Athena, let your son have a small square. He's been good all morning."

"I think Athena wants some Greek custard, too," Case said, pulling out his wallet. He eyed the luscious custard squares and added, "Make that three."

"Coming right up." Selene turned to dish three squares onto heavy cardboard plates.

Case picked up our desserts, passed one to Nicholas with a wink, and we moved on to the booth after Delphi's, where the sign said: *Save Our Dunes Nature Walk.*

"Today we're giving a short lecture on the native plants as we hike a portion of the trail," a man in matching khaki shirt and pants told the crowd. "If you enjoy nature, you'll enjoy this. Our first walk starts in half an hour."

"Let's sign up," I said to Case.

He looked dubious. "It's hot today. Are you sure you want to hike?"

He was looking for a way out. "Come on, this will actually be interesting," I said, writing our names on the list. "And we'll have time to eat our dessert beforehand. Let's go find a place to sit."

"Interesting?" Case muttered. "Right."

"What?"

"Tables are *right* over there." Case pointed across the wide lawn to a grouping of bright green wooden picnic tables.

As we sat down at an empty table facing the

water, Case held his hand up to shield his eyes from the bright late-morning sun and glanced around. "This *is* beautiful land."

"You should have seen it twenty years ago. My family used to come down here with a picnic lunch on Sunday afternoons. I have fond memories of playing in the sand and swimming in the lake with my sisters. I'd really hate to see it destroyed."

As Case took a bite of the soft custard dessert, I asked, "How is the *galaktobourekos,* by the way?"

"You were right. It's delicious. But I'm not even going to try to pronounce that."

"Just say *Gah-lacto-burekos.*" I finished my dessert and sat back with a sigh. "The Greek language is a challenge, which is why I skipped a lot of Greek school."

"I have an idea," Case said, sliding his arm around my waist. "Why don't we skip the nature hike and take the boat out? Just you and me. Out on the water. Alone."

The idea was tempting. It seemed as though Case and I hadn't been able to spend any quality time together in weeks. Ever since he'd started working toward his P.I. license, all of his free time was spent studying, researching, and taking classes. Not only that, but the summer rush was in full swing at the garden center. Between that and spending time with my son and family, there wasn't much room for romance.

"Athena!" someone called. I looked around and saw Elissa Petros Reed, a talented artist and wife of city councilman Pearson Reed, walking toward us.

"Hold that thought," I said to Case.

A full-blooded Greek, Elissa was a petite woman

with thick, short dark hair, an olive complexion, dark brown eyes, and a generous mouth. After inheriting the Victorian house and property from her father, Elissa and her husband were responsible for renovating the mansion and turning it into a well-regarded art studio and tourist attraction.

I'd known Elissa since we were both gawky preteens. We'd become friends through summer camp and had stayed friends until college, when our paths took us in different directions. Now that our sons had become friends, we looked forward to seeing each other regularly. "It's good to see you," I said.

"You, too. And who is this handsome gentleman?"

I introduced her to Case and told her we had signed up for the nature walk. "Case is really excited about it."

He stared at me as though to say, *I am?*

"Good," she said. "You'll understand why we love this land so much. In fact, my husband and I are the ones who started the Save Our Dunes group. I hope you two will join. We need more members."

"I'd love to join," I said. "I'm all for turning the lakeside back into a park."

As Case ate the last bite of the soft custard dessert, he glanced past the dunes to where the trees started. "What about the forested area?"

"If a business bought the land," Elissa explained, "it could be razed or ignored. Either way it'd be a shame to see it go to waste, and it would completely ruin the view from our studios. That's why Save Our Dunes was created, to convince the city council this land should be rehabbed as a public park again."

"What's the latest word from the city council?" I asked.

"According to my husband," she said, "there's a company that wants to build on the land, with a parking lot on the southern end and an industrial driveway that would run alongside the property here. Supposedly it would bring in a good chunk of money in tax revenue for the city. Unfortunately, it would also devastate the dunes and more than likely put my studios out of business."

"That'd be awful," I said. "This is such a beautiful property and a great old house."

"Yes, it would be awful," she said. "This is one of the oldest homes in Sequoia. Have you taken Case inside?"

"Actually, we have time to do that now. The nature walk doesn't start for another twenty minutes."

"Then I'll leave you to it," she said with a smile. "Let's meet for lunch soon and catch up." Then she turned to talk to someone else.

"Let's go," I said, dragging Case from the bench. "We'll have just enough time to take a fast tour."

"Am I excited about that, too?"

We walked around to the front of the huge Victorian mansion and went up the stairs to the spacious front porch. Inside the foyer we found a list of artists who rented space in the building to create and sell their artwork. We took the staircase to the second floor and toured the former bedrooms that were now studios. Just as we were about to start down the curving staircase, Elissa's eleven-year-old son, Denis, came trotting up, out of breath, his bookbag bouncing heavily on his shoulders.

"Hello, Denis," I said.

He seemed surprised to see me and muttered a quick, red-faced hi.

"Niko's at the Saint Jacob's booth. If you're looking for something to do, why don't you go find him?"

"Thanks. I will," he said, and kept going up the staircase to the third floor.

Case and I did a fast sweep-through of the main floor and exited just in time to walk back to the nature trail booth and join the group. Our guide was a tall, solemn-faced man in his forties who introduced himself as a professor at the local community college. "Does anyone know why native plants are so important to a region?" he asked as we hiked over the dunes toward the woodland area.

"Because they're more resistant to disease?" I answered.

"Very good. That's one reason. Actually, native plants require less water, less fertilizer, less pesticide, and less care and maintenance. They also provide a habitat and food for many birds, insects, mammals, and other wildlife. This is why we're so dedicated to preserving this land. We don't want to lose all the benefits of this beautiful sanctuary."

He paused to point out some thorny shrubs. "Please be mindful of these barberry bushes. You'll find them all over the woodland. They can cut into your clothing and your skin very easily."

As we walked along, he pointed out flowers, shrubs, and trees that were native to west Michigan. We also saw perennials such as butterfly weed, black-eyed Susans, showy goldenrod, and blue coneflower, as well as an assortment of ferns.

"This is more than I wanted to know," Case said quietly as we walked along.

"I think it's interesting."

"That makes one of us."

"Over here we have a perfect specimen of a black cherry tree," our guide said. "And on your right a type of bush called the—" He stopped suddenly and then gasped. As everyone crowded forward to see why, he pulled out his phone, putting out one arm to hold us back.

I craned my neck to see what everyone was staring at and saw a pair of a man's legs sticking out of the underbrush.

"Yes, hello," the guide said. "I have an emergency."

"Oh my God," someone cried.

Case pushed through the crowd to get a closer look, and I followed. "It's Hugo," Case said, "and it looks like he's dead."

While everyone stood around gawking, I took out my cell phone and quickly snapped some photos.

"We'll have to stay here until the police arrive," our guide said after ending the call. "Let's move back to the dune area to wait."

As we followed the guide back up the trail, Case said, "*Now* it's getting interesting."